CONFIGURED

Book 1 of the Configured Trilogy

JENETTA PENNER

CONFIGURED

Book 1 of the Configured Trilogy

By Jenetta Penner

CONFIGURED

ISBN 10 : 154811308

ISBN 13 : 978-1548114305

Printed in the U.S.A.First printing 2016

To Ohana and Lynn.
Without you this book would not exist.

And to Emma, who didn't get the chance to read
nearly enough books.

CHAPTER ONE

My own mother is ranked beneath me. Incompatible.

Joy is the name she gave me seventeen years ago. Sometimes I imagine it as an invocation, a gift entrusted to guarantee a happy life, no matter what. But it's inappropriate to question a name I barely use—given by a mother I barely know. Avlyn, the name I go by now, suits me much better.

My final meeting with her is scheduled in a few days at our once-a-year meal together on the other side of Elore, in her meager Level One apartment. She'll prattle on about the weather and avoid the topic of Ben, my twin brother, or our bio father. Her chocolate-brown hair, the color we share, worn long and loose, makes her lower-level distinction obvious. When I leave, she'll remind me she's proud of my status and give me a tight hug I've little practice in returning. Thankfully, I wasn't raised by her.

Reassignment by Direction to a compatible family is an honor. Especially if it's an upgrade.

Lark is my compatible parents' last name, as well as mine now. The name is compelling, of a bird, supposedly with a cheerful song. I've never heard one. People are few, so are birds, and the meaning strikes me as ironic for a Level Two compatibility family. The higher your Intelligence Potential, the more you're required to stay focused, display less emotion.

Today is configuration day. It's my seventeenth birthday, and the last day of university. My career, which I have no choice in deciding, begins tomorrow.

"This should be your day, too, right Ben?" I mutter. He doesn't answer. When does someone who lives in your mind ever respond?

Butterflies fluttering through my stomach, I run my hand under the mattress of my bed and find it. A flat, hidden package wrapped in brown paper. Paper went out of general use years ago. I take it and rub the unfamiliar texture between my fingers—rough and old. A scrawl of childish letters adorns the surface.

I love you.

The backward y brings a smile to my lips, but then disappears with a gulp at the forbidden words.

A single piece of tired, opaque bonding material holds the fold of the paper together. I flick it open, and out drops a tiny pendant attached to a chain—a simple gold heart. Because outward appearance is considered irrelevant, people don't wear jewelry. And a *heart* shape? Shocking.

But also pretty.

I stroke the smooth metal, then shake my head. No… it's out of place, from a time long past and gone forever, and yet something about it being my birthday makes me slip the charm into my pocket. That, and it makes me feel close to Ben. It'd been a gift from him on our fourth birthday, likely stolen from our biological mother, Bess. He lived with her at the time. Of course, I'd never wear it. If seen, Direction may pry into my personal life. If they ever found out I still thought of Ben, let alone *talked* to him, I'd be sent in for re-education. Probably demoted to a Level One. But safe in my pocket, no one will ever know.

I shove the paper back under the mattress, push up from the bed, and step toward the sliding bedroom door, turning back to look at my room. For a second, I close my eyes and take a deep breath, just like Father taught me, but the ache in my stomach I woke up with still bores inside me. I slip my hand over the sensor and move through the open doorway into the hall.

A faint auto light fades on to guide me through the vacant hall. My parents rise early, and I figure they're already waiting for me to talk of the career configuration meeting later today, or worse, something dumb like spouse pairings. I'm dreading being chained to another person for the rest of my life more than any aspect of my citizen configuration.

Passing through the living room, I shuffle toward the kitchen, expecting the familiar busy motion of Mother in the dining area. Instead, I'm met with a blinking memo on the personal message screen alongside her image. Darline Lark, always put together, with sandy-brown hair cut in a short, crisp bob, the same as mine, but fairer in color. Sometimes, for a fleeting moment, her face looks kind, even warm, but here she only displays her standard, composed demeanor.

I tap the screen and the image flicks to life.

"Avlyn, your father and I had to leave early this morning," her image says. "Remember your appointment at the medical station at university first thing. One last physical before the meeting. Lunch is on the counter."

Mother pinches her lips together and the vid pauses. With a tap, the screen goes black.

I roll my eyes. She still orders my lunch every day and puts it on the counter for me to take to training. Silly. I'm not five. And besides, I won't even need a lunch today. My position will start tomorrow, not primer school. I must have asked her twenty times to stop doing it, but every morning it sits on the counter. She doesn't trust that I'm capable to do it myself. She never has.

My stomach groans. I touch the screen on the food printer to order my favorite, a blueberry muffin, ignoring the flashing green alert signaling the printer will need to be refilled soon. No sooner than I hit send, it makes zipping and whirring noises, followed by a beep. I release the door and grab the plain, printed plate, holding the fluffy, blue-splotched muffin. A sugary aroma wafts from the opening, making my mouth water.

I've watched informational vids on fresh food and pictured myself picking the fresh fruits and vegetables shown in them. I pick out a blueberry and pop it into my mouth, tasting the sweet, tart juice.

Wonder if the food from the printer tastes the same...

Despite the sweetness, I only manage to choke down a few bites of muffin before tossing it and the plate into the recycler to be remade into food and plates again. I pack a satchel with my handheld Flexx and the lunch Mother put out, just in case.

In the living room, an alert flashes on the media viewer. An official Direction message addressed to *AVLYN JOY LARK.*

My heart stops. On configuration day, besides a designated career, citizens also obtain the contacts of suitable spouse pairs. I've never even been on a date—courting hasn't been allowed for over thirty years—but now strangers deemed perfect for me will come calling.

A shiver works its way up my spine at the thought. This day is already happening too fast, and it's barely started.

Most look forward to the opportunity to be paired, but instead, I ignore the message and hold my breath until I'm out the front door and into the corridor. Almost tripping, I sidestep a hefty package with a Nutra Enterprise logo stamped on its side, our weekly order of food printer refill.

I release the breath and take out my handheld to reach my friend, Kyra.

Flexx 682AB1-ALARK: Want to walk with me?

Kyra and I often meet up on the way to university, and since today is my last day, I really want to see her. Who knows how much interaction we'll have in the future? Probably none, since after the transition period, communication with childhood friends is highly discouraged.

The vibration of her response comes quickly.

Flexx 35D52G-KLEWIS: I'm downstairs.

Today the elevator sounds too confining, and I need to work off this nervous energy. Each footfall echoes and booms as I take the seven flights of stairs down. For some reason, the noise is satisfying, turning up the corners of my lips. At the bottom, I spot Kyra through the sparkling glass of the foyer, vacantly staring at her Flexx. Her straight, blonde hair is pulled in a low ponytail, and her plain, light gray clothes are as utilitarian as the bleak khaki outfit I chose. Somehow, she always looks amazing, with her naturally tanned skin and aquamarine eyes. In contrast, my pale complexion and hazel irises are common, but looks don't equal intelligence, so it's stupid to care.

Once at the entrance, the door drifts open to the street and lets in a rush of cool, fall air. A fluid, pearly Aerrx delivery drone floats through and hovers past me, metallic tentacles clutching a delivery for a resident in the building.

The gigantic media screen affixed high on the building directly in front of ours flickers, and up comes Brian Marshall, the morning newscaster, with salt-and-pepper hair and a stern expression.

"Level Two and Three births are at an all-time high, and outpace those at Level One by fifty percent. This extraordinary news has come in time to commemorate thirty-five years of Compatibility Pairing and Birth Reassignment," Brian reports.

He goes on to announce an interview tonight with an expert on disease, and why the vaccinations are necessary to ensure a worldwide pandemic like the Collapse never happens again. This evening, Director Manning will make an announcement regarding the newest inoculation roll out.

"Up next," Brian says, "we'll take you to the Elore Detention Center for an update on the latest rebel activity and arrests."

The Direction emblem, a world wrapped in a swooping arrow pointed north to remind Elore to focus on forward thought, spins onto the viewer, and then fades, revealing an overhead view of the city. Above the screen is the spectacular dance of the Aerrx and Guardian drones as they shoot across the sky. The display never fails to impress me. An air shuttle passes over too, making me shiver at the thought of flying. Not my thing.

Kyra breaks my concentration, saying, "Configuration day."

"Huh?" I ask.

She shakes her head and gestures for me to walk toward university while folding up the thin, transparent material of her Flexx and snapping it to her wrist.

"Oh, yes," I confirm in a low tone. "First the med checkup, then the meeting."

An uncharacteristic glimmer lights up her eyes. "Did you read your official message?"

The message? *Nothing* in that message would excite me today. All "configuration" means is that everything is changing. After our transition period, I won't even be allowed to see Kyra anymore. She's not much, but she's all I have.

I've known her since the age of ten, when I got overly emotional one time at school. At the end of the day, she waited out front and walked me home. Kyra, an overachiever, believes she can "fix" me. She's even told me so. She knows everything about me. I slipped up at twelve and told her that sometimes I *talk* to Ben, my dead twin. For some reason, Kyra never breathed a word.

"I forgot," I lie.

She stops and rests her hand on her hip. "You *forgot*? You're not even curious about your pairings? With a good pair, you could secure a fantastic apartment right next to a Level Three sector with a view of the whole city. Not to mention anyone *worth* pairing with is going to get snapped up immediately."

Not that any Direction pairs would be of interest to me anyway.

"What if I don't *want* a pairing?"

"Of course you want a pairing," she huffs. "Otherwise you'll end up alone and unable to fulfill your obligation of children to society." Kyra shakes her head. "You never think these things through."

But I have thought this through. Being on my own will be easier.

I keep my head straight and continue walking without answering her.

"Oh, come on," she insists. "You'll be fine."

We hike the remaining blocks, nearing university. The smooth sidewalk continues as we pass the front of Level Two residences and the companies where we receive configuration. In an hour, I could be assigned to any of them.

"Sorry," I whisper, drifting toward her. "I'm nervous. So much is changing."

She gives me an expression of understanding. Her turn is Monday.

"Do you still think you'll be placed into government?" I ask.

Kyra shrugs. "All my scores are pointing to that division, but I overheard my parents trying to pull some strings for the actual entry position."

"Can they do that? I thought everything was decided in the testing system?"

"Probably not, but they want their union to produce a *superior* Level Two citizen instead of offspring influenced by an 'overly emotional friend.' Their exact words."

I flush, well aware she means me. Kyra has been a good friend, but her tact could use some work.

Another building's giant media screen flickers into view.

"Elore is a thriving metropolis, largely due to the hard work and continued focus of its citizens." An unseen woman's smooth voice narrates as the scene shifts to people working. "Societal Configuration allows citizens to concentrate their efforts away from emotions for the benefit of all—"

Hurried citizens pass by. A woman shepherds a little girl to drop her off at pre-primer school. Others gaze at handhelds or move to the line for the driverless taxis.

As we stop on the corner of Seventy-eighth Street, a motion across the road catches my eye. A teenaged, sepia-skinned girl pulls her curly hair loose from a ponytail and drops the dark coat she wore to the ground, revealing bright red clothing and standing out from the sea of neutral like illumination on a dark night. Something about the fabric appears soft and comfortable, in contrast to mine, which is more or less functioning as a uniform. She races down the sidewalk, and the blur of color streams around her like a flag.

A rebel. I should have known.

Kyra stares, her mouth falling wide. Some citizens from the crowded street gawk while others continue on with their business, each with eyes glued to their Flexx devices.

The runner stops and pulls out a small, matte black weapon from a bag slung over her shoulders. My eyes grow wide. Not that I've seen many weapons this close before, but something is unusual about it. She slides the top of the gun back and it emits a high-pitched whine. Barely thinking, my arms shoot out and I force Kyra to the ground. Other people duck behind anything substantial, even if it's just the person in front of them, or sprint the other way.

The rebel points the weapon at the nearby building, causing me to crouch further down. The little girl I saw earlier screams and points at the rebel clad in red. The rebels will only destroy our way of life, and that child knows it. The mother tries to cover her child's mouth and assures her that the Guardian drones will take the bad lady away.

My heart pounds at the mother's words.

Don't take her away.

I quickly correct my thinking.

They must take her away, for the protection of all of us.

I cover my ears, expecting a loud blast, but it doesn't come. Instead, it's more of a crackling. There's no damage to the building other than a set of words emblazoned across the surface. The hair on my arms stand at the sight.

PEOPLE OF ELORE, BREAK FREE

I look to the rebel girl again, now staring right at me. My heart nearly leaps from my chest. The corners of her mouth lift to form a tight smile, and she raises an eyebrow.

Why would she smile at me?

She tosses the graffiti gun and bolts, but the red clothing makes it impossible for her to hide. A group of Guardian drones swarm the girl. As they do, I clench my fists and grit my teeth. She stops and immediately throws her hands into the air. The rebel just gave up. No fight, nothing. Because of it, my body feels drawn to help her, to help her fight off the drones and make a daring escape. I picture the whole daring scene in my mind.

My legs push up from underneath me and I feel a hand grab the back of my shirt. I whip around to find Kyra staring back at me, her eyes panicked.

"What are you *doing?*" she whispers.

I fall back into a crouch. *This is ridiculous.* I'd be throwing my future away on some crazy rebel I didn't even know.

I imagine her smile again. I take a deep breath as she crumbles to the ground, tranquilized. Her head hits the sidewalk with a sickening *thwack.* A Guardian drone's metal tentacles snake from its form and wrap around her. It lifts from the ground to take her away for judgment, maybe even re-education, but in my heart I know that that's not true.

Worker drones buzz in to remove any evidence of the words she wrote on the side of the building. Citizens return to their business, acting as if nothing out of the ordinary happened. The woman and child, the one who was screaming, rise and move along. Nothing witnessed made any impact. If she had wanted to make a sacrifice, it was wasted.

Kyra and I stand there for a minute or two longer, eyeing one another before we leave.

Not a word is spoken between us for the next block. The university comes into sight, as does the colossal screen displayed on the face of the school. Looking up, I squint at the end of a Direction Initiative notice, swallowing hard at the words.

REMEMBER YOUR FUNCTION

Chapter Two

My knees still feel weak beneath me at the university entrance, and I silently order them to get it together. I square my shoulders and clench my jaw. Kyra inhales deeply and nods. We enter through the sliding glass door.

Inside, the fawn-colored, antiseptic halls are filled with teenagers. No rebels. You'd think there would be whispers of the attack we just saw, but no. Only seemingly oblivious students walking with handhelds folded out into tablets, shoes squeaking over glossy floors. Occasionally, teens hang out together here, but it's a race to the top, and we only have until the day we turn seventeen to prove ourselves. Focus is essential.

We're told *it's essential.*

Fixating on a girl pointlessly sacrificing herself to momentarily deface a building is useless and they know it. So do I.

Kyra sticks to my side, keeping pace.

Twenty-one trainees had been in our group over the last five years, all coming of configuration age within a month of each other. Four have been assigned already, but I know none of them well enough to ask how everything turned out. My turn comes today, and Kyra will be placed on Monday. If Ben would have been a Level Two instead of a One, we might have been in the same class, placed on the same day. Today.

But he's dead, so it's just me.

Loneliness for my twin rushes over me when Corra Bradley targets me from the side and mutters something. I glance at the lanky, skinny girl. Her blonde hair puffs up in the back like she just rolled out of bed. Corra's grown taller, but other than that, little has changed over the years.

"What did you say?" I ask.

She leans in, smelling of bacon and whatever else she ate for breakfast. "Any idea about your career placement, Avlyn?" Before I answer, she adds, "Mine will be at GenTech. I have the highest scores in the group."

Corra likes to talk, mostly about herself, and often brags to the group of her assuredly high position at Genesis Technologies. With scores like hers, I'm sure she's right, but it doesn't mean I want to be reminded of it all the time.

GenTech is the pinnacle of achievement, a high-priority company working as a liaison between Levels Two and Three. They also make VacTech, the vaccines which protect us from any new potential viruses. The projects are so secret that I don't actually know what goes on there. Only the most valuable and loyal trainees in Two are selected, not people who burst with emotion at all the wrong times. Not me.

I shake my head and back away. The social grace most in the community lack is obvious in Corra's interaction with me. Ignoring her bait, I plan a response to appease her enough to go away.

"GenTech is certainly something to aspire to. A placement for the best of us."

It works. She grunts and disappears, probably to do something important.

Kyra mutters words I don't care to hear. Corra is harmless, but it doesn't mean Kyra wants to hang around her either.

The med station comes into view. "Need to go. My appointment." I nod toward the door. "Message you later to tell how the day turns out."

"Sure." Kyra waves me on and gives me a small smile before she continues down the hallway to Lab 102, where the stark cubicle and system station I used for five years will sit vacant until the next group of students takes over the space. Kyra is the only thing I'll miss. She's always put up with me, and I'm convinced that beneath her stony exterior, she's glad for our friendship too.

With a clenched jaw, I turn toward the med station. I step in through the open door, expecting a Synthetic Intelligence nurse to administer the physical. Instead, a man of medium build, auburn hair, and with a slight paunch enters information into a wide, transparent viewing screen.

"Excuse me?" I say. "I'm here for an appointment."

He continues his work, and eventually mumbles, "Yes, I will be right with you."

I stand and wait, canvassing the sterile, white room. The closed glossy cabinets hide their mysterious contents inside. The med nurse, vaguely resembling a featureless torso and bald head with three retractable tentacle limbs attached to its body, sits motionless, charging at a station in the corner, ready to come to life and hover over patients in need.

I clear my throat.

"Oh, yes." The man stops typing and spins on his chair to address me. "Please have a seat." He directs me to a delicate chair with a smooth white finish next to a tabletop. My name already displays on the viewer from my handheld's university auto-network function. "Avlyn Lark, correct?" he asks.

I nod, and he unfolds thin Flexx material out into a tablet and places it in front of me. The surface of the table shows right through the screen. "I'm Medic Snyder. Answer the questions on the questionnaire to the best of your ability."

The basic information should already be in the system. I don't understand why I need to fill out the data again. Even so, I enter past medical procedures, MedTech, and exercise habits, among answering other redundant questions that could simply be downloaded from my nanos. Medic Snyder has my file on the main screen, and studies the records. He enlarges the facts and swipes each into the files on the screen with a finger when done.

Without turning, he says, "When finished, please place your right hand on the screen and keep still. The pad will take a reading of your body."

Why do the medics tell us this at every exam? The nanos injected into your body at birth assist your DNA and bodily functions to keep you in optimal working order... blah, blah, blah.

A slight vibration resonates in my hand and through the rest of me. Does the scan measure the nausea in my stomach from this morning's events on the street, or my apprehension about the meeting?

My stats, vitals, and ID image come on the screen. Average. Height: 5'5". Weight: 119 lbs. Hair: Dark brown. Eyes: Hazel.

Yep, ordinary keeps me invisible, along with any of those "subversive thoughts" that seem to pop into my brain when they're not welcome. I'm smart, but choose not to appear *too* smart in order to remain low key. The only thing I can't hide are the freckles scattered across my nose. It's silly, but I've never liked them. The spots make me feel childish, Level One, and I prefer them hidden, but there they are on the gigantic viewer, completely exposed.

The medic doesn't seem to notice them. After a moment, he reaches into a drawer alongside his seat and pulls out an object, keeping it concealed in his closed palm.

"Avlyn, your health is optimal other than some elevated stress levels," he states in a flat voice. "But those are likely due to your upcoming career configuration. In a few weeks, if this remains, you may obtain stress reduction MedTech. When you log in to your new citizen account, you will see the instructions to order them."

Everyone says the anti-stress tech is fine, but something about it never sat right with me. Even my father, who's never had a rebellious thought in his life, thinks one should control their stress naturally, although I think he just likes the challenge.

"Thank you," I say.

"And lastly, Direction has updated the disease vaccination. Some official citizens may opt to receive it today, in phase one, or elect to wait for a later phase. If you choose to do it today, you will receive one hundred additional credits in your account."

Deciding for myself, without Mother and Father, is a new concept. Until now, any health choices have been theirs, as is the case for every child before seventeen. A warm burn spreads in my chest and crawls up my neck. I should read the update, but the temptation to make my first grown-up decision taunts me.

I slip my hand into my pocket and find Ben's necklace. The same necklace that, if I were to wear it, would expose me and make me stand out from the crowd as the woman in the bright clothes did.

Undirected. Unfocused.

All the urges I need to repress.

I sweep my fingertips over the polished heart shape while my own heart forms a lump and rises into my throat. I swallow the lump and, without another thought, blurt out, "Sure. I'll do it."

He pokes the object hidden in his hand into a port on the side of the tablet.

The words *VACTECH TRANSFER COMPLETE* splashes across the screen.

"Place your hand on the screen," he says.

I obey, pressing my fingers against the smooth surface.

"It will only take a few seconds. Hold still. You shouldn't feel a thing."

The tablet beeps, alerting us that the nanos have accepted the upload.

I turn to the man and gather my bag. "Where do I go now?"

He returns to the keyboard. "Hmm? Oh, the Career Counselor will hold your meeting in 510."

As I stand, my hand tingles and a flash of white bursts over my vision. I shake my head and stumble toward the door, catching myself on the doorframe. But as soon as it comes, the feeling is gone.

That's never happened before.

"Is there a problem, Miss Lark?"

I right myself and turn back to him.

"Uh... no," I mutter as I leave the sterile room. Must have been the VacTech upload.

In the empty hall, my footsteps echo on the hard surface of the floor. Moving toward the stairwell, the clear lab doors come into view, exposing students working in front of viewing stations in cubicles. Inside, Synthetic Intelligence Staff hover over them.

As I run up the stairs, the burn in my calves at the fifth floor tells me I'm alive. The feeling is an excellent reminder of life before I turn over to an existence of function. Once, Ben and I ran through the park and accidentally tumbled down a hill, laughing all the way, before our parents caught us and ushered us back into the privacy of Bess and Devan's apartment. The corners of my lips turn up at the memory.

At the top, an echo of footfalls meets my ears. I turn back, expecting a student. Instead, a young boy of about eleven, with dark hair and a freckled nose, follows me.

My whole body clenches.

Ben?

As I open my mouth to say his name, the boy flickers snowy white and dissolves, leaving me alone on the stairs.

What's wrong with me?

I shake off the vision, but my hands continue to tremble.

He's dead, Avlyn. He died when he was four.

To the left, 510 shows on the directory. Passing the other offices, their doors closed, I find the way to the correct one. Inside is a cramped waiting room with a large viewing screen displaying the Direction spinning globe emblem. Another door sits to the left of the screen. I assume this is where the meeting will be held. A stiff couch waits off to the side, but I have no idea if I'm supposed to sit or not, so I just pace in front of it, still shaken from whatever I saw on the stairs.

"How can I help you?"

I turn to see a plump-cheeked woman on the screen.

"Uh, my name is Avlyn Lark. I'm here for my career appointment."

"Yes," she replies. "Rest your right hand on the identification pad next to the screen."

I spot the pad and walk over to lay my hand on it, bracing for anything unusual to happen again.

"Leave it on the screen until I inform you to remove it."

I do as she says. When I feel nothing, my body relaxes.

"Miss Lark, have a seat. Feel free to attend to tasks on your handheld while waiting."

The screen goes blank and returns to the globe.

A distraction from the impending meeting *would* be good. I bring out my device, unfold it, and sit on the couch this time. The memory of the pairing message from this morning makes me groan. It will still be available in my citizen account, along with any other official messages I've received today.

The same logo from the giant screen splashes across my small one, and I'm instructed to lay a thumb on the screen for identification. I push down, and my account details display. On the left are the one hundred extra credits I received at the med exam. Excitement wells in my chest. I've never had any credits of my own before. Not that there's much to order in my citizen account, but I might get a new pair of running shoes.

The thought makes me feel a little better about the meeting. A green button in the right corner of the screen informs me of two new messages. The first is a *Welcome to Citizenship* message, and the second is the spouse pairing one I'm avoiding.

I tap the welcome message.

> *Ms. Lark,*
>
> *Welcome to Direction citizenship.*
>
> *In this account, you will find the instructions for your new housing requirement, spouse pairing information, using and earning credits, and regulation obligations.*
>
> *You will be graced one month to complete certain requirements. During this time, you will obtain housing. Full-fledged citizens are advised to break contact with any childhood relations during the transition to complete societal configuration.*
>
> *Review the information and confirm that you have read and received this by completing the exam found in your account details page within one week.*
>
> *If you have any additional queries, use the search feature on any page in your account, or review the Direction FAQ. If questions cannot be answered through either, connect immediately with a Direction representative.*
>
> *Maintain Forward Focus.*

I close the account without checking the spouse pairing message. What's a few hours to wait to make *this* grown-up decision?

Ugh, why do I always think that way?

The door opens; my parents come through. Mother's green eyes brighten, but I know it's not for me. She's only hoping for an opportunity to show me that she was a good parent, that she did her duty. In my mind, I pretend she wants to come over, hold my hand, and discuss what to expect during the meeting, but she doesn't.

Father, with his browned skin and neatly cropped hair, throws me a look that I can only take to mean *don't mess this up*. He utters a quick hello before the emblem disappears again to reveal the woman. She gives them instructions like the ones she gave me. After they complete the tasks, they both sit on the couch.

I ache to ask Mother if I made the right choice with the VacTech, and to tell her of the rebel I saw on the way in, but I say none of it. Instead, we sit in silence as Father completes work tasks on his Flexx handheld. Nervous energy works its way through my body, making my head spin.

The door by the viewing screen opens, a lean woman with graying hair stepping out. "Avlyn, Mr. and Mrs. Lark," she greets. "Come in."

From the dizziness, I grab my mother's arm to steady myself as we stand and follow the woman. Mother glances at me, then the spot I grabbed, but if I let go, I'm sure to fall over. Even so, I take in a breath and release her. Three padded chairs wait in front of an enormous wooden desk. The desk is an odd sight. It's old, antique, and stands out from the functional, sleek appearance of the rest of the office. I take the first seat, my parents following behind. Some of the lightheadedness passes.

The woman rounds the desk and sits, introducing herself. "I'm Claudia Alder, and I will handle your career configuration today, Avlyn. Your parents will serve as witnesses and listen to the information to assist if you have questions during the transition period from living under their care to becoming responsible for yourself."

I rub my palms over my thighs. The hand I took the MedVac in tingles again, as if an electric pulse is running through each of my fingers. I turn over my palm to find that it's glowing.

What is going on?

I blink and the glow is gone.

I'm just nervous.

Maybe I'm not ready to live on my own. Somehow, the idea of the spouse pairings is growing more and more appealing.

Ms. Alder continues to speak, but slowly, her mouth forming words I can't hear. My hand burns, and the room rotates in slow motion. Everything in the space glows white, then falls away; the desk, my parents, and Ms. Alder. Replacing them is a tall, thin boy with shaggy, chocolate-brown hair, dressed in a navy short-sleeved shirt and tan pants.

He stands off in the distance and reaches his hand out to me. I squint. It's Ben, the way I've pictured him a thousand times in my head... if he hadn't died.

Confused, I reach toward the apparition, but just as I do, the vision dissipates. So does he, sending me back to reality with a jolt.

I twist toward Mother and Father and blink several times.

Did you see that?

Instead, they both exhibit satisfied looks and nod toward Ms. Alder. If I didn't know better, I'd even think they were almost smiling.

Is the meeting over already? How is that even possible? Didn't we just sit down?

Mother looks toward me and we lock eyes. She mouths my name, then again, except this time I hear her. "Avlyn, do you have any questions for Ms. Alder?"

"What?" I yelp.

"Do you have questions?"

I didn't hear a single thing during the meeting. What questions *should* I ask?

Deep breath, hold it, and let it out.

Keep control at all times.

When I was six, Father walked me to primer school. Out of nowhere, a malfunctioning auto taxi launched itself on to the sidewalk twenty feet in front of us. The taxi hit a woman, pinning her underneath it. Blood spilled onto the ground from a gash on her head. My screams caused as many people to stare our way as at the bleeding woman. It was as if electrical pulses in my legs were telling me to run toward her. *Why was no one helping that woman?*

Father had squeezed my hand so tight I thought it might explode. Bending next to me, he pulled my chin up until I stared into his placid, brown eyes.

"Look at me," he soothed. "You *must* be able to keep control at all times. It's essential."

Tears pooled in my eyes as I kept trying to dart my eyes back to the scene, but his gaze stayed locked with mine.

"Avlyn, focus."

Then he started breathing. Deep breaths. He held it in, then let it out. I followed him while time froze.

He breathed with me for a long time, and when we finally finished, the lady and taxi—as well as any other sign an accident

23

had even happened—were gone, taken care of by drones and security vehicles. I still don't know whether she lived or died.

I curl my fingers together and squeeze until I gain control. *Just breathe.*

"No." I clear my throat. "But I'm looking forward to beginning tomorrow." I rack my brain, trying to remember the meeting, but nothing other than the vision of Ben comes.

"Well," Ms. Alder states and rises, "if you *do* have questions, today's meeting is recorded in your citizen's account for review."

My parents stand and nod to Ms. Alder. I follow their lead, afraid the dizziness will return, but it doesn't.

Father goes to the door and gestures for Mother and me to walk through.

I tail them but turn to check for Ben again. He's gone. The top of the wooden desk displays a viewing screen. I spot my name, and beside are two words: Genesis Technologies. The top company you can be placed at as a Level Two, and the place I fear the most.

I pull my bag against my body and force myself around and out the door.

CHAPTER THREE

Out the main doors of the university, clouds have blanketed the sky, and the cold breeze bites through my long sleeves. The desperate need for air rattles my whole body, but I can manage only short gasps. My parents walk in front, and I trail behind.

How can this be true? I did everything right, blended in, acted ordinary.

"That was unforeseen." Mother's eyes gleam with uncharacteristic pleasure as she glances back at me. "Genesis Technologies was not an option we expected."

It shouldn't have *been* an option at all. I wanted an average job where I could blend in. GenTech is not for people seeing things, losing time... having a mental breakdown.

"Avlyn, go to the apartment to review the meeting," Father says. "Since your position begins tomorrow, you'll need time to prepare."

He stops to order an auto taxi with his handheld. Within seconds, a tiny white vehicle with barely enough room for three passengers arrives.

"Father, something's wrong..." I say.

"We'd take you home, but Mother and I are due at our assignments. This conversation will continue tonight."

I nod in agreement. I shouldn't have tried to tell him anyway. Father wouldn't understand.

After a few minutes, which drag by like an hour, the taxi pulls up to the front of our building. I get out, my bag still over my shoulder. Mother nods a good-bye, and the vehicle pulls away swiftly.

Whatever energy is allowing me to stand drains away in an instant. I become heavy, standing alone on the sidewalk, the only person without somewhere to be. Inexcusably, hot tears attempt to form, but I will them away, burning the back of my sinuses. Around me, the world seems to spiral. *What's going on with me?* I'm usually so good at keeping everything in. The burning in my hand returns, reminding me of my need to get to the security of the apartment.

Safe inside the elevator, I thrust my hand against the cold identification pad, and my hand stops tingling. As always, it knows where to take me. The door slides shut, and I turn to rest against the rear of the cab.

The time between the open elevator door and the security of my bed blurs together. I wish Ben were really here, and assigned Level Two instead of staying with Bess and Devan. Of course, Direction would never allow us to be reassigned together, since twins are often too emotionally connected, but maybe he wouldn't have died. I've seen the report at least a hundred times. Death due to Virus 3005B. Level Ones are the last to receive VacTech updates, and several hundred Level Ones had died over the course of twenty-four hours before they finally received the update that would have saved them.

"Why'd you have to die?"

I wait for the vision of him to return. It doesn't.

As I stare at the smooth texture of the ceiling of my room, my tears dry. This is ridiculous. How am I ever going to work for GenTech if I can't control myself? It's a waste of time to mourn for someone thirteen years later anyway. Ben is gone.

Keep your focus forward.

Move on.

Slowly, I inhale and search for my bag. The spouse pairing message alert still blinks on the media viewer. I ignore it and find the bag on the couch, plopping down next to it. Inside, I dig for my Flexx, resting beside the uneaten lunch, and launch my citizen account. My heart thumps as the emblem emerges and spins slowly on the screen. I press a thumb against the pad to open my account.

CREDITS: 10,100

My heart skips. Two times greater than expected, and I'll receive that monthly. It's more than I'll need even after moving. Maybe GenTech isn't that bad after all.

Among the messages is the vid of the meeting which includes the greeting I remember and plays through everything I missed when the vision began. I scan the recording for any sign that what I saw was real, but Ben never appears. It was only a meeting, like any other. The whole thing was in my head.

Instead, the counselor informs us of a new Direction advance, which pinpoints desirable characteristics for career configuration beyond training scores. She doesn't delve into the science, but it makes me curious. This information, coupled with my scores, decided my future at Genesis Tech. The actual position doesn't shock me—Information Security. At birth, my anticipated strength was for network systems. At age five, a confirmation test sealed my general career path.

Always wanting to keep attention off myself in training, I've hidden my ability to find security vulnerabilities in the system coding. To me, they stand out like a light, just like that girl in red stood out among the citizens in gray, black, and khaki. I guess it wasn't enough though. The testing software saw through the ruse anyway.

Why GenTech though? I wanted a position at a mid-grade company, one that was essential, but not elite. Direction will be watching me too closely there.

I shake my head and grab my lunch from my bag. The usual— a sandwich, apple slices, and peanuts. I pop a peanut into my mouth and finally check the spouse pairing message. It's merely a distraction. If nothing else, it will stop the incessant flashing of the message alert.

> *Miss Lark,*
>
> *Congratulations on Direction Citizenship. One privilege is access to spouse pairings. Four top choices are listed in your account, and as more become available, they will be added.*
>
> *As a benefit, you have two complimentary trips to any Direction-sanctioned Level Two café for a potential spouse pairing meeting.*

A spouse pairing contract must be agreed upon and officially registered within one year of turning seventeen. Otherwise, you will not be paired.

If you have any additional queries, use the search feature on any page in your account, or review the Direction FAQ. If questions cannot be answered through the FAQ or search function, connect with a Direction representative at any time.

Compatibility Perfects Us

I grit my teeth and select the link.

Here goes.

The display lists names with their matching photos. A partial description of why each is an acceptable pairing flanks each image, but I will need to individually select them to view all of the information. A quick scan of the images reveals them to all be complete strangers. Seven other universities run in Level Two, one in each Sector, and these potentials did not attend my school.

The only one who looks vaguely interesting is someone named Aron Barton. There's something kind about the expression on his face, where the others are all far too serious. Plus, his blue eyes and blond hair remind me of Kyra.

I log out. Maybe I'll look at him more later, and at least I can tell Kyra I checked if she messages later.

The sandwich sits by me, uneaten. I gaze at the perfect, frilly lettuce hanging over the sides of the soft white bread, no browning or bruises on the vegetable's surface. Food from the printer is impeccable. Optimal nutrition, yet it's not real.

None of this is real. Not me, not the spouse pairings, nor the career placement.

My stomach turns at the thought, but I lift the sandwich and take a bite. It's what I'm supposed to do.

I startle awake. The half-eaten sandwich skates from my lap, and I snatch it before it hits the floor.

Father's at the door. He places his bag on a hook and walks toward the couch.

"Napping?" he asks, a touch of disgust in his voice.

"Yeah, I guess I was." I sit up and smooth my hair.

He just stands there. "Your mother and I were shocked by the assignment. Pleased, but shocked."

"Father, when are you ever shocked about anything?"

"I'm shocked when my daughter who barely *deserves* a Level Two rank is assigned to one of the most important companies available. That's when."

A flush overtakes me. If I didn't hide my skills with systems, he would never think this. I guess I didn't conceal them well enough.

I gather my mental strength. "I'm moving out. Tomorrow."

He stiffens, probably expecting something else from me, then relaxes his stance. "Good. Maybe you will assimilate better than we expected."

More sounds come from the hall and the door opens again. Mother.

Father glances toward her, announcing, "Avlyn's moving out."

Mother turns and hangs her bag on the designated hook. Before she speaks, she straightens her grayish shirt.

"Good. You have a very respectable career placement, and will have moved well before the month grace time. This will be noted as positive on your Father's and my records."

I stand and go around her. The sandwich is still in my hand, ever perfect and fresh. I work on finishing it while I walk to my room.

I don't say another word, and I doubt they care.

At my desk, I tap the viewing screen and access my account. The instructions for GenTech tomorrow are already available, detailing where to go and what to expect on my first day. Since I'll walk there, I browse through and memorize the route to take and the layout of the building, a classified facility. I don't even want to discover what happens if I become unassigned from them. Of course, I could review the rules and regulations, but the walls seem to close in and squeeze me. I need air, and I'm not getting any in here.

A run. A fine excuse.

While changing into my running gear, the necklace from Ben falls from my pocket and onto the floor. *What to do with this thing?* I have no clue.

I snatch it from the ground, lift the mattress, and stuff it under again alongside the paper. I slip on running shoes, and fold and snap my handheld to my wrist after disabling the message function. A healthy body supports a healthy mind, so says Direction. I shouldn't even tell Mother and Father I'm going, not that they care anyway.

As I make my way through the living room, the smell of roast beef and mashed potatoes meets my nose.

"Headed to run," I call. The door closes behind me, muffling whatever Mother answers.

I burst from the building and make my way through the blandly-clad citizens returning home after the long workday. The sun has already worked its way behind the buildings. Normally, I try to run during or after training, since it lets out earlier than when citizens usually leave from work. Not all the streets are as bustling as the one in front of our apartment, so I head west on Ninety-sixth toward one offering a less congested route to the middle of the city.

The fact the park exists still amazes me, since most green spaces have been replaced with steel and concrete. Father scoffs that many people aren't ready to let go of humanity entirely. Whether I believe that to be true is another issue. Most seem ready enough to me, but the park, and a few rights, like still allowing us to birth our own children, even if we might not be able to raise them, keeps the illusion hanging on.

True or not, I'm glad it's still here.

While I jog the blocks, I pass a gym I use if I want to swim or forget to work out at training. Director Manning's face flickers on a media screen high above. His sandy hair has just begun to turn lighter at the temples.

"Curfew begins at eight p.m. For the safety of all citizens of Elore, you are required to return to your housing units by this time. Rebel attacks are on the rise..."

I check my handheld for the time. 6:14 p.m. Plenty. Manning's voice drones on.

On the next block, I pass a Direction-sanctioned café. I've never been in one. The cafés are used for meetings outside work that must be done in person. Inside sit a few couples, probably spouse pairing candidates.

Sitting with coffee and food in front of them, a girl yawns, and the guy at the same table stares out the window. If love isn't part of the mix, unlikely for those two, you at least want assurance that you don't loathe the person outright. Breaking a spouse contract is rarely permitted. It upsets the focus and training of any children involved. Choosing a spouse wisely is crucial.

Finally at the park, I breathe in deeply. The earthy smell of the grass and trees lifts my spirits. Everywhere else in the city just smells like bland concrete.

Giant evergreen trees block the view of the Level One part of the city on the other side of the park. Bess Winterly, my bio mother, lives in Sector C. I'm scheduled to meet her in a couple days.

I pant for air and slowly take in the earthiness of the grass. A familiar stone bench on the far side of the park beyond the trees welcomes me. I take a seat, resting on it, closing my eyes and clearing my mind.

Take what's offered. I'm lucky. More than lucky. Most have less.

But in an instant, my VacTech upload site begins to sting again and my eyes fly open to check my palm. Other than the sensation, it seems normal, but as I stare, a tiny flickering starts at the tips of my fingers and begins to work down my whole hand, turning it a radiating white.

I gasp and look up for help, but I'm no longer in the park. Instead, I find myself in a small room with eight incubators, lined up in two rows of four. Two of them have babies inside. The panic that just filled me strangely disappears as I walk toward the containers.

The cooing babies inside are bald and pink, swaddled in fuzzy blankets. Confused, I reach toward the first one and realize my hand has returned to normal. From behind, the door to the room clicks and whooshes back. My heart leaps as I scramble for a place to hide. There's nowhere to go though, leaving me exposed in the middle of the room.

Two female medics dressed in white step in, but ignore me. I stand frozen but quickly realize that they don't see me. I let out a long breath of relief. The first medic reaches into her pocket and pulls out a curious object, a syringe. I only know it from my history studies. As the woman approaches the child, it begins to fuss. Disgusted, she recoils her hand.

"They do that every time," says the second woman. "You'll get used to it. Most of them don't last long anyway." She takes the syringe from the first woman's hand and plunges it into the infant's arm.

The child wails, and as if on cue, I clutch my arm, now screaming in pain. A sharp cramp works through my limb. The other child joins in the chorus of screams, as does the sound of a chime. A heaving gasp of air escapes me and my eyelids fly open, relieved.

Until I see utter darkness. The sun should only be about to set.

Panic zips through my belly. City curfew. I check for the time on my still chiming Flexx, but instead find the words:

Lose your life and you might find it.

But time is running out.

What is this? There's no Flexx ID. Forgetting the vision, my hands go clammy as I frantically poke the screen, flicking my messages to on and displaying the clock. I suck in another breath, realizing I won't make it home in time for curfew. *Why did I go to the far side of the park?* If I'm caught by a Guardian and held for the night, I won't get to GenTech. A missed curfew will go on my record. It's only a first offense, but it could mean reassignment to an undesirable position, and all my new credits could be drained.

Or worse, what if a rebel attacks me?

Think, think.

The rising moonlight gleams across the skyline of Level One.

Bess. I can make it to Bess's apartment. Barely. It's a risky choice, but my options are limited.

A shadowy figure races past me in the same direction I need to go, making my breath hitch, but they quickly disappear from view through the trees.

Lose your life and you might find it.

The words intertwined with my horrific vision tumble through my mind as I race across the grass, into the streets of Level One.

Chapter Four

Level One citizens scurry into shabby apartment buildings. These people are under an identical Initiative as us, but expectations are lower, and Direction often leaves them to their own devices as long as there's no trouble.

A man ushers his spouse and a child into a building. He lays his hand on the small of the woman's back. A tiny gesture I've never seen anyone in Level Two indulge in, not in public.

As I round a corner and the family moves from view, I notice something peculiar. A boy close to my age leans against the brick wall of Bess's building. Light from an auto lamp that's just flicked on illuminates the side of his face, accentuating his square jawline. A tiny tuft of wavy hair, just slightly longer than worn by most men, peeks from the hood of his dark fitted jacket, pulled over his head. Even with the jacket, his broad shoulders reveal he's more muscular than the typical male citizen.

Despite the hustle of remaining citizens to get into their dwellings, he looks like he's waiting for a taxi in broad daylight. As if curfew didn't apply to him. The boy reaches for the cuff of his sleeve and pushes it up with his palm, revealing an antique watch.

Odd. I've seen them in my history studies, but no one wears them anymore because the Flexx is so much more useful.

I pass him and his dark eyes meet my stare. They lock onto mine, making my breath hitch. I slow to a crawl, and his lips appear to move in slow motion.

"You're late?" he asks.

"Jus… just a bit," I stutter, trying not to give away that I'm in the wrong place.

A soothing, disembodied voice announcing the three-minute warning breaks the trance at the same time my handheld vibrates. Surely it's my parents trying to reach me. They must be unhinged. Father is probably pacing the floor, and Mom's face will be scrunched up like it always gets when she's worried—something that hasn't happened in a long time.

I drive those thoughts aside, ignore the strange boy, and hustle to Bess's. The building emerges, and I give a last push to make it inside before curfew. The doors whoosh open to a modest lobby. Something about the boy bothers me again. I glance behind myself to see if he is still there, breaking curfew, but he's gone.

Thankfully, I've bought a few minutes, but could still be reported for not being inside a unit. Move. I must move. Nightmarish visions about babies in my head are one thing, nightmares in real life of being detained are quite another.

Lungs burning, I locate the stairwell and rocket up to Bess's floor. The door waits ahead, and I wave a hand over the visitor alert before bending over to catch my breath.

What if she's not home?

The thought's absurd. Where else would she be after curfew?

But it's what happened after Ben died. My bio father, Devan, just disappeared. I came for my year five visit and he was gone. When I got older, I asked Mother and Father about it, but they told me it was an inappropriate topic.

After a few seconds, I hear footsteps approaching the other side of the door. It bursts open to reveal a wild-eyed Bess, who catches my shoulders and yanks me inside the apartment.

"What are you doing?" she whispers.

Her mouth hangs open, waiting for a reply, but I'm still out of breath, and all that comes out are gasps as I suck in air. My legs give way and I slump to the floor as she closes the door.

Bess kneels beside me. "Avlyn, you shouldn't be here."

When I try to respond, I freeze under Bess's arms, which have wrapped around my shoulders. Part of me aches to hug her, relieved, but the shock of the embrace paired with the exhaustion cements my arms to my side.

"Bess," I utter, but she doesn't release me. "*Bess!*" I'd bolt if it weren't for the drones waiting outside.

"Sorry," she whispers. "You're not used to that." Bess pulls back and wipes wisps of her hair off her face. "You should be home."

"I know," I reply as unexpected tears form. My voice shakes as I try to explain. "It's my configuration day, and I went for a run, but must have been... distracted, and had no time to get home." Barely making sense, the tears start to flow, and my chin falls to my chest.

Bess cups and lifts my face. "It's okay," she sighs. "We'll figure this out. First, do your parents know where you are?"

My eyes widen. "No. I'm sure they tried to message me." I swipe away the curious words still on the screen from the message I received earlier in the park, hoping Bess didn't see them. Sure enough, I find several frantic messages from my parents. Not frantic as in they are truly worried about me, but as in they worry how it will look on them if I'm caught.

Flexx 682AB1-ALARK: I'm fine. Safe.

My hand hovers over the screen. Do I tell them more? I'm seventeen today, and I don't have to tell them anything anymore if I don't want to, but will they turn me in if they know I'm here? I don't think so. They won't risk it looking poorly on them.

But if they don't know I'm here they might report it since I could have been dragged away by rebels or something.

Flexx 682AB1-ALARK: With Bess.

I send the message and quickly turn off the messaging function for now. After a deep breath in, I look up into Bess's freckled face, much like mine, and the flowing, chocolate-colored hair skimming the bottoms of her shoulders. It's been a year, but she's barely changed.

"Not much we can do now." She gives a crooked smile. "How about dinner? Then fill me in on your day."

After the meal, I try to rise to clear my plate and recycle the picked-at food, but Bess tells me to sit and relax.

How can I relax?

Not only should I be home, but the surrounding room feels tight with loads of mementos she's gathered over the years. Our unit has nothing of the sort. A delicate figurine of a deer with pink flowers painted on it stares my way. Its gaze makes my feet twitch uncomfortably underneath the table. I try to will them to stop, but when I'm not paying attention, they start up again. Bess leaves me to sit alone, gawked at by the knick-knack, and takes the plates into the kitchen.

I break away from its stare and turn to an image viewer, fashioned from a late model Flexx, sitting on the shelf in the living room. The device flips through random still images of nature. Leaves and trees, a sunset image she could have taken from the roof of the apartment.

As I stare, my breath hitches at the next image showing Bess, Devan, and Ben. Devan is handsome, I guess—light skin, straight, chestnut-brown hair, and a shy smile. The opposite of Father, with his dark brown skin and perpetual confidence. Ben must be around four years old in the picture, with short dark brown hair, light skin, and freckles across his nose… like mine. The image must have been taken just before he died.

Bess and I typically don't discuss him much. I've always told myself the silence is for her sake. She's emotional and susceptible. In truth, I'm protecting myself.

"He would have been placed today, too," Bess says, coming back into the room. Bess's thin arms wrap around her torso, and she has a wistful look in her eyes. Usually I'd change the subject, but I can't think of anything else today.

"Bess, tell me about Ben," I whisper, expecting her to cry, but instead, she straightens and takes a deep breath. She purses her lips, and for a second, I'm sure she'll refuse the conversation we've avoided for years.

"He'd turned four a few days before that picture was taken, and a month after that, he... died."

She eyes the viewer, maybe remembering that day in her head. When she continues, her voice is shaking.

"Devan and I took it after your yearly visit, since it wasn't appropriate to take the two of you together." She pauses for a beat and looks away. "You aren't mine, but I thought it would help me remember the day better... and that you two had a nice time."

My chest tightens with her words. It's the same day Ben gave me the necklace.

"What was he like?"

"A lot like you, even though he was determined Level One." She sighs. "Reserved most of the time, unless with you."

With this, my mind sparks with a memory... or a vision? Everything goes white again and the two of us are together, just Ben and me. Such joy. Laughter. The scene vanishes and I'm left with despair. I can't see his face anymore, but a child's cry shrieks in my ears.

As fast as it came, the vision and cries dissipate.

"Did he ever cry when we were together?" I choke out.

"Oh, no." She shakes her head. "He was so happy to meet you each year, even the first time. The two of you understood each other. That's one reason we never had our meetings outside the home. You were impossible to contain... like that time in the park when you two rolled down the hill." She clears her throat. "Neither of you ever cried when the meetings ended, as if you knew you'd come together again."

The memory gnaws at me. "Are you sure?"

Bess's eyes lose focus. "I'm not sure. Maybe I've forgotten. Anyway, he always followed the rules. Ben was a good boy. The best behaved at pre-Primer school, so his teachers said. Devan and I enjoyed... raising him."

She's choosing her words carefully, I realize, avoiding the word "love" or other emotional ideas. It could be for my benefit, but maybe she doesn't trust me, or thinks I'll report her. From the watering of her eyes though, I can tell how she really feels.

She forces a smile and steps closer. "What else would you like to know?"

A million questions flutter in my mind, all out of reach. "I don't know," I lie. "That's all, I guess." Desperate to change the subject, I rack my brain for a new topic. "What time is it?"

Bess checks the time on her handheld. "Eight fifty-eight. Oh... a Direction address is on tonight regarding a new MedVac announcement. Would you like to watch it?"

I shift and rub my palm where I took my MedVac this morning, then nod. She turns on the media viewer and the two of us move to the couch.

Director Manning, a Level Three science expert, steps up to the podium. Manning must be sixty years old by now, but his body barely shows it. Medium in height, he still appears strong, and his hair only shows a small amount of gray.

"Greetings, citizens of Elore," he booms. "Tonight, I'm here to announce an exciting update concerning the latest MedVac."

I'd swear some of the tingling is back in my palm.

Manning reminds us that over one hundred years ago, the human race risked extinction from a deadly flu the government called Aves, which crossed from birds to humans. Only a limited amount of both species survived the Collapse. Scientists refined a series of vaccines combined with technology, and these have continued to keep us safe from new threats ever since. I've heard the spiel hundreds of times.

"Under Direction Science, a new, more powerful version has been developed to fight specific viruses and help build a super immune system. This newest version will make a permanent bond with your internal nano system. It is designed to evolve, as needed, to protect against any future threats. Vaccination schedules over the next two weeks will be determined by each person's Level and assignment. Citizens are required to report to assigned medical facilities or test stations for inoculation. This information is already available in your citizen's account."

His droning makes my eyelids droop but pop back open for a stern "Maintain Forward Focus." The scene shifts to Brian Marshall and an interview with a pandemic expert. A replay, I guess.

"Well, that was interesting." Bess flicks off the screen and we sit, not speaking, for what seems like a very long time.

She attempts to make small talk, and I have no desire to do that with her. Bess is weak. Emotional. Everything I'm not supposed to be but often am. I don't need more reminders.

"I'm tired," I say.

"Yes, you must be. Do you need anything before bed?" she finally asks. "I'll bring extra blankets and a pillow for the couch. It's not great, but there's no bed in the office."

I dart my eyes to the office door, the room that belonged to Ben. I have no idea why she keeps this two-bedroom. Maybe she can't bear to leave the home where he lived.

"No," I answer. "I'm set."

She rises and disappears into her bedroom, returning with the bedding.

"It's late, and I'm sure you need sleep. I'll be here if you need me."

I nod and take the bedding from her. "Thanks for tonight."

"Sure," she murmurs and returns to her room. To my relief, she doesn't give me another crazy hug.

I toss aside the linens and activate the messages on my handheld. One is from my parents, which I ignore, the other from Kyra, wondering about the meeting. After arranging the pillow and blanket, I pull the device from my wrist and message her back as I climb under the bedding.

Flexx 682AB1-ALARK: GenTech. Talk later.

I barely hit send before the world goes black.

A Guardian snatches me off the street, then drops me to the ground. I scream the whole way down.

My eyelids shoot open as I jolt and suck in air. The silhouette of the room forms around me.

Not real. Just a dream.

My body slumps with the realization.

But I am still at Bess's. That part wasn't a dream.

I lie back, mind racing with thoughts of my GenTech assignment and the vision of Ben, or some child, crying. Eyes wide, I snag my Flexx from the floor and check the time.

2:14 a.m.

Ugh, I need *sleep*, not this. I swing my legs onto the floor, not moving for a few minutes. Through the window, a limited view displays the Level One cityscape. There are Guardians in the sky, swooping in and around the city. The moon shining across the buildings makes the shadowy world outside seem like a dream.

Or a nightmare.

Searching the room, differences stand out from my functional Level Two apartment. I'm unaccustomed to all these useless items displayed on her walls and shelves: a framed painting of an unrecognized location, a collection of shells. *Where did they even come from?* You can't order junk like this from your citizen's account.

Across the room, the beady-eyed deer stares again. I walk toward the figurine, pluck the piece from its place, and rub its smooth texture. I return the delicate item to its spot on the shelf after a moment, turning it so it can't look at me anymore.

I wheel around toward the couch, but the office door catches my eye. Ben's old room.

A ghost of a memory seems to hurry past my body and race toward the door. In a blink, it's gone, but the desire to see the room is not. This is my last visit to Bess's, and the final chance to be close to Ben in some way.

On tiptoe, I step toward the office, and once there, reach for the manual handle and twist it. The door opens, revealing a desk pushed up against the wall with an active system on top, providing the only light in the room. A few plastic boxes are scattered about.

I step in further and hunt for any evidence of Ben, but it's not there. Most of the boxes are empty, and those that have something in them turn out to just be more junk.

I rack my brain, trying to remember him more clearly. Not the made up version from my head, the *real* Ben. But we were only four, how much could there be to remember?

Disappointed, I sink into a squat in front of the desk and rest my face in the palms of my hands.

Just let it go.

I wipe my eyes and start to rise when I see something peculiar. Under the desk, the baseboard of the wall is cracked. I don't know why I care. Everything in Level One seems to be shabby. Even so, I push away the chair and trace the crack with my finger.

Pull it.

I pick at the flaw with my fingernail, and a chunk of the baseboard comes free, revealing a cavity barely larger than my hand. When it does, a memory floods my brain.

This was Ben's hiding spot. That morning, he pulled the wrapped heart necklace from the hole. His little hands clutched the gift as if it were the most precious possession in the world. Ben's palms opened and he thrust the parcel into my hands.

"Hide it," he whispered. I'd quickly stuffed the unopened package into my pocket and ran out of his room back to my parents. Our visits were always quick, and only out of obligation. Direction wants us to know where we come from so there are no questions that get in the way of our focus once we become citizens.

I force my hand into the small space and feel around. To the right is something soft. I pinch for it and pull it out.

It's a stuffed creature, no bigger than my hand. From its long ears and short tail, I think it's supposed to be a rabbit, but I've only seen rabbits on the net as a past food source.

Gently, I place the rabbit aside and feel to the left inside the hole. From there, I pull a stack of folded papers, tied together with a string. It's the same brownish paper my heart necklace has always been wrapped in. I brush my fingertips over the crinkles and untie the string, then flip through the pages.

Personal letters. Before I open any, I crane my neck, looking out the door of the office to make sure there's no sign of Bess.

With trembling hands, I switch on the light of my handheld. The notes are from Devan to Bess when they were first paired. As I read them, a strange warmth fills me. In one, he confesses to Bess how nervous he is that she was pregnant with twins. Nervous, but excited with the possibilities. He loved her so much. So why did he leave?

The letters have obviously been read many times, folded and refolded into place. Some brittle edge pieces fall to the floor. The last in the stack is dated much later, right after Ben died. The writing is sloppier than the others, almost unreadable.

Bess,

I at least owe you a good-bye. Virus 3005B offered the escape I needed, one which should have been taken long before now.

Don't worry. I deleted all the files, and you will no longer have to think about what happened. I know you cannot leave, so it's better this way.

On your own, you have enough credits saved to last you. I'm sorry, but you won't hear from me again.

Devan

Virus 3005B? That's the virus from which Ben died. *Were they glad it killed him? Released them of their duty?*

What's wrong with them?

Bess acts like she cares for Ben, and even me. And Devan... he made some emotional choice and look where it got him. No doubt eaten up by wild animals, or killed by a virus in the Outerbounds.

My breath catches. This is sick. No way is love worth this. I flip through all the letters of him declaring his love, then what? *This?* They were *glad* when the virus took Ben? The whole thing disgusts me. Attachments are dangerous... Direction is right.

With shaking hands, I restack the letters, barely tie the string back around them, and stuff them back into the hiding spot, sweeping in the paper scraps that fell on the floor. Using the broken piece of baseboard, I cover the opening again.

My hands grip the lip of the desk above me and I pull myself up.

I deleted everything.

I stare at her desktop system, a very out-of-date model. Does it even still work?

Pulling back the chair, I plop into it. If there's something left on this system, I'll find it. I always do. Ben at least deserves that.

I activate the viewer and link my Flexx. Years ago, out of boredom, I programmed a data recovery program and hid it on my device, just in case.

The program runs, downloading the information to my handheld. The file I want would be old... from thirteen years ago. Most of them that old appear overwritten, but if he was really in a hurry, maybe he forgot.

I scan the recovered list.

PROGRESSIVE RESEARCH PROGRAM
WEEK 10

The words jump off the screen, and for a split second, the sound of a scream fills my mind and is gone with a jolt. I gasp and shake off the shiver threatening my body, tapping to open the file.

Test Subjects: Joy (Subject 23) and Ben (Subject 24) Winterly, Fraternal

Joy Winterly was my name before I was reassigned to the Larks.

Age: 10 weeks

That can't be right. I was assigned to the Larks upon birth, after my immediate establishment as a Level Two.

Treatment: 10 weeks of human genetic engineering to increase intelligence potential. Weekly Injection of Serum 528a to modify alleles to raise cognitive ability.

Suddenly the room grows too warm. My breathing becomes rapid, but I continue reading.

Result: Subject 23, moderate increase of fifteen points. New classification Level Two. To be reassigned.

Compensation: 100,000 credits for the successful upgrade of Subject 23.

Result 2: Subject 24, slight increase of three points. Continue with testing.

Compensation: 10,000 credits per agreed on testing round.

At the bottom is an electronic confirmation signed by Bess and Devan, allowing the testing on Ben to continue.

I was born a Level One?

The sound of a familiar whimper permeates my mind and grows into full-blown shrieking. Without a doubt the crying is Ben's. Somehow I *know* it's the same crying I asked Bess about earlier. The vision--no, *memory*--from the park overwhelms me, and I throw my hands to my ears to force the sound to stop, but it won't. I've balled up, pulling my legs from the floor onto the chair and hugging myself, rocking back and forth.

What was it the medic said?

"None of them last long."

Eventually, the sounds in my head dissipate. I let out a long sigh and quickly close out the file. I continue putting together the puzzle with quick, shallow breaths.

Direction put Ben and me through some sort of horrific study, and Bess and Devan allowed it for credits. Then Ben died from the virus, and Devan probably couldn't handle the guilt of what he'd conceded to and ran away.

Fury smolders in my center.

Noise from outside the office gives me a start, and I quickly log off the system and unlink my device. I flee to the safety of the sofa, throwing the blankets over my head.

I'm done sleeping. I've been asleep far too long.

CHAPTER FIVE

The light streaming through the living room window can't arrive soon enough. Curfew will lift soon, and I'll leave before Bess wakes. I fold the blankets and look down at my slept-in running clothes, making my heart drop. With everything that happened last night, I hadn't considered the need to go home and change before the first day at GenTech.

I check the time. 5:30. Not enough time remains to chance the extra stop after curfew lifts at 6:00, not for my first day. I'll have to borrow something from Bess.

Feeling trapped, I rub my face. I've spent years hiding emotions though. Hiding my anger with Bess shouldn't be a problem.

As a distraction, and because my stomach is growling, I walk to the kitchen to order breakfast. When Bess finally comes out, I have somehow managed to order bacon, eggs, toast, and orange juice from the food dispenser. I don't know why I ordered food for her as well as myself.

"Morning, Avlyn," she chirps. "I hope the couch was okay."

I wince but muster out an "Acceptable." Countless questions race through my mind, and I ram them away. "I ordered breakfast."

"I see that." She smiles. "What a treat to have another person prepare a meal for me."

Then we stand and stare at each other, the air sucked from the room. This is my standard relationship with Bess. Last night, I let my guard down.

My eyes tighten before she breaks the silence with a "Thank you," paired with a quizzical look. She walks toward the table to sit while eyeing my clothes. "You know, we're close to the same size. Want to borrow an outfit?"

I hesitate, but I'm paying the price of staying out too late. It's either take her offer, or arrive at GenTech in running gear.

"Yes." I sigh and wave her away, not looking.

She stands and goes into her room, returning with a smoke-gray outfit similar to the style I wear. I take it and sit, gulping my meal in silence.

"I need to get ready," I say after I've finished.

Bess looks up from her plate. "Sure. You can use my bathroom. The shower's broken in the other."

I snatch the clothes and my bag and head back through her room. Inside, I undress and stuff my dirty clothes into my satchel, then fiddle with the shower controls. The water's cold for some reason, so I make quick work and hop out to brush and dry my hair.

Shivering, I pull on the clean outfit. It's itchy, but a perfect fit. I tug at the collar. The pair of shoes Bess left is a different story. I squeeze them onto my feet, but the toes pinch. Running shoes will have to do.

After finishing, I quietly slip through the bedroom where Bess, her back to me, chooses her own clothes from a drawer. Invisibility would be a superb trait right now.

If only.

Instead, I keep my attention to the floor and tiptoe through the open bedroom door into the living room.

"Oh good! The clothes fit," she announces from behind.

I don't acknowledge her as I grab my handheld from the couch. Without warning, the media viewer bursts on with a morning auto-play of a Direction Initiative Broadcast concerning the function and relevance of each Level. I whip toward the screen and stare for a moment, transfixed.

Ask her about the experiments. About Ben.

The thoughts swirl mercilessly in my head.

"I… I need to leave," I stammer. "I'm counting last night as our last meeting."

As I turn, the corners of her mouth droop. A pang rips through my gut, but I clench my Flexx tighter. The rush of hot blood through my neck urges me to turn and bolt out the front door, but not before I get one last look at the door to Ben's old room.

I take the stairs and sprint out of the building, pausing outside to compose myself. In the daylight, the cracks in the sidewalk and the faded and peeling paint on the buildings show clearly. This part of the city is partially left over from before the Collapse, with few of the upgrades found in Levels Two and Three.

For a moment, I stand, shaking and panting. A man bumps my side. "Sorry," he mutters without turning back.

Half expecting Bess to have followed me out, I check over my shoulder, but she's not there. I turn to move, but the way to work has slipped my mind, despite memorizing the route yesterday. The recovered files and thoughts of Ben continue to spin through my brain instead.

I rub the back of my neck and exhale, long and steady. Reason returns.

I need to get to GenTech.

I lift my Flexx to order an auto taxi and go to scroll for the app, but find it's already open.

Strange. Must have launched it accidently.

I push my finger to confirm. An electric surge moves from the screen up my hand and arm. Everything goes white, and I yank my hand back, but the pain and white is gone. With a gasp, I glance at my hand and the citizens passing me to check if they saw anything, but they only pass as if the morning is like any other.

I gingerly tap the app again. No shock, but it doesn't open.

"Figures," I mutter as a public air shuttle whooshes past. I shudder at the thought of flying. Father took me on it once when I was small. Despite his urging, I screamed until we got off at the next stop. No thanks, the handheld can guide me just fine.

Overhead, the Guardian and Aerrx drones whirl, no longer spectacular. More like jailors. I push past any Level One citizens blocking my way, the scratchiness of Bess's clothes burning my skin.

As I walk, sweat pours down the back of my neck. I wipe it and check the map on the handheld. Suddenly I don't feel well at all, but if I keep focused, the trip to GenTech should take approximately thirty minutes at this current pace. There are forty-five minutes until I'm late.

Staring at the blurry, spinning screen, I make headway through the masses, but bodies seem to press into mine and push me back the other way. Everything takes on a white, hazy appearance.

Where did all these people come from?

My throat tenses. Gasping, I try to yell, "Stop, please!" but nothing comes out. Their eyes avoid mine, and people continue to press on. I stumble to the ground, but no one stops to help, so I pull in my limbs to avoid trampling feet. Attempting to stand, a hand grabs my upper arm and yanks me against the corner of a building.

I hear a muffled "Avlyn, what's wrong with you? You shouldn't even be here."

I spin to look up at my savior, the boy who was leaning against Bess's building last night. He's still wearing the same black hooded jacket, and his concerned eyes, nearly as dark as the fabric, pierce mine. Behind him, the crowd has disappeared.

I bob to see past him. "Where'd they go?"

"Who?" he asks.

"The crowd of people."

He squints slightly, giving me a confused look. "Avlyn, you need to get to work."

"Wait... you know my name?"

The boy smiles widely. "I gotta go. You'll be fine. GenTech is the right place for you."

He turns and I watch, still stunned, as the tall boy with wavy brown hair rushes down the street. He turns and taps the ancient watch on his wrist.

"You're late," he mouths.

I whip back toward the street leading out of Level One. The pedestrian traffic seems normal. Heavy, but not the same crushing mass of people as before.

Did I imagine the crowd?

Something in me wants to follow him, but he's right. I have to leave.

After a beat, I make it about twenty feet when a crack like thunder sends me flying to the ground again. Hard. With a smack, my device hits the concrete and my hands rake over the sidewalk, stinging my palms. When I look up, I'm not the only one seeing chaos this time.

Two bodies litter the ground around me. Both breathing... not dead. The scent of acrid burning fills the air, and my eyes sting. Heat brushes at my back and shoulders, and Guardian drones swarm the area. Turning, I spot the lobby of a workplace, blown apart, and three, no, at least four large drone units lying on the ground in front of it in flaming pieces.

A bomb?

All around, citizens scramble. Screams break through the ringing in my ears. Across the building behind the drones are the words:

YOU'VE BEEN LIED TO

I swivel my head around to assess the scene. I can't be here, not in Level One. There will be questions. Direction might think I'm involved.

My head clears and I look down at myself to make sure I'm all right, noticing a tiny tear in my pants on the thigh. My back and knees protest from the fall, but the chaos provides me with an opportunity to dash out of Level One. There's no one here to stop me yet.

I grab for my Flexx and bolt.

The buildings streak past, and I check the time again. Ten minutes. I speed up to avoid being late and having to explain being in the wrong part of the city.

The map on the screen marks GenTech at 164 feet away. Right on time. Sweat soaks the back of my shirt, the chilly air nipping at my skin.

Finally, when I bound through the front door, I slow to a stop. Air fights to satisfy the burn in my lungs, and when I decide I'll still live, I walk toward the open lobby.

Sterile walls reflect the polished floors; the scent of antiseptic fills the air. The ceiling extends at least twenty-five floors, and the glass walls and elevator mean there's nowhere to hide. Aerrx delivery drones float through the exposed ceiling and floors, some clinging to packages. Both humans carrying weapons and drone Guardians speckle the room. At this point, I'm unsure if they make me feel safe, or terrified.

The check-in station line waits, and I head toward it. My head pounds with each step, and my body is aching to crawl into a corner and curl up. In the reflection of a mirrored wall, I catch sight of my face, flushed and sweaty. I smooth my flyaway hair and wipe at the streaks of dirt staining my pants. Anyone might think I'd been through a war zone. Perhaps I have.

When I reach the front of the line, a petite woman gives me a once-over, eyebrows raised. I straighten and cover the tear on my thigh, meeting her gaze. Without a word, she turns back to the line. Waiting, I keep my head held high and avoid staring at any one person for too long. A floating Synthetic Intelligence attendant instructs me to touch a pad for an identity scan. Fortunately, SI don't have eyes, and *it* doesn't concern itself with my appearance.

"Avlyn Lark, please proceed to Suite 846 for orientation," the attendant says.

Immediately, my handheld vibrates, and the screen displays the identical instructions, including directions to 846.

A man behind me clears his throat, prompting me to slip out of the way. I straighten again and move over to the elevator to wait with several other employees. The transparent doors open, and we enter and begin the ascent. At floor eight, I exit the cleared doors, met by a viewer screen ahead displaying an arrow pointing to the left.

NEW PLACEMENT ORIENTATION, SUITE 846

I follow the corridor, running shoes squeaking on the polished tile. I groan and clench my teeth, then pick up my feet the rest of the way.

Inside the room, a young man sits at a table, hair combed perfectly. I don't recognize his face, and assume he must have attended another university. The boy with impeccable caramel hair stops working on a handheld and turns to me, raising an eyebrow.

A viewer screen at the front of the room displays the company logo and slogan:

GENESIS TECHNOLOGIES:
MAKING LIFE BETTER

With no place for my hands, I drop them to my side. "Is... is this the place for the orientation?" I ask.

Narrowing his brown eyes, the boy stares at me for a moment. "It is," he replies, then blinks and returns to his Flexx.

After a sigh, I find a seat across from him and try to appear busy on my device, but if anyone looked closely, they'd see I was dragging my fingers across a blank screen. I can't focus. After finding out about the experiments performed on Ben and me, and then the attack I'd just witnessed, it's no wonder. But if I look busy, I look normal.

With a flicker, the logo disappears from the screen and a man with creases around his eyes appears on the viewer.

"Greetings, new citizens," he announces.

We snap straight in our seats and repeat in unison, "Greetings."

"Daniel Carter?" the man reads.

"Present."

"Avlyn Lark?"

I swallow. "Yes."

"Welcome to your first day at Genesis Technologies," the man on the screen says. "We are pleased you will join us in aiding Direction in *Making Life Better*. My name is Neil Waters, and I will walk you through today prior to meeting your SI assistant for the week."

Making Life Better? My life could certainly get better.

A few hours later, I not only know the complete history of GenTech, but also what happens if I break their nondisclosure agreement. If found guilty, I'd be labeled undirected, re-educated, and demoted to Level One permanently. We may remove none of the system hardware from the GenTech building. Anything we used during the day must be returned to its proper place by end of day or, at minimum, we will be fined for the loss, or, at worst, relieved of our job.

Daniel looks almost bored from this morning's orientation. He probably did the research I should have. None of this is new information to him.

"Lastly," Mr. Waters says, "as the newest members in Information Security, the two of you will be competing for advancement in the division over the next thirty days. The loser will work without pay for one week, and then your salary will be reassessed. You will not be informed of the specifics, but be aware that your performance is under scrutiny at all times." Mr. Waters' face grows even more serious than it's been all day. "Keep in mind that we do not take false accusations lightly. Sabotage will not be tolerated."

The viewing screen returns to display the GenTech logo, and Daniel straightens and turns to me. "Avlyn, right?"

I nod.

"Up for the challenge?" He smirks. A calculating look washes over his face. This guy is the last thing I need right now.

"Daniel, after my morning, working here will *not* be a problem."

I don't know why I even said it. It's like it wasn't even my voice.

His eyes rake over me, making any bit of bravado shrink back.

"Let's see who gets the promotion then, since you are so confident," he replies.

I open my mouth to respond, but the SI attendants arrive to escort us. Daniel and I silently continue to the Information Security Division. The eight inches he has on me, coupled with the thick air of superiority hanging around him, makes me step to the back of the elevator. Direct competition was never part of my training at university, and now I have one more pair of eyes focusing on me.

We step from the cab onto the InfoSec floor, SIs floating alongside us. Our guides direct us to a room of drab cubicles. Daniel locates his station near the front. I'm a few cubicles down. As I move past him, his stare burns into the back of my head. I never should have responded to him that way. Remaining invisible is my way of life, why slip up today?

The other workers sit with headsets on, completely oblivious to the new girl. At least that's something.

My cubicle consists of a viewing screen with a projected keypad in front of it. To the side is a sleek, gray headset for Virtual Reality live coding tasks. I sit on the chair in front of it and connect to my new GenTech account, affixing the headset on top of my eyes. The VR activates.

INFORMATION SECURITY DIVISION DRILLS FOR A. LARK runs along the bottom of my vision as the InfoSec suite disappears and is replaced by a single stark desk with a viewing screen and keypad. No window, no other people, just me and a crude, digital version of my AI assistant. From university, I'm well aware the VR increases our productivity, but I've always hated it. It's so lonely, but that's the point.

"For the first three days, you will learn the Genesis Technologies system through practicing removing network security threats," says the assistant. "Each drill today evaluates your ability to find potential security breaches. Testing will be on speed and accuracy. Additional instructions may be found within the program. After that, you will move on with the primary Information Security team, working to keep the server mainframe protected. In addition, as a new team member, you may be required to perform physical information security. If you need assistance, you may page me." It adds, "You may take two allotted breaks a day, and a thirty-minute lunch. I will accompany you at all times for your first week."

"Thanks," I mutter, not that politeness matters when you speak to a SI. It disappears from the artificial room.

Apart from two awkward bathroom breaks with the SI outside of VR, and my first use of credits on a turkey sandwich from the eating area on the main floor, I stay locked in the mock workspace all day.

Day one of a life of lonely monotony.

After my shift, the reality of being back on the street floods me with thoughts of Ben and the knowledge that my parents are probably livid with me. The ache in my back returns.

"Avlyn!"

I swing around at the familiar voice to see Kyra jogging toward me.

"What happened?" she pants as she eyes me. "Long day?"

I'd almost forgotten about my appearance. During one break, I tried to smooth my hair out, but it didn't help much. I push a clump of hair behind my ear while heat slithers up my neck.

"Yeah, intense," I reply. "It was stupid. I... I fell on the way to work and didn't have time to go home and change."

Daniel rushes past, sending a shiver down my spine. I turn to watch him get into a taxi.

"Who's that?" Kyra asks.

Trouble.

"No one. Can we just walk?"

"Of course. I wanted to make sure you were settling in." She gestures and starts in the direction back home.

"You mean spying on me," I say, catching up.

"Spying?" Kyra gives me a look of indignation, but we both know it's true.

After our month-long transition to citizenship, we will not be allowed to see each other on a friendly basis. Direction doesn't exactly forbid it, but doing so would publicly announce our disloyalty toward the Initiative. Over the next month, our lives will diverge. Soon she'll become a memory of childhood and nothing more.

I change the subject. "I'm getting my own apartment."

"You are? Well, that's good news. Maybe there's hope for you, yet." Kyra cracks a small smile. "At least my work over the years wasn't wasted. When's moving day?"

"If I choose a unit tonight on the network without a viewing, then… tomorrow." I own little, and since the units come basically furnished, all it takes to move is packing a few bags and leaving.

"Make sure to message me an image after securing a unit," she says. "So… GenTech? How much are the credits for working there? Big, right?"

A tiny bit of tension enters her voice. Kyra has always dreamed of a top tier unit so she could imagine she was a Level Three. This is the first time I've potentially outranked her, but we'll know for sure on Monday after her configuration day.

I blow it off to make her feel better. "It's not as much as you might think."

"I figured it was only a childish rumor. I mean, why would you have been placed there otherwise?"

The comment stings, but in the end, it's my own fault. I'm the one who hid my skills all these years.

She means well, but Kyra needs some manners.

CHAPTER SIX

At the door to my unit, I close my eyes, take in a long draw of air, and release it slowly. Inside, Mother springs up from a chair in the living room, and Father comes from the kitchen. As they rush over, my muscles tighten, bracing myself for the onslaught.

"Sit down."

The words are simple, but the tension in Father's voice tells me the lecture I'm about to hear is anything but.

I slink toward the sofa, reluctantly sitting on the edge of the cushion. Mother still stands near the door, arms crossed as Father keeps his distance several feet away.

I raise my lowered eyes and make contact with Father's face.

"Well?" he finally says.

Thoughts of everything that has happened over the last twenty-four hours intertwined with excuses, swirling through my head. None of them are going to make this situation better.

"I'm packing tonight."

"Good," Father huffs and turns to walk from the room.

"You risked our reputations as upstanding citizens, Avlyn." Mother speaks in a low voice. "Don't let us hear of anything like this in the future, or we will not hesitate to report you. Your father and I will be keeping close tabs on your progress over your transition period."

She turns and leaves me with nothing to say, only a hollow in my stomach.

I have no one.

I view my unit options alone in my room late into the night. In the end, my chosen apartment is impressive. At least, I think it is. I'll know for sure when I see it in person. Of all the ones on the housing infosite, this one has the loveliest view, and is in extra-safe sector E, right next to Level Three.

After what happened yesterday in Level One, I'm glad I'll be far away from there. If I'm to succeed, I need to know I can focus on the right choices, not worry about Bess or events in Level One that are none of my business.

The few bags I have are packed and pushed into the hall. Mover drones will come retrieve them later this morning. A relief, since my back is still killing me from yesterday and my knees ache anytime I bend.

Still tired, and avoiding my parents, I sit on my bed and mull over the room around me. It's not much. Bare walls, no decorations or keepsakes. Little more than the bed and a desk that sits with a chair in front for working.

I stroke the plain bed covering. It's soft enough, but still only functional. Meant for warmth, not comfort. Nothing to miss here.

Pushing from the bed, I remember Ben's necklace, and an ache fills my chest. I kneel and run my hand under the mattress, finding the gift he gave me what seems like a million years ago. I pull out the paper and the charm falls into my hand. A lump forms in my throat as I think of what we went through, what he must have endured for four years. If the pain I felt in my vision was any indicator...

The necklace and wrapper find its way into my pocket for safekeeping.

Gathering my courage, I slip my satchel over my shoulder and leave my room. The other bags are gone.

Mother and Father are in the living room watching a news report concerning the explosion in Level One. Rebel attack, multiple injured, two dead are the words I pick up from the hall.

It could have been me that died. Would they have cared, or only been horrified to be associated with me?

From what I hear, nothing is mentioned about the words I saw graffitied on the building. *YOU'VE BEEN LIED TO.*

I straighten and make a beeline for the door. If my parents wanted to say good-bye, which I highly doubt, I don't give them the opportunity, but the ache in my heart follows me.

❈ ❈ ❈

A blast of wind blows from behind me as the taxi pulls away from the curb, and I'm left alone on the relatively deserted sidewalk. The building before me is towering and smooth, practically liquid, built in the last few years. Anyone would be glad to live here, and now I do, in unit 2438.

A willowy girl with long black hair approaches the entrance and goes inside. I take it as a cue to follow. Once inside, I fall in line as she waits at the elevator.

To pass the time, I stare at the light above the doors.

"New in this building?" asks the waiting girl.

At this, I flinch. Why is this person talking to me? I lived in my parents' apartment for seventeen years, and I don't believe I knew one of the other families that lived in our building, let alone would recognize someone new to the building.

"Um, yeah. Moving in today." I flick a glance her way, and she stares back with kind, russet, eyes. A nervous pang in my stomach makes me turn away. I don't need distractions.

Focus.

With a chime, the elevator doors finally open. Inside, she lays a hand on the pad and I follow. Both for floor twenty-four. Shaking my head, I wrap my arms around myself and lean on the back wall of the cab. When the doors slide open again, my legs want me to bolt out, but I let her lead. No need to be followed.

I check the directory for my unit number and spot it. It's the same way the young woman is headed.

Of course.

Trying to disappear, I clutch my bag against my body and put one foot in front of the other, keeping a safe distance. Eventually, she stops, opens her door, and disappears inside. I check for mine and suppress a laugh. It's right across the hall from hers.

Shaking my head, I go to open my unit.

"Congratulations on your new apartment," the girl calls from behind me.

I jump as her door shuts, leaving me alone in the corridor.

Safely inside, I turn and rest against the door while pinching the bridge of my nose. Finally peering up, an astonishing view of the city greets me, and I forget about the girl.

My unit is close to the top of the building, and allows me a wide-angle vista of Level Two. The Representative building, taupe with a white domed top, is in plain view, and behind it is Level Three. Level Three has the tallest and most spectacular buildings of all, their rooftops glaring in the sun, making me squint. A view isn't necessary, but still a welcome, private perk. Kind of like a birthday gift to myself.

Below, the sidewalks are nearly emptied of citizens. If Elorians don't work on the weekend, many of us remain in our apartments, safe.

I drop my satchel on the dining table and notice my other bags have arrived. The unit is modest and functional, but cozy. I'll enjoy curling up here after a long day at work, if the neighbors leave me alone.

I stuff my hand into my pocket and find the necklace Ben gave me. The mattress provided a good place to stash it before, so I shove it under the one in my new bedroom.

Kyra wanted an image of the unit once I arrived, so I flop on the bed and swipe the screen of my device to send her one from the listing.

Lost time is never found again.

My eyes widen.

What is this?

It's another message like the one I received at the park. I just want a normal life, to do what I am supposed to, but a report could bring attention on me, and I am *not* normal. They may find out I spent the night at Bess's.

What if they discover I'm having these visions? Direction could bring me in for testing again.

Ignore it. Act ordinary. Be an exemplary citizen.

I swipe the words away, unfold the device into a tablet, and find the spouse pairing section of my account. Something normal, and better than weird messages, nosy neighbors, and seeing my dead brother.

Four choices await me. Two have already sent invitations. I ignore the first one, but the other's from the guy named Aron Barton, the one I noticed when I first checked.

5'10"

Five inches taller than me.

Blond hair

Blue eyes

And he has the same tanned skin as Kyra.

Career Placement: Syn Corporation

Division: Electrical Engineering

Compatibility: 98%

Like GenTech, SynCorp is another high-ranking company, but specializing in drone manufacturing.

He seems okay. Why not?

According to Direction, he's 98% perfect. I select the *AGREE TO MEET* button, *No turning back now,* and hide the other invitation. Then I flick off my handheld, fold it, and snap it to my wrist. My right leg bounces with energy, despite my stiffness from yesterday. I crave a run, but my bruised knees have other ideas, like staying in on my couch. Despite the view, being cooped in here lacks appeal.

A walk. That would work.

My knees concede to the idea, and I pull my running shoes from one of the packed bags in the living room. They're scuffed, probably from my fall yesterday. I make a mental note to order a new pair. The scuff isn't a big deal, but the memory is, and I can afford them now.

On the street, the warm afternoon air brings new life into my lungs. The sunlight slides over the buildings, and seeing the rays turns up the corners of my mouth. Just to be sure, I check my Flexx for the time. Hours and hours before curfew.

"Do you have the time?" a familiar, deep voice asks from behind.

My stomach clenches as I whip around to look at him. Our gazes lock, and I'm certain it's the guy from Level One. Tall, muscular, eyes so dark they're nearly charcoal.

I step back. What if *he* was involved in that attack?

"You weren't hurt, were you?" he whispers.

I shift and march away from him, but my leg muscles stiffen. As his footsteps close in, my heart picks up speed. A woman across the street pauses to watch, but then moves on. This has to stop.

I swing around to find his body inches from mine.

"What? What do you want?" I whisper. I long to scream at him, but it would draw too much attention.

He raises his eyebrows and shifts back, but then his lips curl into a smile. He's wearing the same drab clothes everyone else wears, but he's different, charming. Something about the sparkle in his eyes draws me in.

I tilt my head and will the thoughts away. My fists tighten. "You find this funny? Are you sending these messages?"

"No, no... it's not funny. But yes, I did send the messages." He smiles again. His straight teeth beg me to punch them.

"Why are you bothering me?" I demand lowly. "Did *you* have something to do with that explosion?"

"We had nothing to do with that." His hands slip into his pockets and reveal the top part of a black watch. Peering toward the ground, he murmurs, "I *helped* you when you were freaking out."

He did, and I'm grateful. To be honest, he seems sincere. Something in me begs to trust him.

No... concentrate. This guy may be a terrorist.

With a sudden burst of bravery, I square my shoulders toward the boy. "In no way does the favor excuse you following me. *Stalking* me."

He doesn't respond to the statement. Instead, he gestures down a different sidewalk. "This route is safer."

A security vehicle passes and I lower my voice even more. "Safer? What do you mean *safer?*"

He tips his head. "I mean less surveillance, Avlyn."

"Maybe I want *more* surveillance." I don't, but he doesn't need to know that.

He rolls his eyes and crosses his arms. A Guardian's whirring sounds above the building, reminding me of the need to end this conversation quickly.

"You need to leave me alone—whoever you are."

"Meyer. My name's Meyer."

I turn, and those knees that didn't want to run earlier change their mind.

Fortunately, I'm wearing running shoes, even if they are scuffed.

CHAPTER SEVEN

"No, stop!"

The words whirlwind in my brain, and a scream grows in my throat, but no sound comes. My lungs refuse the air buffeting my face and body. My heart threatens to escape my chest through brute force.

A Guardian hovers above, its long, unending metal tentacles snaking and squeezing around me. I rip at them, but my wet palms slip from their surface. I writhe through the freezing air as I'm carried hundreds of feet over the city. The hair on my arms and neck pricks up over my skin. Tightness spreads over my back, and I try to wrap my arms around myself to stop my shaking, but they're trapped.

The stone detention center I've seen on the newscasts whooshes into view. Blazing orange flames consume the building, and swarms of drones drop other people into the inferno. One swoops past, clutching the rebel girl with the brown skin from the other morning. Her bright fabric has become flowing, and streams across the sky like a crimson banner. She screams and flails as the

Guardian dumps her. The blaze devours her body and greedy flames kick into the ash streaked sky.

I recoil when the scent of black charcoal mixed with sulfur assaults my nose.

Burning people. Burning rebels.

"Not me! I do what I'm told." The words eventually escape my lips, but the uncaring, unhearing drone does its job. Disposing of me.

"We have to take care of you like we took care of Ben," the drone says in a mechanical voice.

My handheld buzzes in my pocket, and I wrestle to slip it out. My eyes sting and water from the soot, but I make out a blurry **Avlyn, you are running out of time**.

I scream, my legs pushing out against my bindings. A pop and crunch compels me to strain harder against the loosening restraints until they give way.

I surge upright, screaming, "Get off me!" I gasp and rip and claw at the tentacles still coiling around me...

Except no metal exists. Only fabric. Only my sheets.

I finally kick the cloth off and fall back into the bed. My veins threaten to explode from my racing pulse, and a caustic scent still works its way around my nose. I roll over and curl up, hugging myself. My teeth chatter, synchronized with the shudder traversing my spine.

My shaking slows, allowing reality back inside. I push up and rest against the headboard. I don't even know how I got to sleep after that boy... Meyer, tried to corner me on the street earlier.

Do what I'm told. Ignore the undirected.

I swing my legs off the bed, then get up to activate the system on the desk. I spot my account link and swipe the screen.

ONE NEW SPOUSE PAIRING MESSAGE

Yes. A perfect distraction.

MESSAGE FROM ARON BARTON

Avlyn Lark,
I request an initial spouse pairing interview. It has been determined we are a 98% match for producing Level Two or higher children. This is a favorable percentage.

I scan the rest. Ah... a normal guy. A normal guy without a watch. One that doesn't give me nightmares, looking to meet for dinner tomorrow at a nearby Direction café.

In front of the café, I check the time. Early. Why my stomach is churning like a whirlpool, I don't know. The meeting isn't about love, right? This is only to talk. A duty. Who cares if we're not a fit, it's what I should be doing. Forgetting the past. Forgetting my twin.

When I step in toward the door, it glides open. Two of the tables are occupied with couples. No one's waiting for their appointment.

I should leave, message whatshisname... Aron Barton. Tell him I'm sick.

No. You can do this. You work at a prestigious company and are an upstanding Direction citizen.

"You're an early bird, too?" a tenor voice asks.

I turn to the same face and electric-blue eyes from the spouse pairing account. Aron's face is kind, still boyish, but handsome. He has a runner's build.

I wouldn't hate looking at that every morning.

I blush at these new feelings.

His eyes squint as he smiles. "It's a positive quality." I must look puzzled, because he leans in and whispers, "Being an early bird."

"Why do people even use that phrase?" I say, gazing toward the sky. "See any birds?"

It's a dumb reply and I know it. He looks at me quizzically for a moment, raising an eyebrow. "Let's go in." He gestures toward the door, allowing me to go first.

I suck in air and walk to the reporting station to check in. We find the assigned table and sit on well-stuffed seats in a similar blue tone as the walls. Aron grabs a menu screen from a rack on the table. The thin, sturdy viewer displays the dinner choices. I remove mine, but lay it in front of me.

"So, your job configuration's at SynCorp?" I get right to business.

Aron nods, but goes back to the menu. He must find me boorish after my comment outside. I know the answer to my question from the spouse pairing account, but need to get him talking so the meeting isn't a total loss.

"What department are you in?"

He glances up from the menu. "Engineering. You're in InfoSec, right?"

"I am. Did you start with training drills too?"

"Yeah. For the next couple days, drills are my life." He relaxes and grins, showing off a dimple in his right cheek I didn't notice in his spouse pairing image. It adds to his boyish appeal.

For the meal, I choose a chicken salad with star fruit, and he orders a turkey club with an aioli sauce. Aioli hasn't been an option on the home printer. We barely have time for two words before the server drone delivers the meal.

"Miss Lark, Mr. Barton," the SI server says, "please let us know if you require anything else." It places the plates in front of us, then hovers away back into the kitchen.

"Well, this looks intriguing," I say, eyeing my plate and then Aron's.

He checks out the salad. "Ever had a star fruit?"

"No, but the name accurately describes the shape." I poke at the produce.

"What do you guess it tastes like?"

"Here, take one," I offer.

Aron hesitates but takes the piece from me. He turns it over, inspecting, and then smells the yellowish fruit. "Think food from the printer tastes comparable to grown food?" he asks.

I smile. "Aron... I've thought about it more times than you can imagine. To be honest, I've even had a few weird dreams about it."

He raises his eyebrows. "Okay, you try it first."

I pop a piece into my mouth and crunch on the sweet, tart fruit. I give him a smirk.

"Good?" he asks.

"Find out yourself."

He munches on the fruit, cerulean eyes sparkling with some sort of mischievous thought. I thought I'd find Aron to be stiff and boring, but he's not.

He leans in and signals for me to do the same. I hold my breath and bend toward him, wondering what he's going to do.

"Tastes like... star fruit," he says. He shrugs, then raises his sandwich and takes a bite.

I chuckle and push my back into the chair. Maybe the whole spouse pairing system is not as bad as I thought.

During the rest of the meeting, I learn his parents were bio, and he attended the university on the opposite side of Level Two as mine. He has lofty goals of working up the ranks at SynCorp.

"The drones have always fascinated me, even as a child," he says. "So when I received a position at Syn, it fulfilled a lifelong dream. I'll be creating new drone technology."

"How was it on Friday after the... uh... *incident* in Level One?"

"Oh, interesting. The other recent placements and I were tasked immediately. We didn't have the training introduction until end of day. How did you know?"

I try not to react, but my face burns red. "I saw the story on the news."

"Yeah, the news." Aron shakes his head. "To tell you the truth, it was chaos at Syn. The whole day was spent working on upgrades to prevent an attack from happening again. Somehow the rebels infiltrated a Guardian drone and made it into a bomb. In the end, we upgraded the security. It could have been much worse."

"What do you mean?"

"If the attack had happened in Level Two or Three." He shrugs nonchalantly. "It's only Level One."

A knot pulls in my stomach at his opinion, but his attitude doesn't surprise me. It's how we're taught, and I've had similar thoughts. Bess is ranked beneath me, and right now, any thoughts of her make me grind my teeth. Maybe she is of less value, but Ben? Was he?

My stare bores a hole into the table.

"Are you ill?" Aron asks.

"Those are *people* you're talking about," I reply softly. "They could have *died.*"

"What, did you know one of them?"

"Not that day, but yes. My twin brother died from Virus 3005B because his sector was one of the last to get the MedVac update."

"You had a Level One twin?"

I smack my hand over my mouth. I've never told anyone outside my family about Ben except for Kyra.

"Well?" he asks.

I shift in the chair. *Is it really hot in here?* The girl from the next table looks up from her meal and stares my way. Did she hear me too?

"Well, I enjoyed this," I lie. "Thanks for requesting the meeting, but I have to go."

I rise, wave a backhanded good-bye, and turn to leave. As I bolt for the door, he says something I can't hear.

❈ ❈ ❈

"Well, that was terrible," I mumble, hugging myself tighter as I walk. I ruined my chances with a guy I could stand, possibly even care for. Sure, he thinks the Level Ones are inferior… and I guess they are. Aren't they?

The rest of the way home is a blur until I round the corner of the block of my building. My Flexx vibrates on my wrist, so I stop and check the message. For a moment, my heart does a little dance. Some chance remains the pairing meeting didn't go as lousy as I'd thought.

Sorry.

The word makes my pulse speed. I'm right. But then I notice the lack of Flexx ID. Meyer? My fluttering heart drops to my stomach.

Sorry I scared you, but I need a chance to explain. If you don't like what I have to say, I won't contact you again. I found a safe way to meet. Check your spouse pairing account.

I scroll to my citizen account and locate the report suspicious behavior page. I stare at the words… and then navigate to my spousal account.

ONE NEW SPOUSE PAIRING OPTION ADDED.
CLICK HERE TO VIEW.

I grit my teeth and select the link.

Kian Martin.

Whose wavy brown hair, light skin, and piercing, charcoal eyes look a lot like Meyer's.

Apparently Meyer, at least as Kian, is now a perfect pairing.

CHAPTER EIGHT

After seeing Meyer's face in my account, I rush from the street and into my unit, stunned he hacked into the system and assigned himself as one of my pairings.

The nerve.

Inside the door my handheld buzzes, and without looking, I rip it from my wrist and hurl it across the room, hitting and knocking over a lamp.

Fantastic.

Whatever's on the screen, I can't deal with it. Tomorrow, I'll go back to a normal life at GenTech, but right now, I only want sleep, even though it's barely after seven. I stand, shuffle to my bed, and try to forget today ever happened.

Hours later, unable to sleep, I pull myself up and press my back against the headboard. The scene out the window appears lovelier at night than during the day. If I strain, I can even glimpse the trees at the park backlit by moonlight.

The beauty almost makes me forget about my terrible day. Almost.

I swing off the bed again and pad over the carpet into the living room, where the fallen lamp still waits next to my flashing device. I reach to retrieve the lamp, but grab the Flexx instead. Biting my lip, I swipe the screen, then relax. The message from Meyer is gone.

TWO NEW MESSAGES ADDED.
CLICK HERE TO VIEW.

I tap the link, finding the messages are from Kyra and my mother.

Good job throwing it across the room for nothing.

Flexx 35D52G-KLEWIS: I'm so nervous for tomorrow.

Even Kyra, in all her perfection, is afraid.

Flexx 682AB1-ALARK: It will be wonderful. Let me know how it turns out.

Although, I'm not really qualified these days to say everything will turn out wonderful. However, it's a lie I can live with, for her sake.

I swipe Mother's message next.

Flexx 813JK9-DLARK: We are required to assess your progress. We will complete this obligation next Friday at dinner.

Then their duty to me will be done. After, they'll take on more rigorous work schedules or raise another child or two. Kyra was her parents' second child. Mother and Father are still fairly young, but I never asked which route they'll take.

Flexx 682AB1-ALARK: Dinner at 6:30 p.m.

My first week on my own goes smoother than expected. According to the news, nothing of interest happened in the entire city. I was even able to keep the thoughts of Ben at bay, and there were no other visions. I'm beginning to think it was all nerves.

GenTech is unremarkable. Training drills wrap up, and I move onto the primary InfoSec team. My current responsibility is to make sure the lab department is archiving research daily in the mainframe. As a new placement, my responsibilities remain limited, but I'm at least trusted enough to find my own way around the building. No more bathroom breaks with the Syn Intelligence.

Kyra received her career placement on the Level Two Direction Government staff, a surprise. It's an entry-level assistant position, but still exciting. We were sure she'd be placed in the Legal Services Division, not government. Maybe her parents *were* able to influence the choice. Her first week must have kept her busy though, as Monday was the last time she checked in.

I've adjusted my schedule to that of my weird neighbor, successfully avoiding her and keeping to myself, but there's still nothing from Aron after our disastrous meeting. I'm sure he finds me a lunatic, but he hasn't removed me from his contacts.

One more time, I check to see if Aron sent a message.

ONE NEW SPOUSE PAIRING MESSAGE ADDED. CLICK HERE TO VIEW.

My heart vaults as I swipe the link, but the message is not from Aron. Instead, a face with a chiseled jaw and striking eyes stares up from the screen. Kian Martin, or rather, Meyer.

His image displays right next to the message:

KIAN MARTIN REQUESTS TO SCHEDULE A SPOUSE PAIRING MEETING. ACCEPT OR DECLINE.

I tip back from the screen, wrinkling my nose. There's not one good reason I haven't deleted his whole profile already. Curiosity is the one thing holding me back from the life of an upright citizen, but I can't click the X on the options. Each time I consider doing so, I close out the account.

I sigh and close it. Again. My parents will be here in thirty minutes. Now is the time to tidy up, order dinner, and stop concerning myself with mysterious boys *not* acting as model citizens. I have to show them I'm capable.

The meal waits on the table by the time the door chimes. They're right on time, as always. I stand at the door, hand poised over the sensor, mulling over all my answers to their impending grilling, but the possibilities are endless. I'll do my best to satisfy them, but it's unlikely it will be enough.

My touch releases the sensor and the door whooshes back. Mother and Father stand at the entrance. She's made of stone, and Father's buried in his Flexx. All tonight means is the ability to tick off their obligation to me, regretful they ever agreed to raise a child born to a Level One. I'm sure they have no idea I actually began life ranked as a One either.

I gesture for them to enter. Mother steps inside first. "Hello, Avlyn," she says coolly.

Father is even more aloof than usual. Probably still working, as he hasn't even looked up yet.

Mother darts her eyes around to take in the room and view. Somewhat satisfied, she relaxes and turns back to Father, still standing in the hall, swiping at his screen.

"Michael, come inside."

Father glances up. "Oh, yes," he mumbles as he returns the handheld to his pocket.

"Dinner's ready," I tell them. "Why don't we eat, and then I'll give you a tour?"

"We won't be here long," Father says.

Mother turns toward him. "It might be fine to stay for a meal."

Father narrows his eyes. "No, we are here to finalize the end of our contract with Avlyn."

"It's fine," I sigh. "Have your look around and complete your duty."

Father eyes me, but says nothing. Mother avoids my face altogether. I plant myself in the unit's entrance and motion for them to take a look around.

After a few minutes, they return, Father with his Flexx as a tablet and the contract on the screen. He points to a spot to push my thumb to confirm my agreement. The device beeps, and he quickly folds it up and slaps it to his wrist.

As they turn to exit, an auto broadcast flicks on the screen of the large media viewer in the living room.

"Citizens, please wait momentarily for a required message."

Father sighs and turns back to the screen.

"Citizens of Elore," an unidentified male voice begins. "As you well know, a terrorist group who has yet to identify itself has increased its attacks on our great city."

An overhead view of a busy morning street scene shows on the viewer.

"We implore anyone who witnessed any of these recent attacks to come forward for questioning. Doing so will help Direction ensure the safety of its entire people."

My heart skips. Footage from the morning of my configuration day shows, when the girl in red graffitied the wall with *Break Free*. I don't even hear what the announcer is saying, watching the moment right before the Guardians take her down, the moment she gave up without a fight.

I wanted to help her, but didn't. I wait for her hands to fly into the air as the drones surround her, but they don't. Instead, she does the opposite and reaches for her bag, swiftly pulling out a small, matte black weapon. She points it at the drones, the same weapon she graffitied the wall with, as my mind races with confusion. As she does this, the drones swarm, never letting her get a shot off.

"That's not what happened!" I yell at the screen.

Mother whips toward me. "You were *there?*"

I freeze. "The morning of my meeting."

"Why didn't you inform us of this?" Father demands. "You must come forward."

"And tell them what?" I snap. "That the footage is all wrong?"

Mother stands, shocked at my outburst, and Father tenses, trying to maintain his control.

"Avlyn," he says in an annoyingly too-calm voice, "you are letting your emotions get away with you. Direction's actions are for our protection. This terrorist group wants to take away the success we have built, probably for themselves."

"You must have been frightened and aren't remembering correctly," Mother adds. The look on her face and her words don't match though. For some reason, part of her believes me.

The broadcast has ended and the room goes silent.

I square myself. "You have what you came for, now please leave. You are no longer responsible for me."

Father locks eyes with me for too long, but then looks away. "Let's go, Darline."

Mother falls in line behind him as they exit my unit.

When the door slides shut, I release a long breath. My mind drifts back to the rebel girl, her striking red outfit, her browned skin, and wild, curly hair.

I know what I saw. She *was* trying to make a statement, but it wasn't through violence. The rebellion is not what Direction is making it out to be. If they're lying about this, is there a chance that the rebels causing the explosion in One could be a lie too?

Who am I to question Direction?

I slump and rub my hands over my face. No answers and no one to confide in.

Except...

I pull up my citizen's account and access my spouse pairing options. There's still a request to meet from someone who just might be able to answer my questions.

I poise my finger over the link as nausea wells inside me.

I accept it.

At least I know who I am.

I'm a traitor.

CHAPTER NINE

Somehow I fall asleep, but my dreams fill with images of my parents being taken away. I'm dragged out of GenTech in front of Kyra and Aron. Mother and Father are questioned and then charged with treason. My fault, just like they said. Aron screams he knew I was damaged and holds a weapon to my head.

When I awake, I'm the one screaming.

If I was normal, a good citizen, Aron would be the perfect pairing Direction has deemed him. Sure, it would be a life of duty and unanswered questions, but I'd be safe. Maybe I'd be happy, too.

I shuffle out of bed to wash my face. The dim auto light flicks on, and I squint and tug at the purple tint under my eyes reflected back in the mirror. If this keeps up, I'll need to order the anti-stress MedTech from my citizen account.

Instead, I wander into the living room for some relaxation exercises Father taught me. Keeping calm will be my best defense. The flowing motion and steady breathing of the exercises help, and I'm able to settle again, but not enough to sleep. I sit and watch a rerun of the news story on the thirty-five years of Compatibility Pairing and Birth Reassignment.

"A young and upcoming Level Three scientist named Colin Manning is working on an exciting project to pinpoint intelligence potential," a female narrator says. The vid flips over to a man in his late twenties in a white smock. Director Manning.

"Our current endeavor exhibits great possibility for the future of Elore, of humanity," young Manning says, his gray eyes shining.

I fast-forward through the rest to a section showing two members of the Direction Council stepping down. Two women stand at a podium. One speaks.

"This evening, Director Fisher and I will be voluntarily resigning from the council."

I tap her face. *ADRIANA RUIZ, FORMER SOCIAL RIGHTS DIRECTOR* pops up on the screen.

"I know I speak for the two of us when I say it has been a privilege to serve Elore, but a season of change is necessary."

Director Ruiz glances at Manning. He nods, and she returns to her notes.

"Colin Manning has tirelessly worked on advancing the Direction Initiative in the science division of Level Three. Over the last five years, he has worked on many different methods for advancing our healthy society, but the one with the most promise is called the Birth and Compatibility Measure. Because of this new course of action, Colin Manning and Lewis Patel will replace us as additional Science and Engineering Directors."

Maybe I already knew this had happened, but this information is usually glossed over in university. Always forward focused, rarely looking at the past. I can't even remember Fisher and Ruiz being mentioned. And Patel? He works under Manning now.

I flip away from the vid and find reports on both the graffiting rebel girl and the drone "incident" in Level One. Both are inconsistent to what I remember, and there's no mention of the words on the buildings either time. It's like Direction is trying to hide that part and only focus on activities they label as terrorism.

I log off and switch over to the spouse pairing account.

ONE NEW SPOUSE PAIRING MESSAGE ADDED.

My stomach lurches when I see it's from Meyer.

Thank you for accepting my request. Meet at Direction Café D at 9:00 a.m.?

Nine? He's assuming I'd even check for a message tonight and then be available so quickly. I inhale deeply and keep the response short.

Yes. See you then.

I wave the screen off and stare at the blank viewer for way too long.

Out the window, one of the screens on a nearby building catches my eye. The globe of Direction's logo spins, and under it display the words: **STAY FOCUSED.**

If I only knew *what* exactly to focus on.

The Saturday morning news means Brian Marshall is reporting again, detailing recent rebel arrests. The girl from the street who graffitied "Break Free" on the side of the building might be among the detainees shown.

These types of people are typically incarcerated at the edge of the city and re-educated. After, they might spend the rest of their lives working in a factory, but Brian announces upcoming changes in the Direction policies, and to stay tuned for a special report and announcement from Director Manning on Monday evening. When it ends, I try to turn it off, but a Direction Initiative Auto Broadcast plays and I can't. I walk into the other room.

Thirty-two minutes until the meeting with Meyer.

On the way to the café, I yank on my black, stretchy top and straighten any potential wrinkles at least five times, although the fabric doesn't even crease. The streets are mostly deserted, since few citizens work on Sundays. Still, a few pass on the way. Are they loyal, or imposters like me?

Everyone has secrets.

A woman with chestnut hair hanging too far over her eyes glances in my direction. I feign my attention the other way.

At the same Direction Café I met Aron, I peek through the window to check if Meyer has arrived. He hasn't, but if I need to make a getaway, it will be easier from out here. I keep my gaze on the ground. No more gawking at people passing by.

8:59 a.m.

My breath grows shallow, and I grit my teeth. I could go, change my mind. No one would ever have to know I came.

"Hello," a low voice says behind me. Meyer.

I look up at his tall frame. Pale skin, but slightly darker than mine. Short, inky-brown hair that's slightly wavy. It's the first time I've had more than a few seconds to really get a good look at him.

"Um… K-Kian?" I ask.

He tips his head and gives me a crooked smile. "Yes. Avlyn?" He holds out his hand for me to shake.

My lips tighten, but I take his hand and grip hard, continuing to stare straight into his slate eyes. The smile widens, giving me the sudden desire to punch him again. This is meant to be serious, not funny.

"Should we go in?" I ask through clenched teeth.

His hands slip into his pockets. "No. I never confirmed the reservation."

"What?" I check to make sure no one is watching. "You're the one who asked to meet."

"Yes," he answers in a whisper, "but it's not safe. We need to go somewhere else."

My feet seem to sprout roots and grow into the sidewalk. I have no idea who I can really trust anymore.

"I want to be out in the open."

Shaking his head, he says, "Oh, not a problem. I know all the spots." He walks quickly down Fourth Avenue and signals me to follow.

I reluctantly uproot, calling, "Hey, slow down."

He does so I can catch up. "Sorry, I'm just ready to get away from here." He stuffs a hand in his pocket again, but keeps walking. "This way." He nods toward the road leading to the park, a route I generally take on runs.

"The park?" I ask dubiously. I'd presume Guardians would keep a close watch in such a place.

"You'd be surprised at a few of the locations where they're lax," he says. "Direction believes they're doing what's right for Elore, and that people will simply fall in line." He turns and grins at me. "It will be fine."

Fine? Right. The thought of following him nearly paralyzes me, but not knowing what he has to say will drive me crazy. It's already hard enough to sleep.

"Lead the way."

Our feet hit the soft grass, and a strange mix of both anticipation and relief rushes through me.

This is almost over.

He leads me under a tree and slides down against the trunk. Lifting up, he pulls a Flexx from his back pocket and swipes at the screen a few times.

"There." His eyes meet mine. "We're secure. Have a seat a few feet away. Just act like I'm a spouse pairing you barely care about meeting."

"Which is sort of true... right?" The only reason we're meeting is his fake account.

He ignores me, but he's right. If we're casual, no one will even care. I settle on a spot with sun coming in from the branches above us. After a few seconds, I turn to the side enough to see him. Let's start this thing.

"First, I need you to tell me why you're here," Meyer says.

Nervousness sweeps over me.

Why am I here?

Is it the experiments Direction did on Ben and me, the weird visions, or seeing the changed coverage of the girl rebel? What if I imagined it and she really did reach for another weapon? She could have been trying to kill us all. What if the visions just mean I'm crazy? Instinct urges me to run, but I lock onto his face instead, and a strange calm befalls me. His expression is genuine, like he truly cares about what I have to say.

"Um…" There's no way I can tell him about the visions. "Last night I saw something on the news. It wasn't right."

Meyer cocks his head in interest. "What was it?"

I mull over the scene on the viewer and compare it to my memory. "On my Configuration day, on the way to university, I saw something. A rebel… attack. But it wasn't. The girl didn't do anything but graffiti a phrase on a building, but…"

Meyer winces slightly, then nods for me to continue.

"When I saw her do it, I even thought, 'She's not going to fight'. And she didn't, she gave up easily. But last night… the broadcast showed her pulling out some sort of weapon before the drones took her down."

"And you are sure that's not true?"

I pause for a beat and run the two scenes through my head again. "I'm sure."

Meyer lets out a long sigh. "Okay. I sent the messages to your handheld. My assignment is to bring you into a group called Affinity, who wishes to stand up against Manning and his lies."

They want me *to be a rebel?*

"Why?" I ask. "What's special about me?"

"I'm only the messenger, but something tipped them off that you'd be a good fit." His dark, probing eyes meet mine, and something about their intensity makes my stomach flip. "Were they wrong?"

Embarrassed that he might sense my feelings, I break eye contact. "No, they weren't wrong, but..."

On some level, I've always wanted more than this existence, knowing things were not right. Even as a child, I knew if Ben had lived, I'd want to be allowed to see him more than once a year.

"But what?"

"I don't feel as if I have much to offer. And the risk..."

"I can imagine it's a difficult choice when this is all you know."

I swing around to face him. "Wasn't it for you?"

"I never really had to make it," he replies, shrugging.

"Why not?"

He sighs. "We're not here to talk about me."

I shoot him a sarcastic smile, but quickly hide it. "How else am I supposed to trust you?"

Meyer pinches his lips together, giving me a frustrated look. "Fine. I'm not a citizen. In their eyes, I don't exist. I was born in the Outerbounds."

The Outerbounds?

My ears perk up.

"My parents escaped Elore and lived outside the city. They were killed fifteen years ago. A man named Jayson was heavily involved in Affinity as he raised me, so I kind of became a child of Affinity."

At this point, I feel somewhat guilty I'd even asked. I'm no stranger to the effects of having someone you love die.

"I'm sorry," I say. "It must have been difficult to grow up without a stable home."

"Thanks, but don't be. The past made me the person I am, and to be honest, I'm honored to be involved. Sure, I wish I knew them, but I imagine they'd be proud of who I've become. My parents gave their lives for this cause."

His last words smart. Would I die for Affinity?

"People live outside the perimeter?" I ask. "I thought outside the city boundaries were dangerous."

His eyes snap to mine. "*Direction* is dangerous."

Questions reel in my mind. I know Direction is lying, but how bad is it? "But why did Affinity attack Level One?"

"Affinity wants to *free* people, not kill them." He snaps up, his stare boring right into me. "The demonstration was only the words on the building. The bomb wasn't us."

I frown. "Why would Direction injure their own people and damage property?"

"To blame it on Affinity. If everyone hates us... *fears* us, Manning can ensure the rebellion is crushed." His voice is tight. "He can look like the savior."

The confirmation stings, but incites me to want more. "Last night I watched a vid showing Director Manning, before he became a Director. He's done good things. Elore is growing. We are safe--"

"And what else did the vids tell you?" Meyer interrupts.

"I... I don't know. I just don't understand how they went from helping people to killing them?"

"Avlyn... Manning has *always* been killing 'undesirable' people," he says, looking back at me seriously. "It just wasn't out in the open."

Shame and fear floods over me. "What do you mean?"

"Manning has been quietly purging the so-called 'undirected' for years. Anyone who doesn't fit into the mold might go missing.

A knot twists in my stomach. He's right. There was a boy in our group at university that didn't quite fit in, who got in trouble a lot. He used to have a cubicle next to mine, and I don't even remember his name. One day, he stopped coming to class. I asked the AI teacher if he was coming back.

Reassigned.

I was told he was reassigned, and without a thought more about him until now, I'd accepted that answer.

"And don't even get me started on the experimental projects."

I spin toward him. "What?"

"Sometimes Level Ones are recruited with promises of credits and potential level upgrades to take part in experimentation," he explains. "They're told it's a good thing, their duty and a privilege to take part. The only reasons they give the rewards are to make sure people keep quiet, and in case Direction wants to use them again."

My palms dampen, and I rub them over my pants. I hadn't even considered what happened to Ben and I could be more widespread.

What if I was wrong about Devan and Bess's part in it?

Maybe they had no choice.

My head reels. I can't quite process the idea, and struggle to change the subject. "The... the leadership used to be structured differently, right?"

"Yeah," he says. "There used to be eight on the council. When the initiative shifted, the first to go were Cynthia Fisher and Adriana Ruiz, the Directors of Social Rights. The reports indicated that they stepped down voluntarily. Soon after, the others stepped down as well, leaving Colin Manning as the sole Director."

A woman passes by a little too close for comfort. I lean in. "It was *reported* as voluntary? Are you saying it wasn't? Ruiz seemed content enough to step down on the vid I watched."

"I *know* it wasn't."

A Guardian drone floats overhead, but Meyer ignores it.

"How?" I ask.

"Adriana Ruiz leads Affinity."

"A former Director leads the rebellion?" I whisper.

"That surprises you?" he asks.

I nod. "And Fisher?"

"Ruiz is confident she received threats," Meyer says. "Ruiz received them too. It's part of the reason she's our leader. She escaped the city and quietly began a rebellion. It started small, mostly transferring people out of the city who were unable to obey Direction laws, but it's grown. Fisher hasn't been heard from though. There's only rumors that she fled the city."

A thought sparks. Did Devan have help out of the city?

Meyer continues. "People want to marry who they love and keep their children, basic rights they are not allowed. Not everyone fits into the standard Direction mold, and these people will take risks in order to make their own choices. Safety and security is not most important to everyone. People have a need for freedom. Happiness."

"I want freedom too. But I have a good job, a nice apartment… a *future*. What you're saying changes that."

He sighs and glances toward me. "So you would rather see people die while you sit on your nice sofa?"

I pull my knees up, then bury my head between them, confused if the burning in my gut signals me to say yes or no.

Meyer lets out a sound of disgust and pushes up from the ground, leaving me to myself as he hustles across the grass.

Chapter Ten

I haven't budged. I'm a coward. Everything is moving too fast. Coming out here, having not a clue as to what I was getting myself into.

I just wanted answers, not to overthrow the whole government. But I've gone this far, and I know in my heart that I can't give up, especially after the confirmation that Ben and I were not the only ones experimented on, that Direction may have used Bess and Devan.

I scramble to my feet and sprint after him.

When I reach his side, Meyer's shoulders relax. Silently, the two of us work through a maze of somewhat unfamiliar city blocks, since I usually only stick to the areas I need to be in. My stomach churns the whole way while Meyer fiddles on his handheld. Surprisingly, our destination is in a Level Three sector. We must have taken the long way. Meyer did mention that some routes were safer than others.

He takes me through the front of a neutral-colored apartment building and motions toward the elevator. I was expecting a darkened alleyway in Level One, not a pristine Level Three building.

We enter the elevator, and Meyer waves his hand in front of the panel. The cab moves—*down*. I shake my head. I'm on the base floor, but we're headed into the ground?

"Down?" I ask.

"Yep. A few buildings funded by supporters of Affinity conceal... secrets," he whispers.

"But we're in Level Three."

"You'd be surprised how many supporters exist in Three."

"I already am."

When the doors pull open, they reveal nothing but a concrete hallway. A low auto light near the floor illuminates our way. This location's definitely secluded, and is a lot more like the back alley I'd pictured. I follow closely behind Meyer, close enough to duck behind him if I need to.

He leads me through three empty hallways. Right, left, then right again. I keep track in case I need to escape. It makes me feel better to know how to get out of here.

Toward the end of the third corridor, Meyer stops in front of a door. He swipes a few times on his Flexx, then pushes his hand to a security pad on the wall.

He smiles. "Here we are."

My hands clench into fists at my sides, but I creep toward the now-cleared door panel.

No turning back.

Inside, the room is dim, empty except for two deserted cubicles along the walls.

"Pretty impressive, right?"

My cheeks burn. I spin around to meet Meyer's eyes. "Is this a joke?"

"Stop worrying. Someone will be here in a minute." Meyer motions to the ceiling. "He's upstairs."

"What is this place anyway?" I ask.

"It's a bunker we don't use much anymore. Affinity tends to move around. My contact thought it would be a good place today."

Then the door opens again. A man close to Father's age, barely showing gray at the temples, steps through. Standing out is his wide smile, similar to the one Meyer regularly displays.

What's wrong with these people? Who has this much to smile about?

"Meyer," smiling man booms, "it's been a few months!"

Meyer goes toward him, arms out, and pulls the man into an embrace. They exchange a serious look, but pat each other on the back, then turn to me.

I stiffen. It's *not* my turn.

"I brought a friend. Jayson, meet Avlyn."

"Avlyn, it's a pleasure." His serious expression returns to a smile. "I've already heard about you."

Smiling man—Jayson--has heard about *me?* What has he heard? I shift my eyes between the two.

His smile softens. "Sorry. I'm being rude." He extends his hand. "The name's Jayson. I raised Meyer. I'm also here to give you the information needed to join Affinity." He smiles again, this time wider, and drops his unshaken hand. "And… *I* won't hug you, but I might consider advising Meyer here to at some point in the future."

What? No. Warmth flushes over me.

"Jayson!" Meyer's deep voice scolds. "Avlyn is my *assignment.*"

Jayson's gaze falls on me in a rather fatherly way. He shrugs. "Your loss."

I can't tell if he's speaking to Meyer, or me. His eyes twinkle, and the fear I initially felt toward him melts away. Maybe this is how fathers act in the Outerbounds.

Meyer stands off to my side, hands stuffed in pockets, giving Jayson a slightly perturbed look. "Sorry about that," he whispers.

"Let's get to it, kids. You two can take a chair... or stand," Jayson says while unfolding his handheld into a tablet. He hands it to me, and already on the screen plays a familiar newscast of rebel activity, the kind we've been hearing about for months. As I watch each one, they increasingly get worse. A woman is attacked by a rebel, but escapes. The next shows a group of insurgents taking a child. The scenes go on, all the way up to the Level One bombing, then it pauses.

"None of that happened the way they're showing it," Jayson says. "See that flicker?" He points to the screen and pauses the vid. "That's when they switched the footage."

I stare at the screen. "How do I know *you're* not the ones lying?"

"You saw it yourself on the street," Meyer says.

I glance up from the pad and lock eyes with Meyer. "What else are they lying about?"

Jayson chuckles. "Well... that's going to take longer than we have."

"Here's one," Meyer says. "Remember that last viral outbreak that killed a bunch of Level Ones?"

"3005B?" My heart races. That's the virus that ultimately killed Ben thirteen years ago.

"That's it. The one they use in all the broadcasts to remind citizens how important it is to get your MedVac updates? It wasn't an accident."

We were always told a virus swept through Level One because they hadn't gotten their updated VacTech yet. Hundreds of people died in the day it took to get everyone up to date.

"My brother died because of that." Everything I've found out over the last week suddenly grips me with fear.

This can't be real.

My breath shortens, and suddenly my head starts slowly spinning. Everything goes blurry. Then black.

❁ ❁ ❁

"It's all right, kid," a distant voice, which must be Jayson's, echoes in the back of my mind. The room swirls around me. Their faces blur in and out of focus. "Meyer, get her."

Blinking a couple of times, I try to sit up. I guess I fell. Meyer's warm hands rest on the back of my neck, my head in his lap.

"Don't stand. You could pass out again," he says. He helps me sit up. "Are you okay?"

"No, I'm not okay," I mumble. "This is too much." I feel like I should be crying, but I'm not. The reality is that the anger I feel is so much greater than any sadness.

Neither Meyer nor Jayson speak, and let me mull over what I've just heard.

"Why did they do that?" I eventually ask.

"Two reasons, kid," Jayson says. "To cull the Level Ones, and to scare Elore into taking the VacTech. If viral outbreaks are still a threat, no one questions it, and continues believing inside the perimeter is the safest place for them."

"I'm sorry about your brother," Meyer says as he stands, offering me his hand. His words are genuine, filled with the emotions of someone who has also experienced loss.

"I hate to end this," Jayson interrupts, "but it's time to go."

Meyer eyes Jayson, and then me. "I understand if you're not ready, but you need to choose soon. Within the next few days."

I take his hand and pull myself to my feet. Words catch somewhere between my heart and throat. The old me wants to tell them to get lost and to never bother me again. It's so risky.

Then again, I can't stand by while Manning and Direction kill people to keep us in the dark. Joining is the right thing to do. Feelings I've never experienced before well inside my chest, and I long to shout, *When do we start?*

Instead, I stuff them down and stare at the ground.

Subtle pressure squeezes my hand, bringing me back to the present. I never let go of Meyer's hand. How long have we been like that?

He releases my hand as he mutters and steps back. The heat from his touch still flickers on my skin.

You didn't have to go.

I clear my throat and turn toward Meyer. Our eyes lock. "I've already decided," I tell him. "I'll do it. For Ben. Direction caused his death, and there's no way I'm standing by and letting them do this to more people." I barely recognize my own voice as I ask, "What do I do?"

A slap hits my back and I choke. Jayson. "Atta girl. Meyer and I knew you had it in you."

"Jayson, you have to give Avlyn some time." Meyer steps toward me and holds his handheld in the air toward Jayson. "I'll bring her up to speed."

"Sure thing." Jayson throws his hands in the air and walks to the other side of the room.

"Sorry," Meyer murmurs. "Jayson is pretty… overwhelming. At least until you know him. Even then…"

"Oh, it's fine." A white lie. "He's a nice guy. Now, why don't you tell me the instructions before I change my mind." My bravery might only last so long.

Meyer chuckles. "To be honest, it's probably not much yet. Affinity keeps its members on a need-to-know basis." He swipes his screen and pokes it a few times. "There. I've activated the account, and instructions will be sent to your device. They're secure, and can't be monitored. I've also deactivated your device for any possible tracking, setting it to always appear that you're in the proper locations."

Panic floods me. My eyes widen. "What about that night in Level One?"

"Don't worry. I deactivated the tracker when I saw you on the street. Unless Direction suspects you of something, you're safe—and they don't yet. It's just a precaution. Also, you can debug your apartment as needed from your handheld. This makes the work you do in there and on the network invisible."

The instructions are simple. I form my own password, put my thumb on the screen, and download an app. Easy. The app launches, and I scroll through the instructions.

MISSION INSTRUCTIONS FOR

AVLYN LARK: TBD

To be determined?

I turn to Meyer. "I'll have a mission?"

"Everyone in Affinity trains as a soldier and potential intel. Of course, you'll be tested for your specific skills. They may give you a simple job as soon as tonight." He gives me a tight grin. "Make sure to memorize your password."

"Already did." I close the app.

"Oh, the one thing I can tell you now," Meyer says, "is that you are to have no contact with anyone out of the ordinary. Doing so would only attract Direction's suspicion."

I guess that means I can't contact Bess to try to find out about what happened to Ben and me.

Meyer waves to Jayson. "Time to go. We're headed out."

Jayson stops poking at his Flexx screen. "Good meeting you, Avlyn," he calls. "See you soon."

I nod, and Meyer takes me back up to the ground level.

"Forgot something downstairs," he says. "It's time to split up anyway. You can map the route home."

Before I have time to answer, the doors to the elevator shut and he's gone.

The closing of the doors has a sort of finality to what just happened to me. Terror builds in my gut, but I push it down.

No. This is what I want.

If nothing else, I can help make Direction pay for what they did to Ben... to me. I belong here. I've *never* belonged. A sense of excitement starts to grow, replacing the terror.

My handheld vibrates.

INSTRUCTIONS FOR AVLYN LARK: COMPLETE

My heart leaps and I click the link.

Initial Test Mission Instructions:
Contact Aron Barton for a second spouse pairing meeting.
Mr. Barton has potential usefulness to Affinity. You will
work to gain his trust and potentially create a contract with him.
This message will delete upon closing.

What? Potentially create a spouse contract… with *Aron?*
The terror inside me makes a reappearance.

Gathering my wits, I activate the desktop system in my bedroom from my handheld, go to the citizen's account, and select the spouse pairing option. Aron's face stares at me from the account.

He's nice to look at, with his caramel-blond hair and deep blue eyes. His expression is serious on the profile image, but I zoom in and make out where the dimple on his right cheek sits. If I wouldn't have told him Ben was a Level One, I'd probably still like him. He might have liked me.

I suck in a breath. Adrenaline has made me brave today, and I select Aron's profile to request a second meeting.

Even though our first meeting flopped, care to try again?

Before I commit, the memory of Meyer's warm hand on mine trails across my skin, making the hairs on my arm stand on end.
Pairings are about duty.

I throw off a ridiculous disappointment that the message isn't addressed to Meyer. Maybe someday I will enjoy the freedom of choice, but today is not that day.

Meyer is not a pairing. Aron is. And Aron is also my mission.

I send the message and head home.

This whole rebellion thing is not nearly as exciting as I hoped. Over the next week, Affinity sends me a barrage of coding tests to take every day after work, basically doubling my workload and making finding time to sleep incredibly difficult. The whirlwind of emotions quickly dissipates. Sadly, I don't even hear from Meyer, and Aron doesn't respond to my invite.

As I wind down for the evening and prepare for GenTech tomorrow, my handheld buzzes with a message.

UPDATED INSTRUCTIONS FOR AVLYN LARK

I tap the link and hold my breath for the news.

Mission instructions: Monday morning, link your Flexx as usual at your GenTech workstation. When doing so, an invisible program will launch into their net to gain access and gather intel. There is nothing else you will need to do. The program will work on its own.

This message will delete upon closing.

The download link appears below the message.

While exhaling, my mind reels.

What? So I'm an information security specialist stealing information from my own company?

Pressure wells inside me.

You can do this. You can do this.

I repeat the words over and over.

I sigh, log out, and flick on Direction news on the viewer. There's some sort of activity happening in Sector H of Level Three. I lean in to get a closer look. Through the smoke and flames, drones pull Level Three citizens from a building.

TERRORISM. TEN CITIZENS KILLED.

The words scroll across the screen as the vid pulls back. I squint as if to peer through the smoke on the screen.

Brian Marshall's voice reports over the scene of the incident. "Again, if you have just tuned in, a devastating act of terrorism has just happened in Level Three."

BREAKING NEWS scrolls across the bottom of the screen.

TERRORIST APPREHENDED.

The scene switches to a man's face, his head down and eyebrows furrowed, being escorted away by two burly human guards and a Guardian.

Jayson.

CHAPTER ELEVEN

I check for the fourth time to see if I've received a message from Meyer. Nothing.

If Direction knew I was involved with Affinity, they would be here already, taking me away.

The thought doesn't take away the tension building in my chest.

After a few moments, I review my instructions in my mind.

Link your device into GenTech network as usual. Affinity will gain intelligence from the connection.

If Jayson is detained, how in the world am I supposed to do this?

After securing my desktop system, I link my Flexx handheld and download the program in an attempt to hack into the Affinity spy program. I know it's wrong, but if I could know what it does, how it works, what files it might be transmitting, I would feel more confident.

From the little I can tell, the person who programmed it is an even better coder than I am. I dig up information specific to a project called Chrysalis, but I'm unsure how the program works and what it does. I'm blocked each time I try. Even after attempting to decompile the program, the variable names are all meaningless jumbles of letters and numbers. Frustrated, I shake my head in annoyance at myself. Maybe if I try again later.

Part of me wished I'd never met with Meyer. I should've deleted his message and told him to go away. Personal curiosity is a self-indulgence. A risk.

But it's much more than a curiosity now... so many lives are at stake.

What do you think, Ben?

Again, he doesn't answer due to the fact that he's not alive.

Moonlight creeps over the screen, and I push back from the desk and check the time. Dinner has come and gone. Actually, it's way past bedtime. I unpair my handheld from the system and reset it to normal. There's still nothing from Meyer, and, thankfully, drones still haven't shown up at my door.

Rising, and shaking my head, I drop onto my bed. I should put on pajamas, but instead, I lie there and stare at the ceiling.

Device still in hand, I log into my citizen account and browse through the anti-stress MedTech options specifically for sleep. Knowing what I know about Direction, I don't want to, but living on the little sleep I've been getting can't go on. The med downloads to my account. Instructions pop on the screen.

Place your palm flat on the screen of your Flexx. Hold until the vibration stops.

Before I can stop myself, my hand is touching the screen. When the pulsing stops, there's no change in my body.

The MedTech transmits to your internal nanobots and modifies your bodily function to release the proper neurotransmitters for sleep.

In short, I can get some rest. Finally.

I blink. Nothing happens, but before long, my eyes droop and I barely have energy to dress for bed, let alone worry about Meyer, before a dreamless night of sleep envelops me.

I drag awake full of cloudy, gray memories of seeing Jayson arrested. I run a hand over my face and squint at my handheld. Still no answer from Meyer. Slowly, the natural stress chemicals kick back in and a tightness in my chest builds. I throw off the blanket, spring from bed, and activate my media viewer.

"This is Brian Marshall reporting from Level Three..."

Doesn't that guy ever take a break?

"The body count from yesterday's explosion is now twelve, all Level Three citizens. Names are still unreleased."

The camera pans to the partially destroyed building, sending my heart into my stomach again.

"Director Manning will be taking the podium this evening at eight p.m. for an important mandatory watch announcement."

Mentally exhausted, I flick the screen off and message Meyer again. Nothing. Instead of a response from him, the MedTech screen presents again from my motion, as if the device knew what I wanted and brought it up. I stare at the options. A tightening in my chest forms, making breathing more work than it should be. How am I supposed to do my job at GenTech, let alone be an asset to Affinity, if I can't even function?

The one for sleep worked last night.

Just this once.

So many people take them, and *they* seem fine. With no idea which one would be best, I pick the first one on the list for stress and anxiety relief.

The stress and anxiety relief option will naturally increase your serotonin levels and assist your nanobots in returning your stress levels to normal.

Naturally? It can't be that bad.

I download it and press my palm to the screen. A sick feeling seeps into my stomach.

At GenTech, I make my way to floor eighteen. Along the way, I avoid other employees for fear they might spot the anxiety in my eyes.

When is that MedTech going to kick in?

I clutch my wrist where my handheld sits.

When I link this there's no turning back. I'll have officially begun work for Affinity.

"Evelyn, right?" a voice asks, catching me before I enter the InfoSec suite.

I turn around, clearing my throat. The voice belongs to Daniel Carter, the guy from my placement orientation. He's even taller than I remember, almost a full head. I'd hoped he'd forgotten about me.

He eyes me and blinks twice rapidly. "You look more... together."

He stares as if his eyes are boring through me, remembering my disheveled appearance on our first day at GenTech. Whatever he's doing, I won't play into it.

"It's Avlyn." My focus never sways from his face. "And yes, I am. GenTech suits me."

Stay calm. It's always worked before to keep people from asking too many questions. He'll go away.

Daniel's eyebrows furrow, and he steps uncomfortably close to me. "No… something tells me otherwise, but until I'm sure… We'll see who gets advanced first."

His cold gaze shoots from mine to the InfoSec suite, and he goes around me.

I straighten, but my head spins. From the MedTech? Even so, I whip around to follow close on his heels. He turns for his cubicle, but I can sense his stare as I pass.

What does he know? Nothing. A disheveled appearance one time, albeit on the first day, means nothing. It's just his way of finding a weakness to dig at, hoping I'll slip up.

I activate my screen, then link my Flexx. I shut my eyes and exhale. *It's an ordinary day,* I lie to myself, but my body relaxes, clearing my mind. Things suddenly don't seem that bad. Apparently the MedTech finally decided to kick in.

The device accepts the connection.

Let the Affinity program invasion begin.

I grab my headset and place it over my eyes. After the eyepiece blurs and goes clear, I swipe the screen to activate it. The virtual reality of the headset displays the spinning GenTech logo and the list of today's tasks.

For today the following will be overseeing one another's work:

D. Carter

A. Lark

Ugh. Unless another D. Carter works in InfoSec, Daniel's going to be hanging around me today. Sure enough, his scowling avatar enters my VR office carrying a Flexx formed into a touch tablet. Daniel says nothing and avoids looking my way. To match his, my desktop system morphs into a tablet. The task displays on the screen to investigate an error, checking the other's work along the way.

This sim is nothing like reality. Instead, it looks fake. Generated. Just a plain digital office the VR creates to give us even more of a sense we're alone while working. The avatars are a shadow of what we are in the real world. Cold, sterile.

Maybe it's just Daniel.

When I move to enter our project, the instructions change.

Immediately discontinue current project until further notice.

A high alert shows for a stage-four security breach and my heart races. There's a real emergency. Not a drill. Pain stabs at my gut. I *am* the breach. I knew I couldn't do this. Daniel's avatar eyes me quizzically, then vanishes from the VR room.

Suspicious activity consistent with an intruder reads on the screen.

I squint at my new instructions through the system and rush to start coding. I do my best, and a strange calm falls over me. The MedTech.

You can do this. Coding is what you were made for.

After four hours and forty-five minutes, the breach is contained by the team. From the little I learned last night about what the Affinity spybot does, I'm confident the emergency is unrelated to my hack for Affinity.

But at the last minute, I notice an oddity. A hidden backdoor. It's so tiny and obsolete I should have missed it, but I never miss weaknesses in code. This one's not like a beacon to me, but it's unmistakable. The Affinity program.

As fast as possible, I code a concealment and exit the program. That's when I notice Daniel's avatar. He's in my VR office again, holding his tablet.

"Why are you here?" I ask sourly to cover my nervousness.

He crosses the arms of his avatar. "The breach is secure and we're to continue with the original task. What are *you* doing?"

"Nothing. Just finishing up." I check the time. "I'm headed to eat."

His avatar's mouth tightens. "After lunch, then," he says and vanishes from the room.

Did he see? I wait a few minutes before I pull off the headset, joining the real world once more, and lean over to see if Daniel is still at his cubicle.

Gone.

I stand and unlink my handheld. A shiver runs down my spine. How long are these anti-stress meds supposed to work for? I think I need more.

From a food dispenser on the first floor, I order a sandwich and take it outside to clear my head and the ache in my stomach. As I walk toward the door, I swear a Guardian follows me. I breathe a sigh of relief when it continues off to a corridor on my right.

I hike a couple of buildings down and sit on the curb. The sidewalks have no seating to discourage milling.

Jayson's in custody, Meyer's MIA, Daniel's watching me. What made me believe I'd be smart or strong enough to do this?

As if to answer the question, my handheld buzzes. My heart leaps. Meyer.

I'm safe.

Tears pool in my eyes, and I look up to discourage them.

I don't know if I can do this, I reply.

I move to send the message and delete it instead. With a sigh, I scroll to the MedTech account and press my palm to a fresh download. A sense of calm travels over me.

Back to work.

And I didn't even eat my lunch.

CHAPTER TWELVE

With my shift almost done, I log off the server and gather my belongings.

At least the MedTech got me through the day.

I swallow hard at the thought and check my message center. Nothing new, bad or good. My breath releases in a sigh of relief.

At the top of the stairs, I message Kyra to meet. She's the only person from my old life I have left to talk to and even that is nearing an end in less than a month.

My device buzzes.

Flexx 35D52G-KLEWIS: See you in 5 out front.

I exit the building and spy a petite girl headed toward me down the block, her pretty blonde hair pulled into a high, tight bun.

"Want me to walk you home, or somewhere else?" Kyra asks, reaching my side.

"Home. But let's walk slowly. How's your placement coming along?"

Her back straightens. "Busy... extremely busy. But I enjoy it. It's perfect if you don't mind running around all day."

Kyra's always had a lot of energy. It's what got her so far. She's tireless in getting what she wants.

"I'm second assistant to Level Two Direction Representative Ayers," she adds. "He reports to Manning, but I'm sure you knew that last part."

"Actually, it's terrible, but I don't follow much local government." I grimace. "Guess I should. It's kind of important... and I know a person working there now."

She chuckles. "Well, it's not like I'm making any decisions or recommendations. So far I just run errands for actual important people."

Kyra is a good person. I *know* she is. My hope is with people like her involved with Direction, the situation will change. But it will be a long time before she has any influence.

"You need to start somewhere, right?" I offer encouragingly.

"Absolutely. Legal would have been good, but a government career is the kind I've always wanted." She beams. "What about you?"

"Work's fine, but too much is on my mind lately. I can't sleep."

"You could always take the MedTech."

"Yeah." My face flushes. Knowing what I do about Direction, I can't believe I already have.

We walk the next block in silence. Gone are the conversations of schoolgirls. Our month of transition is nearly up, and we both know it.

Kyra clears her throat. "I met Director Manning."

"You did?" My heart begins to pound. I hadn't even considered Kyra might have access to Manning yet.

"He held an emergency meeting this morning, and Representative Ayers had me come along," she whispers. "The council is concerned with the increasing terrorist attacks in the city."

My heart works to speed up further, but the anti-anxiety meds seem to be doing their job, and it returns to normal.

"I don't understand what those people, rebels, are doing." She shakes her head. "Why do they want to hurt us?"

What do I say to her? That Direction is killing people, not Affinity?

I bite my tongue. The timing is all wrong. Kyra wouldn't understand. Instead, I just shrug and shake my head.

"Manning is so focused and intent. He embodies the Direction Initiative." Her lips form a half smile, but then it disappears and her chin rises. "It really is an honor to work in the Level Two rep office."

And there you go. Direction has officially configured another cog to fit into their machine.

I am next.

Except all my cogs are the wrong shapes.

☒ ☒ ☒

A steady stream of Aerrx drones, ranging from the small 1000s to the commercial 3000s, have flown by my apartment window in the last two hours. Three new messages from Meyer buzz from my handheld on the couch. The fact I never returned his last one concerns him. He's just checking to see if I'm okay. I'm fine, but thinking about Meyer reminds me what I'm doing is dangerous, so I ignore him for now.

Aron still hasn't replied to my request, and Affinity has sent me an additional reminder to contact him again. I don't know what to do about it. Right now I have no desire for establishing a spouse pairing, despite Affinity orders, and if I log on to send it, Meyer's fake account might still be active. I don't want to see his face either since I still don't know how to respond to his last message.

I walk toward the window and palm the glass. My gaze is drawn to a single, rare bird flying over one of the rooftops in the distance. Into the sky it soars, and then dives back to the earth. The creature does this several times before darting off to the horizon and vanishing like a phantom.

Ben's memory permeates my mind. It's almost as if he vanished too.

A chime I set announces a reminder for tonight's Direction announcement, breaking my concentration.

Was the bird only in my mind?

I activate the viewer in the living room and flop on the couch. The program hasn't started yet. Only the Direction emblem displays, flanked by gold and black words:

DIRECTION: ENABLING YOUR BEST FUTURE

The globe emblem spins, and the words transition from black to gold and back in a slow dance.

How do they *know what my best future is?*

I shake my head in disgust. Dread rises at the thought of returning to GenTech tomorrow and all the tomorrows after.

Brian Marshall snaps me from my thoughts.

"Citizens, please stay with us for an imperative announcement from the Direction Council. Director Manning will be taking the podium in five minutes." He moves on to a mini story about food ink production for the printers, and how Nutra Enterprise continues developing perfect personal nutrition.

My eyes glaze over. *Fascinating.*

The segment wraps, and the scene switches to an empty podium where Director Manning steps up. I've seen his stats on the network, and for a man of average stature, he always appears tall. It could be the camera angle, but Kyra's right. He embodies Direction Initiative. His focus and determination are the primary reason spouse pairing and birth reassignment have been so successful in increasing Intelligence Potential.

The vid closes in, his face filling the screen, large and angular. I push into the back of the couch, but his oppressiveness doesn't diminish.

"Citizens of Direction," Manning begins. "On behalf of Elore, I want to personally thank you for your focus and loyalty. Staying on the path of the Direction Initiative to continually build understanding will ensure the survival of our species. Intelligence enacts progress in the Technology, Science, and Medical divisions in a way that is only possible by compatibility pairing. Your allegiance to the Initiative is imperative, now more than ever."

I grip the edge of the cushion.

"Elore has a new threat, one that jeopardizes our survival as the Aves virus did over one hundred years ago. But instead of a microscopic level, this infective agent operates at a macro one, attempting to reproduce and spread, destroying us. Direction sits on the verge of a battle with a group who has identified themselves as Affinity."

A vacuum seems to suck the air from the room and I gasp. I force myself to hear him by getting up to stand directly in front of the screen. It's not new information, but this is the first time I've been on the other side.

"It has come to our attention that Affinity, and the dangers they pose, are a growing problem, endangering the safety and security of Direction. Over the last few weeks, they have orchestrated dangerous, even deadly, events at multiple Levels in the city, including a terrorist attack in Level One in which several Level One citizens were badly injured."

No, not true. I know all this, but hearing the words makes it all too real. My mouth goes dry and I try to swallow, but my throat closes. Gasping for breath, I race back to the couch and grab for my Flexx. The MedTech window is still available, and I scroll to download.

Maximum Daily Anti-Anxiety MedTech Allowance Reached.

I curse and throw the device onto the couch.

"During the latest confirmed Affinity assault in Level Three, twelve citizens died and five more were injured. We have one of their leaders in custody, and he has admitted to leading the operation to murder specific Level Three citizens."

The vid flips to a live feed of a man, probably sedated. His head hangs, but he lifts it a little. My eyes widen when I notice the graying hair at his temples. This glassy-eyed, drawn face belongs to Jayson.

Inching back to the screen, I cover my open mouth and tap his face.

Name: Jayson Brant
Age: 42
Leader in subversive group called Affinity
Accused of the murder and injury of twelve Level Three citizens
Trial: TBD

I jerk my hand back from the screen as if stung, then swipe the words away. The vid returns to Director Manning. He continues explaining how vital it is that Affinity be stopped, and talks about a new app that can be immediately found on handhelds to report any suspicious behavior.

"Citizens, it is your obligation to protect our future."

The Direction logo flashes on the screen again, allowing Elore to stew in their obligations. I stumble to the couch and collapse in the middle. Something pokes my leg, and I pull out my Flexx with the MedTech notification on the screen. I stare at it, but instead of downloading, I take a deep breath, just like Father instructed.

Maybe, deep down, he truly did care about me. Maybe even wanted to protect me. I close my eyes and imagine what it must feel like to be loved, even cherished, by your family. My mind drifts to the words on the paper that wrapped my gold heart necklace from Ben. The childish "I love you" with the backward y. Even at four, Ben loved. Despite everything he must have went through with the experiments, and ultimately died, he still loved.

"I love you, too," I whisper.

Saying the words out loud feels sacred.

Forbidden.

Defiant thoughts roll around in my brain. Why is it that a few people get to decide how we should live? No one should die for the right to love. That kind of freedom is worth fighting for.

"Meyer," I whisper. I let go of any fear and send him a message.

What's next?

The device buzzes a reply.

War.

I make a beeline to my bed. I slide my hand under the mattress and search for the hidden package containing the cold metal necklace. From the paper, the jewelry drops to my hand. My fingers burn as I stroke the delicate chain, then grasp it in my palm. I glance at the clasp to see how it works, close my eyes, and wrap the pendant around my neck. Without looking, I tuck it into my shirt.

The golden heart will remind me that love shouldn't be hidden. It shouldn't be forbidden. It wasn't something to stuff under a mattress.

The thought is better than anything Direction offers, including anxiety MedTech.

As the concealed golden heart hangs near the one hammering away in my chest, I swear it ticks with its own life.

CHAPTER THIRTEEN

I keep my head down as I leave work. Exhaustion creeps over me without any MedTech to keep me focused. The desire to take it still exists, but I've managed to keep it at bay the whole day. The evening wind is chill, and full, puffy gray clouds swell in the sky. The air is earthy and damp. My breath puffs with every step like a trail of smoke, and the long sleeves of my top do little to stay the cold, so I pick up the pace. Any other day, I'd have checked the forecast and worn something warmer, but this morning found me troubled.

Bundled citizens scurry by, some eyeing each other. Since the broadcast, everyone must be keenly aware that any minuscule display of suspicious behavior brands them as a traitor. Turning in conspirators is our duty, maybe even a pleasure for some.

With stiff fingers, I check my handheld, but Meyer hasn't messaged. The Affinity account only says to await further instructions.

A thick drop of water wets my shoulder as more fall to the concrete, speckling the path to my building. By the time I reach it, my shirt is soaked through and my drenched hair clings to the sides of my face and scalp.

"Oh, you poor thing," a female voice says as I enter through the sliding doors.

Busily waving me toward the elevator is my neighbor, the odd girl with the straight, raven hair from the first day I moved in. I hesitate, but make my way across the floor of the lobby and step into the cab, the girl right on my heels. The doors shut, and I turn.

"Leave me alone."

She smiles and flips her raven hair behind her shoulders. "You know, lost time is never found again."

"What?" My voice cracks. It's the same words Meyer messaged me the day I moved in.

"Don't worry. We're safe here. For now," she says. "My name's Lena, and I'm supposed to get you started tonight."

She stares at me as if waiting for me to respond. I stare back at her, arms fixed to my sides.

Started on what? I wasn't told of this.

"Avlyn, put your hand on the pad. Otherwise, we'll be here all night."

I still don't move. Lena chuckles, grabs my hand, and presses it to the pad. I jerk it back, but the scanner has enough time to read the data.

"Listen," she says. "It's a lot to take in, but you will."

The cab stops, and Lena steps out. She waves. "Come on."

When I don't follow, she reaches back and tugs my arm. Instinct says to pull away, but instead, I let her lead me into the hall.

"I'm okay," I mutter. "You can let go. I know the way."

"Of course."

She doesn't.

Inside her unit, the cityscape is just as stunning as mine, only eastward facing instead of west. No view of the sunset, but it doesn't matter. She activates the lights, then dims the glass to black.

"Come in. I need to prepare. If you're hungry, go ahead and get something from the kitchen," she offers. "It's going to be a long night."

She then disappears into the bedroom, closing the door behind her.

My stomach groans, reminding me I haven't eaten regularly over the last few days, and from the sound of Lena's plans, if I don't eat now, I might not have the chance again any time soon. I order and work on a plate of meatloaf and potatoes. When she exits the room, she comes out carrying a bag, a handheld, and a towel.

"Sorry Meyer couldn't do this, but he asked me for help last minute." She smiles, throwing the towel to me and dropping the other items on the couch. "I'm starving."

She disappears around the corner into the kitchen, where the whirring and zipping of her dinner preparations sounds. The fact she mentioned Meyer's name calms my nerves a bit, and I quickly check my messages to see if he sent one informing me of Lena.

Sure enough, there is. Must have missed it when the downpour started.

"Your name is Lena?" I ask while drying my hair. "When did you finish university?"

From the kitchen, she answers, "Yeah, Lena Tran, and I was configured six months ago."

"You're not paired?" I ask, looking around.

"Affinity has arranged a few potentials, but right now it's been easier on my own. I probably won't make a choice until right before my deadline, so I still have almost six months." She steps around the corner with her food and sits alongside me. "I'll be expected to have a child if I make a contract, so I'm holding off as long as I can."

"Even though you're working with Affinity, you'll carry on as usual with spouse pairing and birth schedule?" I ask.

"Of course. Doesn't mean I can't wait until the last possible second though." Lena digs into her meatloaf as if she hasn't eaten in days.

"So what *are* we doing today, other than eating?"

"Mmm..." she says, mouth full and waving her finger. "Operative training... Haven't you been informed at all yet?"

"No. I don't know much." I stab the last bite of meatloaf, frost the chunk with the mashed potatoes, and then pop it into my mouth.

"Generally, in between testing for your specific skill set, they have us learn the ropes in other areas."

"How are we going to do that here?"

"Have you seen Affinity's VR yet?" Lena asks between bites.

"No, but I've used it at GenTech."

She shakes her head. "This is different. The stuff Direction uses for work is to keep you isolated and on task. The version we're going to use is way better."

"Why wouldn't Direction have it then?"

"They do... where do you think we got it? But the technology allows people to meet too easily while not under Manning's watchful eye, so he buried it."

I wonder what else Manning has buried.

"Let's get going. There's only so much time." Lena grabs our plates and takes them to the kitchen, then retrieves the bag and Flexx. "We're diving right in."

She pulls out a clear box and hands it to me.

"Um, what do you mean?" My voice comes out as kind of a squeak.

"We're training tonight. Put on the EP."

"The what?" I crack the box and find a thin, clear object. I squish the small disk between my fingers. "This is really different than what I use at work."

"Yeah, it is." She chuckles. "It's an eyepiece. Stick it in your eye."

"*In* my eye?" I echo, sure I heard her wrong.

Lena nods.

"Which one?"

"It doesn't matter. You'll figure out what's comfortable for you."

I place it over my right eye and gasp as the piece suctions to my eyeball. Both my lids snap shut.

Lena laughs. "You're all right. Open up."

Hesitating, I do as she says. When my lids open, other than the strange sensation of having the eyepiece suctioned to my eyeball, the room looks as it was.

"Everything's the same."

"You need to activate it," she explains. "First, let me grab the rest of the equipment. There's a comm that integrates with your nanos so we can communicate."

She affixes her own EP, then works at something on her handheld. I squint, but I can't even see it in her eye.

"Today's exercises are standard, to let you adjust to the equipment. Basically, it's a VR game, but playing will get you used to it."

"What do you mean?"

"Similar to your VR training drills at work. Not real, so no risk. The weapons aren't real either. And we can do it all right here." She gestures toward the couch. "Can't have you running around breaking my furniture and making a huge racket. The whole exercise will take place in your mind."

A nervous laugh escapes my lips. "Why don't you show me?"

"No time to waste, right? Go sit on the couch or wherever you're comfortable."

I do as she says. She follows behind and swipes at her screen. "Okay, blink twice. Hard. It will activate the tech."

I blink twice. The living room fades and is replaced with a dim, outdoor street scene. It's deserted. In awe, I walk over to the side of a building and graze my fingertips over the bumpy texture. It's all so real, except for an occasional flicker.

Lena's hair is fixed differently in the sim, pulled into a tight, high ponytail. She wears the same tight gray-black uniform I do, complete with gloves and a weapon affixed to our sides. I run my hands over the bodice. There seems to be some kind of harness built into the fabric.

Why would I need a harness?

"How does this work?" I ask.

She motions toward the side of an apartment building, and we move out to the middle of the street. "The EP connects its own network to your nanos and nervous system. If, for some reason, you need to turn off your comm, tap right beside your right ear. And you leave the sim the same as you activated it. Blink twice, hard, or just say 'End sim'.

"The suits are made of the same material the human officers wear, and are designed to work as a light body armor." Lena holds out her hands. "The gloves keep you from being scanned if you touch a sensor. If you run a real mission, you might be given one of these suits, but Affinity doesn't have many."

On the right side of my vision displays the distance to the next building, and if I focus in a new spot, it changes and shows the distance to that one. The left side lists Guardian activity, and all the while, the EP tells me where Lena is, even if I can't see her. There's more, but I don't know what it means yet.

"Today you're training the EP. By your reactions in the sim, the piece will learn. Information overload causes disorientation, so the device will start out slowly and add more as your brain and nanos adjust."

I give her a tentative look, and Lena chuckles, then grabs me.

"Come on. We don't have much time. Make sure to stay out of the Guardian's sight. The EP will help you determine where they are."

Blood rushes to my head and the room spins, but it's only a... What did Lena call it? A game?

"Let's give it a try. I can talk all night about what this will be like, but it can't replace actual training," she says. "If you're injured, your device will alert you. If you die, the sim ends. There's a Flexx on your wrist. You'll need it. We're starting... now."

Still clutching my arm, Lena pulls me and breaks into a sprint. She loosens her grip and lets go of me.

"Are you a runner?" she asks.

"Yeah, almost every day."

"Good. Okay, you should be able to view some of the info in your EP now."

Final Destination: 5 blocks
Approximate time of arrival: 15 minutes

"Sounds easy," she says, "but obstacles can slow you down."

"Guardian drone... sixty-eight degrees to the right, six hundred feet ahead," I reply.

"Yup, I see it. Cover ahead, thirty feet."

The spot illuminates and words flash in my view.

Wait 30 seconds for Guardian to pass.

The two of us jog toward the hiding spot. Lena motions me to wait, and the drone, tentacle arms pulled into its body, continues without stopping. We resume running and take the assigned path directed by the EP. Nearing the last block and standing by for two more passing drones, I recognize the street we're on.

"We're on GenTech's block."

Destination 656 ft. on the right. Genesis Technologies.

"The mission's at GenTech?"

She turns, showing a sly smile. "Yep. We're breaking in."

"Breaking in?"

"Well, we're not taking a stroll. Let's learn something useful."

I seize her arm and pull us to the side of a building. "You said this was just basic training."

"Why do you think we're doing this?" She scratches her neck. "The training is to avoid errors when it's real."

Pressure sits on my chest. In the game, it's easy. Nobody dies. But in real life...

I blink hard, twice, and I'm back on Lena's couch. Lena touches my shoulder and I flinch.

"I don't know if I can do this, Lena. I mean... breaking into GenTech? That's like suicide. I get that today it's just a sim, but what if they want me to do that for *real*? I'm a programmer, not a spy."

She smiles. "Relax. Just do your best. You're capable. Otherwise, you wouldn't have been chosen."

The words are comforting to hear, but it doesn't mean I believe them.

"Anyway, tonight's *not* real," she adds. "Just have fun with it. Seriously? When do we ever get to have fun?"

Pretty much never.

I reluctantly nod and blink twice.

Ahead of me, Lena's already sprinting toward GenTech. She takes out her weapon. I try to hold mine the same way she does, but I'm clumsy and ridiculous. The viewer instructs us to swing around the back of the building, and words flash in my vision.

Entry Point: Service door. 352 ft. on the left.

"We'll enter through an underground tunnel in the apartment building beside it," Lena instructs.

Around the side, the service door comes into sight.

"Go ahead and disarm the security system with your handheld. Shouldn't be any more surveillance until we pop out."

"*Shouldn't* be?"

Lena shrugs. "Sometimes the simulation presents unexpected challenges."

I stow my weapon and follow the instruction on the Flexx.

Success. You may now proceed.

The door opens, revealing a darkened hall. The EP brightens, and the hall illuminates.

"What are you waiting for?" Lena pushes me in. The door slides closed behind us and she resets the security. "Don't be sloppy. Make sure if you change something, you set it back in place. A system left disarmed could tip off our presence."

Lena catches my arm and I ready my weapon again. Our new destination is a service elevator on the right, sixteen feet ahead. Once into the cab, she asks for a boost and slides over a panel on the ceiling. Lena pulls herself up and through.

She pops her head through the opening and reaches toward me. "Grab on."

The EP flashes instructions for grabbing and climbing the sides. Instructions are one thing; actually doing it is another. Even so, I leap for her hand and climb into the opening. I guess the EP and nanos are doing their job.

No words come out, but I must wear a silly grin. Lena doesn't call me out on it. I replace the panel, and she motions to a ladder leading up the length of the elevator shaft.

15 ft. to destination

The supposed entrance looks like solid concrete, but the EP says it's there. Lena punches on her handheld to activate a panel, sliding open. The tunnel is only about three square feet wide and tall, with a narrow metal ledge below. The opening is less than an arm's length from the ladder. With the ledge, we should be able to swing into it. At least, that's what the EP's telling me.

Lena goes first and launches herself inside, followed by myself. The panel shuts behind us, but the EP provides an even brighter night vision, giving us a luminous effect.

We crawl through the shaft and come to a dead end.

"GenTech's on the other side," Lena whispers.

Complete flashes and the panel skates open. We wriggle out behind some storage, and the outline of another person appears in the EP. I grapple for my weapon just as a hand slides over my mouth.

"Ladies, you're late."

I dart my eyes to his face. A glowing, night-vision smile appears.

Meyer Quinn shows in my view.

CHAPTER FOURTEEN

Lena chuckles. "Late?" Then she throws a glance at me. "Eh... she was slowing me down."

"Where did you come from?" I gasp.

He tips his head. "It's VR, remember? We can do almost anything in here."

I shake my head and drop my shoulders. I'd forgotten.

"I didn't know you were coming," Lena says.

"Me either." Meyer walks to the door. "But I finished up early and knew you were in. Had the option to sleep or hang out with you two. Who needs sleep anyway?"

Lena secures the panel, and each of us poise our weapons. The EP has adjusted to show a kind of X-ray outline of the building. I can basically see through walls. A Guardian drone patrols two rooms over, and past the drone stands a human guard.

Meyer turns. "Stay out of their view. The EP will help."

"The stunners are set to immobilize," Lena adds. "We don't want to kill anyone, so never change the setting if you don't have to, even in a sim." She points to the control on the side where the intensity is located. "Only modify if the EP recommends it." She looks at Meyer. "Anything I forgot?"

"No, you covered the basics." He flashes me a smile. "The mission's loading."

Familiarize yourself with as much of GenTech's lab layout as possible while avoiding Guardians and other security.

Begin with floor 10, Labs scrolls across the bottom of my vision.

"It's an easy one tonight." Lena chuckles. "They must not want to push the new girl too much."

I give her a scowl.

"Come on. Let's go," Meyer says. "The drone's gone."

We take the hall and crawl through a tight overhead venting system at the end of the corridor, which pops us out into a service stairwell.

Warning: Guardian Drone Patrol

It passes, then Meyer pulls the vent panel and we slide out. The stairwell is to the right. Three minutes to reach floor ten.

Lena gestures, and Meyer slips through the opening to the stairs. I follow Lena. My heart pounds as I take multiple steps at a time, whipping around the corner of each new floor.

Only fifteen seconds remain for us to catch our breath.

6...5...4...

A shiver nips my spine when I sense Meyer's hand nudge against my lower back. I dart my gaze to his face, but he only looks straight ahead toward our next destination.

2...1...

"Go," he whispers.

Lena sprints down the corridor, lit by dim auto lights, with me close on her heels, Meyer behind. The EP directs us to a narrow alcove approximately thirty-two feet ahead, while the lab is twenty feet after. The three of us squat and wait for the EP to recalculate.

Sixteen minutes to get in and out of floor 10, if nothing in security changes. My heart gathers speed as the instructions load with the countdown. I shouldn't be so nervous, but it feels so real. If I were ever truly caught inside GenTech... everything would be lost. I'd be sent to the detainment center, and now knowing Direction is willing to kill their own, I can't imagine they would treat traitors well there.

I follow as Lena and Meyer bolt onto floor 10.

"Ten-o-eight is up ahead." Lena says. "You take it, Avlyn."

As we reach the door, Lena swipes her handheld to disarm the security, and the door drifts open. The lab is vast and open, dotted with workstations illuminated in my viewer.

Meyer cuts ahead. "I'll take ten-o-nine. Lena, take ten-ten."

I grab Meyer's upper arm. He flexes, then his muscle relaxes.

"It only gets easier, Avlyn," he says. "Until it's the real thing."

Meyer pulls away, and my thoughts snap back to the task at hand as Meyer and Lena leave me and head to different labs. The fact I can still hear them in my comm gives me a little comfort.

I slip into the room, illuminated only by the night vision of my EP. The counters and cabinets have a ghostly look to them, making me more nervous than I already am. The fact that the room is empty and I shouldn't be here only enhances that feeling.

At the back right-hand corner of the lab is an oversized, locked, glass cabinet. Inside, vials of various-colored liquids are labeled with project numbers. I initiate the Affinity program on my Flexx to see if it can break the security and unlock the cabinet. It fails, so I move on.

"You okay in there?" comes Meyer's voice over the comm.

"Yeah, fine."

12 minutes flashes in my vision.

Directly beside the cabinet is a magnifying station and viewing screen. Underneath is storage of glass slides, labeled with more project numbers in a clear, locked case. I crouch and reach out, touching the glass. From my fingers spreads a series of thin, white, electrical currents. I snap my hand back, surprised, and the current disappears. Hesitating, I gently touch the glass again. Numbers and symbols fly past on the bottom of my vision, recognizing it as system code.

I remove my hand again and the scrolling information stops. Is the EP making this happen? Why didn't Meyer or Lena mention it?

As I reach to touch it a third time, I get a strange feeling that someone is behind me and whip around.

A closed doorway, marked 1008b and situated against the back of the lab, glows hot white. I rise and walk toward the door, extending my hand to touch it. As my fingertips press on the cold metal, queasiness seeps through my stomach. The room goes white in an instant.

Not again, my brain screams. It's the same thing that happened at my configuration meeting. The word *Ectopistes* flashes in my vision. As it does, someone touches my shoulder. I spin and find myself looking directly into the eyes of the same boy I saw in my vision last time.

Ben?

Dark hair, like mine. Pale skin, like mine. That same scattering of freckles across his nose...

I open my mouth to speak and the boy and the scene disappear, leaving nothing but the lab as it was before.

"I... I saw something," I gasp.

"You can put it in your report," Meyer says calmly in my comm.

3 minutes

"We need to wrap it up," Lena whispers in the comm. "Meet back in the corridor."

Air escapes my lips as I shake off the vision and leave the lab. Meyer and Lena are already in the hall.

"Did you guys see that?" I ask.

"What?" Lena answers, looking puzzled.

Meyer shakes his head.

2 minutes flashes, then immediately changes to **30 seconds.**

"Something's changed. There's been a patrol shift," Meyer says. "All part of the training."

Lena and I book it to the alcove we used before, but Meyer stays behind to re-arm the security for 1008. When we reach our hiding spot, he still lags.

15 seconds...14...13...

"Come on, Meyer," I whisper.

"It's not working. You both should go."

10...9...8...

Lena grabs my shoulder, but I pull away. "I'm staying. I want to help."

"He'll be fine," she insists. "If it were real, that would be one thing, but it's only a sim."

I shake my head. She clicks her tongue and surges toward the stairwell out of sight.

Stairwell: Secure
Odds of Success 89%

Just then Meyer lets out a shout as if he was hit. Everything suddenly takes on a white, hazy effect, and the nausea in my stomach surges.

Fear grips my chest and I tuck myself further into the alcove, pulling my stunner tight to me. "It's only a sim... it's only a sim," I whisper.

"End sim!" Meyer yells.

But it doesn't end. I bite my lip and peek around the corner.

Meyer lay sprawled on the ground, a weapon trained at his chest, the guard a few feet from him.

I blink hard twice to end the sim, but it doesn't work for me either. My mind races to come up with a solution.

I fling myself toward Meyer, my hands going cold at the sight of the guard. I aim my stunner, but I feel all wrong. I have no idea how to hold this thing.

I depress the trigger, but again, nothing happens.

The guard slowly raises his weapon toward me. His eyes are cold, determined.

Desperate, I blink two times again as hard as I can to end the experience.

"End sim!" I yell. My lids force together before opening a second time to blinding white, replacing the haze. I gasp and throw my hand to the wall, or what used to be the wall. Now it's made up of scrolling code. Where my hand touches it, the spot grows brighter.

I whip toward Meyer and the guard. They're there too, only, just as the wall, made up of code. Not solid matter, but code figures frozen in time.

A tingling runs through my hand and I turn back to it, still touching the wall. The code moves up my fingers and into my hand.

"Something's wrong with the program..."

How it happens, I don't know, but I call up the damaged code and it appears in the wall in front of me. As fast as my fingers will go, I remove the vulnerability.

As if the vision never existed, the white code vanishes, replaced by the corridor.

I turn toward Meyer and the guard, finding Meyer's face is directly in front of mine, brows furrowed.

"Why'd you do that?" he demands.

Air sucks into my lungs, expelled in a squeak.

The guard's caught mid-step, hand still pointing his weapon where Meyer had been on the ground. Frozen.

"Snap out of it, Avlyn. From now on, go with the highest probability of survival. Trying to prove yourself before you're ready gets people killed. Now move."

"But something was wrong with the sim," I say. "I... I fixed the code."

"You fixed the code?" he repeats, frowning. "What are you talking about?"

"My weapon didn't fire... and that guard was about to take you out. You tried to end the sim."

"No I didn't," he says. "I had it under control and stunned him. You trying to be a hero could have gotten us killed. Well, at least in here."

"It didn't look like you had it under control," I mutter. "And something *was* wrong."

"Fine, put it in your report. It's time to go."

Bewildered, I peer back toward the still-frozen guard, then silently follow Meyer into the stairwell to the storage room. Lena's already gone. Who knows if she saw anything either.

"Here's where I take my leave," Meyer says. "Follow your instructions and the sim will end." Then he's gone. Vanished.

In my view, a drone patrol shows one minute away, and I duck behind into the storage room and open the panel. After, I follow the same route Lena and I used on the way in without incident, other than ducking out of sight a few times, all the way back to the start.

Was any of that real? Or am I just out of my mind?

Simulation complete

The street scene disappears, replaced with a blurry version of Lena's apartment. I pull out the EP and blink a few times.

"It takes some time to adjust when you've been in for a while," Lena says from her kitchen. "Especially the first few times."

"So you didn't see anything out of the ordinary in that sim?" I ask.

"Seemed pretty average to me." She shrugs. "Probably just new for you. It was weird for me at first too."

Like seeing impossible things kind of weird?

"You should probably go," she continues. "Make your report, and then grab a few hours of sleep. It will be hard to sleep after that, but I wouldn't take any sleep meds. They're bad news. Direction says their natural, but I have my doubts."

I shift on my feet. What would she think if she knew I'd already been taking anti-anxiety MedTech too?

I hold out the EP. "What should I do with this?"

"Take it with you, and the box. Ruiz wants a few of us to test them out. You can practice in your apartment. Oh, and two things. If you're not wearing it, store it in the box for cleaning, and if you're caught, destroy it if you can. To do that, rip it in half and crush the pieces. The EP will dissolve."

I return the EP to the box and head out the door. "Um, okay… bye." I check if the hall's clear and dart into my unit.

"Bye," I hear Lena call as my door shuts. A low auto light illuminates the room.

A long sigh escapes me.

What if I'm caught with it?

I find the way over to the couch to make my report. The app asks a series of questions, and I document that I thought something was glitchy, and that they might want to check security. Anything more and they will probably question my mental stability.

As I record, my eyelids drift closed, and I pinch myself to stay alert for a second time.

Finally, I enter the last words and stumble into the bedroom. The nanos consistently wake me every morning, but I don't trust them today, and set the alarm on my handheld.

Before I doze off, my fingers graze the chain still encircling my neck, still thinking of the boy with the freckles, my twin, who gave it to me.

The crisp air on the way to work clears away my fog of barely getting any sleep. This is all moving so fast. Me... breaking into GenTech? There's no way they'd really have me do that.

Citizens on the way to their positions perform a mechanical dance, never touching or interacting unless necessary. So orderly, and even more so since Manning's announcement. All the cogs in Direction's machine working as they should.

I check in at GenTech and take the main stairwell, not the service passage from last night's sim. I slip into InfoSec, passing behind Daniel and his slick, sandy-brown hair. He works furiously, wearing his headset and immersed in VR. At least he's dedicated.

Once at my desk, I sit and link my Flexx. In my mind, an imaginary version of the Affinity program engaging with GenTech ignites. The spy program flutters in like a butterfly and grabs the information it needs. I shake my head from the ridiculous vision, but the jitter in my core remains.

No turning back. I'm trusting that my mission is important after all.

I activate my screen, and instructions appear.

A. Lark and D. Carter

One member will report to Lab 1008 to secure system hardware for a physical information security check. After completion, perform maintenance scan of each system to ensure there is no errant code or files which need to be uploaded to the Genesis Technologies Server mainframe. Begin with workstation 519.

In other words, boring, low-level work.

A box waits by each of our names to decline or accept. Daniel has checked the working in InfoSec box.

Of course he did. That's the more prestigious job, and he thinks it will gain him more clout and push me from advancement. I affix my headset and dive in. Daniel's avatar works on the project in VR even more furiously than he appeared at his desk and doesn't acknowledge me.

"Daniel."

"You're working in the lab," he says without turning.

"Oh?" My heart quickens at the chance to go check out if the real lab is like the one in last night's sim. But he doesn't need to know that, so I keep my voice flat. "And why is this your decision?"

"I got here first."

Any other day, I'd argue with him out of spite. I don't know why, I just can't help myself. But it's foolish, and to be honest, I'm thrilled to go.

I pull off my headset, leaving me staring at my system screen. I accept the job, and Daniel's name disappears from the list. Before I leave, I take my handheld and attach it to my wrist.

Once in the lab, I quickly note the similarities and differences between last night and the real thing. The lights are on this morning, of course, and the rooms are not lit with glowing night view anymore. That makes a major difference. But the layout is the same. Cabinets line the walls, and workstations are situated throughout the middle. A door panel labeled 1008b stands between two sizable cabinets, the same door that was glowing in my vision.

There has to be something important behind it.

Chemists are busy ignoring each other and me as they focus on their own tasks. A girl with curly red hair, thin frame wrapped in a white coat, peers into a magnifier at the station on my right. She doesn't look up.

I scan for the workstation numbers; 517... 518... 519. An SI assistant hovers with a chemist. Must be another newbie. Since her back is to me, all I see is her neat blonde hair and white lab coat. I slip to the station.

"I'm assigned to secure your system and account," I say.

She turns, and I recognize Corra Bradley, the nosey girl from my class at university. *Guess her bragging came true.* Instead of her usual messy hair, it's now clean and short. Under the coat, her charcoal pants and fitted matching shirt are neatly pressed. She seems to have used her credits to upgrade her appearance to fit in at GenTech.

A smug expression overtakes her face. "You'll need a lab coat to be in here."

Yes, Corra. You know all the rules here too.

CHAPTER FIFTEEN

During my second day in the lab, I work on the *errant file* part of my assignment, making sure all information is secured in the mainframe. I'm kind of amazed at how sloppy some of these chemists are, there's so many mismatched filenames and formats, but their specialty is biology, not system code, so it's no wonder. In turn, I'm sure I'd be mediocre at their job.

All in all, spending these two days in a different department is refreshing. I've also been able to make more mental notes concerning the lab to use in the sim later. Nothing big, but it makes me feel useful.

Once, Corra stared my way when I yawned a few too many times, so now I try to keep my back to her. As I finish at the last station, voices interrupt the relative silence of the suite. I turn as a group of people donning white coats enters. Margo Yates, the president of GenTech, is first. I recognize her from the vids in my introduction the first day.

She's followed by more faces I'm unfamiliar with—all but one. Kyra. Beside her is a stocky, middle-aged man who must be Representative Ayers. I think I've seen him once on a broadcast.

Ayers leans into her and says something I can't hear. Kyra pulls out a handheld from the bag slung over her shoulder, unfolds it, and taps the screen, then shows it to him. I can tell by the glimmer in her eyes that she's proud of her work.

The group speaks with the lead lab chem, and Kyra again brings up her device and appears to be recording notes. They move over to a magnifier and peer in to take a look. Kyra still doesn't spot me at the back of the room.

More voices waft in from the hallway outside the lab, and the group turns. Three more men enter. Two are tall and burly, similar to the Guardian officers that roam GenTech. Then, a stiff-looking man already wearing a white coat enters.

Director Manning.

Several of the lab chems look up from their work, and I can tell they want to stare, but doing so would give them away as unfocused. However, the occasional glances up give them away, despite their efforts. Even the best of us can't resist such importance.

Why in the world would he be at GenTech?

Manning motions at the lead chem and Ayers.

"Please, continue along with the tour," she says to the group, gesturing to the door. An SI assistant floats in to retrieve them.

Kyra, along with the rest of them, turn and exit. Manning and Ayers follow the lead chem to the back of the room to the mystery door, 1008b. My heart picks up speed. I look around to make sure no one noticed my own staring, but they've either gone back to work, or are doing some gawking of their own.

That lab door has been untouched yesterday and today. If Manning is going in there, something is going on. Something big.

The chem pulls out her Flexx and swipes the screen, then the three walk through the now-open door. I strain to see inside, but it's a bad angle, and I don't want to make a big deal about it. Unable to get a view inside, the door skims shut, and the burly men stand guard. The other chems return to their work, or pack up as if the leader of Direction wasn't even here.

On my way out, I steal a last glance at the mysterious room. Having the x-ray vision would be nice right now.

Once on the street, I message Kyra. Maybe she knows something.

Flexx 682AB1-ALARK: Do anything interesting today?

I wait for a few seconds, but nothing comes back. She's probably too busy for me.

After dinner, I activate the EP and blink into the weapons training sim I was instructed to complete in my Affinity account. Instead of the shooting range I selected, I'm in a clearing, flanked by a forest. Overhead, the sky is a soft blue, the sun shrouded in clouds. Short green grasses cover the ground, interrupted with patches of plants growing tiny yellow flowers.

I bend down and run a stem between my fingers. The blossom pops off into my palm. In my view, the flower name appears: Bur Marigold.

I stroke the flower's petals with my thumb, then bring it to my nose, closing my eyes and taking in its sweet scent.

"What do you think?"

My eyelids snap open and I let out a gasp. The flower falls to the ground.

Meyer Quinn

The viewer informs me of the person who owns the voice a little too late. I need to hack in and change that setting.

"Why do you keep doing that?" I ask.

Meyer circles to the front of me, wearing blue pants and a fiery orange shirt, so different than anyone in the city wears. Of course, he's grinning. It's better than him being angry at me like he was after the last sim. The shirt shows off his muscular chest, and the sight of it makes me turn away, embarrassed I even noticed it.

"Sorry. I saw you were in." He crosses his arms and studies the ground. "I'll set it to alert you before someone new enters a sim."

I lower my gaze, laughing to myself. "Thanks. I'd appreciate it. Did you change the location?"

"Thought I'd help practice," he replies, not answering my question.

"That would be helpful. I'm still not getting a few things."

A small brown bird flies overhead. My eyes follow it as it soars over the trees on the side and disappears.

"It's a lark," he says.

"A lark?"

Meyer bends down to the yellow flowers. "Yeah. I loaded it. It's your last name, and I thought you might enjoy it. And it's also an apology for getting angry at you... it was your first time in a sim."

A blush heats my cheeks. Why is Meyer so nice to me? Must be a strategy to build my trust. Like I'm supposed to do with Aron.

"People thought of them as happy sounding," I say.

"Does seeing one make you happy?" he asks.

"Guess so, but it's not real. Right now, my happiness seems unimportant in light of what's happening."

"Everyone should have the right to be happy. It makes Jayson's capture worth something."

Seventeen years of Direction telling us happiness is irrelevant makes it a hard habit to break, so I ignore his words.

"My friend Kyra came in on a tour of the lab today with Representative Ayers and some other citizens," I tell him. "After they were there for a few minutes, Director Manning joined them."

"Manning?" He raises his eyebrows. "He's never out among the people."

"Yeah, it surprised me too. A few minutes after the rest of the group left, he and Ayers entered a door against the back wall."

I don't mention it's the same one I saw glowing in the sim. Sounds too crazy.

He looks puzzled. "Did you report it yet?"

I smile. "I'm telling you."

"Make sure you note it in your report."

I shake my head. "I'll do it when we're done in here."

"Well, we should get going then," Meyer says. "Load indoor shooting range, scenario ten, then eight."

The scene morphs into the indoor shooting range I had originally called for. A stunner fills my hand

"So you wanted to learn to shoot?"

"Why not?" I shrug. "It's not like programming systems has gotten me a lot of experience in that area. I figure I need the practice."

"Practice is always good." Meyer raises the stunner in his own hands, aiming toward the large black target situated about forty feet from where we are. He depresses the trigger and shoots several times. When each shot hits the mark, it lights the spot.

Meyer's good, near dead center each time. When he finishes the round, the targets vanish, replaced by a closer one, as does his stunner.

"Your turn."

I'll never be as good as he is. Meyer's probably had years of practice. But I won't learn if I don't try.

"Might as well give it a go."

"Okay, first, always hold it pointed downrange," he instructs. "No accidents on my watch."

I do as he says and hold the grip with both hands, my finger just outside the trigger guard, squeezing it so tight it almost hurts.

"Relax," he says. "You don't need to squeeze so hard. It's not going anywhere, and you'll have better control if you loosen up a bit."

My heart flutters as he places his hand on mine.

It's just training, Avlyn. Get a hold of yourself.

Meyer gently removes my left hand and shows me which fingers to place where. I've held the weapon in the last sim, but I really had no idea what I was doing.

"Now, bring your other hand back and steady the weapon in front of you."

From behind, he guides my hands up toward the target and helps me position my body in place.

"Arms a little higher, and bend your knees to control your balance," he says.

I follow his instructions, keeping my eyes trained on the mark, all the while fairly unsuccessfully trying to keep my mind away from the fact that he's so close to me.

"Now move your index finger onto the trigger, and as smooth as you can, start to press."

Without moving anything else on my body, I pull the trigger, anticipating the imminent burst and slight kick. It just gives under my touch, and the blast shoots forward to the target. I repeat this four times.

"Not bad," Meyer comments.

I hit the target each time. Two of them in the center, and the others pretty near the first two. My lips upturn into a smile as the weapon disappears from my hands. In my excitement, I round toward Meyer and throw my hands around his neck. His muscled chest presses against me, and the scent of him, clean and... well, *good*, fills my nose, or at least my brain's mixed with the sim's perception of it. In the split second it takes for me to realize what I've done, I freeze, as does he.

We stay like that for what seems like an eternity, until I finally slide my arms off of his shoulders, embarrassed.

"Sorry," I say as I back away.

Meyer clears his throat. "Avlyn, I want to make sure you don't get the wrong idea."

The pang of my shame worms its way around in my chest, which by this point basically feels like it's on fire.

"Really, I didn't mean to."

"I know," he says. "You were only excited. But you need to understand *nothing* can happen between us. I'm your handler, and that's it."

I pull my chin up from my chest and gaze into his eyes. "I understand."

His face stays serious for a moment, and then the corners of his lips turn up to form a smile. "But your shooting *was* really good for your first time in here. Better than most."

"It was good, wasn't it?" I return his expression, reveling a bit in my success.

Meyer backs off and looks down at his feet. "You should keep practicing, but I need to go."

I nod, and he vanishes from the sim.

Instead of reloading the targets, I plop down on the ground. "Return to the last sim," I say. The shooting range disappears and is replaced with the field dotted with the yellow flowers.

I pluck one and bring its sweet scent to my nose again.

"Ben, why can't things just be simpler?"

If they were, my twin probably never would have died, and beyond that, Direction wouldn't even exist. I know it's too late for Ben, and I may never even know what truly happened to him, but at least I can do some good in his name. Make this world a better place.

I lean back onto the grass and let the fragrance of the earth fill me.

Maybe the lark will come back.
Maybe this time it will sing.
I can always do my report later.

CHAPTER SIXTEEN

URGENT flashes on the viewing screen in my bedroom. I creep from bed, but walk past the screen. Once in the living room, I see the same broadcast alert appear on the media viewer. Reluctantly, I tap the screen. The Direction logo pops up. Not wanting to wait, I continue on into the kitchen while Director Manning's voice wafts behind me.

"Direction citizens, tonight at 8:00 p.m., a required viewing broadcast will air. It is imperative citizens and children over the age of twelve watch. At its completion, you must immediately log in to your citizen's account and answer a series of questions to confirm understanding of the announcement by 9:15 p.m. For each hour that questions remain uncompleted, each citizen will be docked one day's wages. Your cooperation ensures humanity's continuation."

The screen momentarily blanks and the logo returns. I can't remember walking back into the living room, but here I stand in front of the media viewer, heart pounding. A couple weeks ago, this message would have hardly fazed me. Yet citizens have *never* been docked wages for not watching a broadcast. Come to think of it, I can't recall any time-sensitive announcements. The news can't be good.

I tap off the screen.

In the bedroom, another message waits on my Flexx. I swipe to retrieve it. Kyra. Returning mine after I saw her come through the lab yesterday.

Flexx 35D52G-KLEWIS: Yes, I did have an interesting day. Can't say much, but exciting events are happening. I messaged a potential spouse pairing.

Affinity keeps reminding me to contact Aron, but I don't even want to think about him. Maybe he'll delete my information eventually and Affinity will let me move on from that. Kyra always was more excited than me for that part, and she sounds as if she could be looking forward to tonight's announcement. Maybe it's not that bad.

When I access my Affinity account, there's the reminder again to contact Aron. This time it urges me to use flattering language in the message. Says he might respond to it. I log on to my spouse pairing account. A new meeting invitation waits, but I want nothing to do with it, and don't even look at the name. Aron's account is still active in my potentials, but Meyer's fake account is deleted. I hover my hand over the screen where it used to be at the bottom of the list.

If citizens could truly choose, I might elect to find the thoughts behind Meyer's intense eyes. But I don't live where choice is an option. Not yet anyway. Even if I did, Meyer's request was never real, just a hack to allow him to arrange a meeting without questions.

Aron is a near perfect pairing. Direction says so, and even Affinity is pushing me in that direction, wanting me to almost flirt with him.

So why can't I stop thinking about Meyer?

I pinch the heart necklace encircling my throat, pulling the pendant across the chain, lost in the zipping sound of metal against metal and dreams of the freedom to choose.

With a shake of my head, the fog clears. Playing with the necklace could become a bad habit. It's not like it's against the law to wear jewelry, but anything out of the ordinary can make someone appear suspect. I tuck the charm back into my nightshirt.

Anyway, Meyer's only being nice to me to acclimate me to my new life. Just doing his job. In order for me to focus on what needs to be done, Meyer can be no more than a friend... and he knows that too.

There's a slim chance Aron still has interest in me since his account is still active, although, he still hasn't responded to my second request. Affinity gave me a simple assignment, and I botched it up.

Gathering my wits, I ask for the second time to arrange a follow-up meeting. I even throw in a bit of *flattering language*, and ready myself for another day.

At closing time, the GenTech elevator is always packed with other employees. I nearly squeeze in at the last second, but spot Daniel near the back. Because of it, I roundabout and take the stairs. Only a few workers use them, and it gives me a chance to get in a run. Six stories, then rounding the corner to the seventh, I slow for a person at the landing below.

"You looked tired today. How is it you have so much energy?" a smooth voice echoes, wiping away my smile.

Daniel. How'd he get down here so fast?

Before reaching him, I stop. "And what does it matter if I'm tired or not? Maybe I'm just working hard."

"You'd take the MedTech to fix it like everyone else does, but for some reason you must not be." He steps up the stairs toward me and stops at the one below mine.

"Aww... I didn't know you cared about my health, Daniel."

"I don't," he sneers.

"Maybe you should spend less time worrying about me and more time standing out as a model citizen to guarantee your advancement," I snap back.

Before I know it, Daniel thrusts his hands toward me and grabs at my upper arms. I let out a gasp, and just as I think he's going to let go, his fingers grip tighter around the meat of my arms, yanking me down to his level. I clench my jaw and keep my gaze trained on his icy stare.

"I've been watching, and you're not hiding your flaws as well as you think, Avlyn," he whispers, narrowing his gaze, unmoving.

I hold his stare, refusing to let him think he can intimidate me. "Apparently you aren't either. Maybe *you* need some MedTech. Now, why don't you back off before I report you."

I lower my eyes to where he still grips me.

Daniel rapidly blinks and frees me, then turns to grab the handrail and stomps down the stairs. I release a breath, and my head spins a little as oxygen hits my brain again. I shake my tingling hands. It's as if there's electricity zooming through my arms. Either because I can't move yet, or to make sure he's gone—both if I'm honest. I wait several minutes before resuming my descent.

Daniel has been eyeing me since day one at GenTech, and if he'd have actually seen me coding a concealment for the Affinity bug, he'd have turned me in. Daniel knows nothing concrete. He only suspects. Or he's hiding a few of his own secrets, like his anger problem. If he weren't, he'd have turned me in already. At least, that's what I hope.

Outside, golden rays of sunlight spill over my face as I exit GenTech, making Daniel seem less important. It reminds me of warmth and freedom, of the sim in the field with Meyer. It's a sensation I long for more of. Not only in an artificial world, but this one.

I have a lot of work to do before that ever happens.

A voice from behind me pulls me from my thoughts. "So, you made it to GenTech, too."

I stop and turn. Corra. Always ready to talk, most likely about herself, just like at university. Placement at GenTech hasn't changed that part of her, but being that she works in the lab, I'll take advantage of that egocentric nature.

"Yeah, it surprised me. But you always knew you'd be placed here," I say.

She catches up, straightens, and puffs up. Inside, I laugh at her predictability.

"Working in the lab *is* fascinating," she says. "But configuration was not quite what I expected."

Those words shock me coming from her mouth. "Really?"

Corra realizes her mistake and recovers, ignoring my question. "Direction is making so many exciting changes. GenTech is right on the cutting edge with them."

"Yeah, I saw Director Manning in there the other day with the Level Two representative." My heart races. Pushing Corra for information could be dangerous. "Are they often in the lab?"

"I've seen Manning around a couple times. They seem to be working on a project," she whispers. "If I were a couple years older, I'd have been assigned to the project."

"I'm sure it will come together for you." I give her a tight smile. "What do you think is in that secured suite?"

Keep playing dumb. Make her feel smart.

"Not sure, but this is the first time I saw Director Manning and Ayers go in." Her face takes on a serious expression, as if she remembers to mind her own business. Too bad. "I should go."

Without another word, she's gone.

Lena's not home. She hasn't been around for a couple days, and I find myself missing her. Company would be nice for tonight's announcement, which will no doubt be bad news for Affinity. Unfortunately, no answer comes when I knock at her door. I sigh and head into my unit.

Before the door shuts, my handheld buzzes. I pull it out and swipe the screen.

Meet me at 6:45 p.m.

Attached are sim coordinates from Meyer.

Briny air with a hint of sulfur wrinkles my nose in the simulation. Under my feet is earth, but not dirt. It's too pale and fine. I bend to sweep my hand through it. The rough grains sift between my fingers back to the earth.

Ahead of me is water as far as I can see. Not still water. Instead, the sapphire waves swell and churn as if lapping the sky for air, forming silvery foam before they vanish, then appear again in the distance and repeat the cycle.

I rise and walk closer to the shoreline, wind blowing my hair back from my face. Water rushes over my shoes and then pulls back, leaving the earth darker and denser. Again, I bend to scoop a soft clump and form it into a ball in my palm. It's like clay.

"Magnificent, huh?" Meyer's voice sounds from behind me.

I turn to find him walking toward me. Once again he's wearing completely different clothing than I'm accustomed to. Short khaki pants, a white short-sleeved shirt, and no shoes.

I peer at my typical black uniform, then back at Meyer. "Should I be dressed differently?"

He laughs. "I didn't want to assume... but sure."

I shrug. "What else is available?" My clothing has never varied from practical and utilitarian. I have no idea what to ask for.

Meyer pulls his handheld from his pocket, makes a few motions on the screen, and my clothing shifts. The bottoms of my now-bare feet sink into the damp earth, and I wiggle my big toe into it. But then a gentle wind swirls my legs.

The hem of emerald-green fabric falls at my calf and hangs loose around my lower half. I'm no longer wearing pants, but clothing called a dress I recognize only from history research at university. They went out of fashion long ago. It's a stark contrast to the form-fitting pants I always wear. The top half of the outfit hugs my chest, and the sleeves— nope... no sleeves, only thin straps. I hug my exposed arms and rub the bumpy flesh under my fingers.

"Um... I'm a bit... naked."

Meyer's cheeks flush, and he pulls out his Flexx again. "Sorry. I thought I'd give you a taste of something other than Direction's stuffy clothes."

He swipes at the screen, and a long-sleeved stretchy white top with buttons on the front appears over the dress.

His face is sheepish as he asks, "Is that better?"

"A little... I'll adjust," I reply, but it's a white lie.

He folds and returns the handheld back to his pocket and joins me where water meets land. "I'm dreading tonight's announcement, so I thought I'd show you this instead of training."

"Training is more important."

"It is, but we won't have a chance again for a long time, if at all." Meyer's eyes focus down, and he pushes the grainy earth around with his left foot.

As we walk on the shore, I tell him the little I learned from Corra today and about Daniel's bullying.

Meyer bristles as I share what happened in the stairwell with Daniel. "You know, if you wear the EP, it can alert you if he's near."

"Wear it all the time? I didn't know if I could."

"They're undetectable." He pauses. "It's how I tracked you in One."

I cross my arms. "And how you knew when I was in sim?"

"I know. It seems like a privacy invasion, and it probably is, but you were... *are* my assignment. Sorry I didn't explain it to you sooner. All I see is your position in relation to me, your vitals, and if you're in a simulation, nothing more."

I relax and let my arms fall to my sides as I gaze out over the rolling waves. "Where do you live now, Meyer? In Elore, or outside the city?"

"All over. If I have business in the city, I'll stay in a safe house for a few days. If not, outside city bounds."

"You can travel outside city bounds?"

"Until recently, Direction has mostly used Guardians to patrol the borders, and our people on the inside have gotten us past the electro perimeter. But with human security increased, it's not as easy anymore."

"Where are you located now?"

He gestures for us to walk. "In the city. To stay near."

Near to what? Me?

I blush. That's ridiculous, he must mean rebellion activity. Meyer is on assignment, nothing more.

"Where did you grow up?"

That's not the question I wanted to ask.

"In the Outerbounds..." he replies stiffly. "With Jayson."

"Really?" I study his face. "Tell me what it's like."

His coal eyes gaze toward the horizon, and the stubble growing from his chin fascinates me. So much so that I have to stop myself from reaching over and touching it.

My face warms. Men in Elore never grow facial hair. Most even have their nanos programmed to slow the growth so it only has to be removed occasionally.

"I can't... I'm not allowed."

My shoulders sag. "What *can* you tell me?"

He shrugs while running a hand through his thick, dark hair. "Only that what Affinity does is worth it. It's imperfect outside the city, but I've experienced both lives, and the freedom far outweighs the security and advancement Direction offers." He checks the time on his antique watch.

"Why do you wear that?" I chuckle. "You see the time in your EP, or you could just wear your handheld."

"Time fascinates me."

"Should have guessed. A bunch of your messages were about it. Remind me of the second one? Lost time is—"

"Never found again," he finishes.

I stop and turn toward him. "That's it. What did you mean by it?"

"Oh, it's an old quote from a person you won't find in official Direction history."

"Who?"

"A guy named Benjamin Franklin, a leader from a long time ago. You'd be surprised by the information still beyond the walls of Elore."

"Surprises are overrated." I sigh, thinking of Ben. "I just want to know now."

Meyer smiles. "Then I don't really need to tell you what the quote means."

That smile is definitely growing on me.

The sun sinks, casting a pinkish orange hue across the sky.

He checks his watch again. "Care to view the broadcast with me?"

"In here?"

"Sure. It will auto play on your media viewer in your unit, but we have access in here, too." He gestures to the dry earth behind us. "Have a seat."

"I'd rather watch the sunset, but I guess that's not an option," I grumble lightly.

Meyer laughs. "No... no, it's not."

I plop onto the ground and tug at my skirt in an effort to cover my ankles. Meyer doesn't notice. He's messing with his Flexx to bring up the announcement. As he joins me, the view changes into a giant Direction logo.

My stomach sinks. The sky looked better without it.

Direction's logo blips out of sight and Director Manning's face fills the sky, making me draw away. The camera pans back, and he sits at a sleek, white desk with a sterile white background. He's clothed in a white smock, a nod to the fact he's a Science Director. A smug expression reminds us he knows best, that he's the Director, the top tier of intelligence, and should not be questioned.

His icy gray eyes peering down over those watching send a shiver down my spine.

"Citizens, it has been Direction's goal for over thirty-five years to focus on strengthening intelligence, since our world population was robust enough to do so. This has meant sacrifice for the greater good. Fortunately, developed intelligence has evolved our nano and MedTech, providing optimal health and stability for our society through the sacrifice of pruning our population."

Manning's fingers gently tap on the desk and he forms balls with his fists to stop them.

"We have reached the point again where adjustments have become necessary due to dissenters who plague the population of Elore."

My hands dampen as he speaks of Affinity. I look over at Meyer, whose wide eyes stare toward the vid.

"We will not allow the Affinity terrorist group to destroy the exceptional future Direction lays before us. As of this afternoon, the latest round of vaccinations was completed at each level. Not only does it protect the citizens from the potentially life-threatening viruses spreading outside our city—"

"A lie." Meyer shakes his head. "No serious viral threats have surfaced in the Outerbounds for over ninety years."

Before a couple weeks ago, I'd never believed Manning to be outright lying to us.

"Each citizen's and child's internal nano system has been upgraded as a safety precaution. The new technology has the ability to control the nervous system, and as a result, those suspected of consorting with any terrorist group will be unable to move, or will remain 'suspended', until a team can arrive to retrieve them."

Fear cyclones through my body. I have this tech inside me.

"Affinity has forced our hand, so we do this for the safety of the people of Elore. We must begin a draft. When curfew lifts tomorrow morning, Level One citizens and children will have ten hours to report to a dispatch center on each block within their sector. From there, they will be evaluated to either join the Direction Preservation Force, the DPF, or will be sent home to await future instructions."

On the screen flashes a digital image of multiple male and female soldiers in tan, camouflage-style uniforms. Displayed on their chests are letters DPF.

"Level Ones, we thank you for your sacrifice. As a show of our gratitude, if you, or someone in your family, is chosen for the new DPF, you will receive a fifteen percent wage increase. Levels Two and Three will continue as usual, following prior instructions to report any suspicious behavior via your citizen's account or app until further notice. Guardian drones will assist in Level One to maintain order. Until further notice, any business or scheduled family visitation is prohibited in Level One for Level Two and Three citizens."

Then he repeats the instructions from earlier in the day, that we must all log in to our accounts and answer a series of questions concerning the broadcast.

"Cooperation is the key to humanity's advancement."

The vid blanks and returns to the logo. I turn toward Meyer, numbness setting into my limbs. "What does this mean for us?"

His breathing is quick, and by his expression, I can tell he's trying to work through the news. "They're using the VacTech to control Level Ones and turn them into an army. Their goal has always been to phase out those with lower Intelligence Potential anyway, and this is an easy way to fight Affinity and rid themselves of Level One at the same time."

I gasp. "Is that true?"

"They did it with the viruses."

"Bess," I whisper. The thought pierces me. I still have a hard time letting go of the fact she allowed Ben and me to be a part of the experimentation to raise our intelligence potential. My head knows she probably had no choice, but my heart wanted her to fight harder for us.

"Your bio mother? Is she a Level One?"

"Yeah, but I can't see her being made into a soldier. She's not that strong."

"SI's aren't running everything yet. Direction still needs Level One for lower-level jobs. Hopefully, it can buy her time. But if I'm right... I don't know." He starts to dart his eyes around. He must see something in his EP I can't.

"Are you safe?" I ask, my heart racing.

Meyer frowns and touches my shoulder lightly with his hand. "Avlyn, I may not see you for a while, but I meant what I said the first time I contacted you."

I rack my brain. "Lose your life--"

"And you might find it," he finishes. And then he's gone.

My body quivers with the thought.

I'm ready to find a life worth living, because it's not this one.

And now... time really is running out.

CHAPTER SEVENTEEN

I pace as morning sun paints my living room. I didn't sleep a wink after that announcement last night. Thoughts and feelings swirl through me, churning with visions of going to war.

My head throbs. At least the beach sim was vast and peaceful. I should have stayed in there last night. In the real world, I'm confined to this cramped apartment with nothing to do but imagine how I'll die. Even the view does nothing for me now.

Lena's not home. Again. There's no reason for her absence lately, but she doesn't answer the door after I try knocking for the second time this morning, and Kyra wouldn't understand. So I can't message her.

I'm utterly alone.

The pacing doesn't settle me down, and I finally resign myself to my generally comfortable couch. This morning it feels like stone, and there isn't a spot worth sitting on. I distract myself by moving into my bedroom to work on the required questions for the broadcast on my viewer. From the living room, my Flexx makes a muffled chime, and at the same time a notification blinks in my EP. My heart quickens. It could be Meyer.

I leap from my seat and follow the sound. Where is it? The chime stops just as I pull the device from inside the couch cushion. My hands tremble as I fumble to see Meyer's message. The screen's blank, and I enter my code for the Affinity app.

My heart plummets into my stomach when I see that the message isn't from him.

> *Affinity,*
> *I come to you with a heavy heart. Direction is advancing their plans more quickly than we anticipated, putting not only Level One citizens in extreme danger, but all of Elore. Time is of the essence.*
> *Today at 8:15 am, we will hold our own announcement. It is imperative that you join us to discuss your futures and how Affinity aims to counteract Direction plans.*
> *Below, you will find sim coordinates for the meeting location. If you do not have access to an EP, the gathering will be available via your Affinity app.*
> *Adriana Ruiz*

I copy the coordinates into the sim program. Still wearing the EP, I blink twice to engage. Who cares if I'm thirty minutes early? The meeting location has to be better than this reality.

When my eyes adjust, I'm met with an amphitheater, row after row of stone benches curving around to form the meeting place. Below is an open grassy space with a podium in the center. There's space for at least a thousand people. It seems like a lot at first, since congregating like this would never be allowed in Elore, but when I think about it, I'm not sure a thousand will be enough. Ten times that could be drafted from Level One, and I don't even want to think about the Guardian drone force.

Even in the sim, the headache I have in real life worms its way through my temple.

How will we be able to do anything against Direction? They have more people... more weapons.

After about twenty minutes, a few people have arrived and are scattered throughout the seats. I squint and lean toward those milling down below, trying to will away my negative thoughts.

Do I know anyone? No. No one's familiar.

From my EP, I see Lena has arrived. On the right somewhere. I turn, spot her, and wave.

"You weren't home last night," I say when she comes close.

"Sorry," she says. "Had official business."

I don't press. "It's okay. I watched the announcement with Meyer instead."

"You did? In a sim?" Her lips form into a crooked smile. "So that's where he was."

The dulcet tone she uses makes me blush, and I'm not sure why. Heat burns up my neck, and I pull at my already high collar. But with thoughts of how Meyer left the last sim in a hurry, the feeling drops to my gut.

"Do you have any idea what Adriana's announcing?" I ask.

"Nope, no clue. But with everything going on, I'm ready to hear it."

More people blink into existence, and the amphitheater slowly fills. I go back to studying them, hoping to recognize anyone, but no one familiar shows up.

"Checking out the faces?"

"Yes."

"I did that too." Lena chuckles. "In my first sim meeting. You won't find anyone unless you're aware a person is part of Affinity and they're on your contact list. The program keeps their avatars unrecognizable."

"What do you mean?"

"See that guy?" She points to a young man with curly blond hair. "He doesn't appear the same in real life. Who knows? Might be a sixty-five-year-old woman."

I chuckle nervously. "A woman?"

"Yeah, the gatherings build a sense of camaraderie and unity, but Affinity still won't risk exposing people. They program the sim to keep identities obscure."

"Lena," I ask, looking around at the crowd, "do you really think we have a chance?"

She gives me a sad smile. "I have to."

"Outerbounders and citizens. Members of Affinity."

Our heads snap forward as Adriana Ruiz's melodious voice rings out into the amphitheater. She's a petite woman, close to Kyra's size, but older, perhaps in her sixties. Her boots are worn over a tan, form-fitting uniform, and she holds her hands behind her back. The jumbled background noise of people's conversations dies out as everyone stares toward her figure in the middle of the arena at the podium. A projection of her face also fills the sky.

"Thank you for joining us on this somber occasion. It was always our hope Affinity could make changes in the Direction Initiative with little to no loss of life. Without the use of violence. Unfortunately, this does not appear to be a reality. Manning is increasingly becoming more dangerous, and is threatening the lives of the citizens of Elore." She pauses. "It's time for us to choose a *new* Direction."

As she says this, the crowd, including Lena, goes wild. People stand, shouting, cheering, and pumping their fists in the air. The chosen phrase is ironic, and she knows it.

Instead of standing, I sink back and grasp at the hollow developing in my stomach. This is so backward from anything I've experienced. Citizens aren't loud. They keep to themselves. They don't throw fists in the air. They keep them to their sides. I'm suddenly dizzy, and my stare locks onto the white knuckles of my interlaced fingers.

From the right, people have begun chanting.

Choose a new Direction.

Choose a new Direction.

Over and over. The arena fills with voices shouting in unison. Affinity has a war cry.

I want to be excited along with everyone else, but with Meyer missing, all I can think about is his words.

Lose your life and you might find it.

I may actually die for a new Direction to become reality. All *these* people might have to die. If Direction is blowing up their own people, there's no way they'll take mercy on traitors. A steady stream of air releases through my nose.

Ruiz raises her hands and a hush falls over the arena. Whispers continue, but then fade as people sit again. Ruiz opens her mouth to speak, but then closes it and drops her chin. After a moment of silence, she breathes again, and she lifts her head. Her face is serious, but her soulful eyes project a sense of bravery.

"But seeing a new Direction come to fruition will take sacrifice. The loss of life could be great, and this reality saddens me deeply. We have asked for assistance from New Philadelphia, but so far they have refused our requests. It's a loss, but one we will handle."

What's New Philadelphia?

"For the time being, those of you in the Outerbounds will meet with your team leaders for instructions. Those working undercover in the city should await further information.

"Affinity holds these truths to be undeniable. Everyone is created equal. They are entitled to certain intrinsic rights, including life, freedom, and the quest of happiness. With the dedication of each and every one of you, Elore can choose a *new* Direction."

At the end of the speech, she smiles tightly and exits. The crowd, including Lena, jumps to their feet again in deafening applause. Echoes of the chanting *"Choose a new Direction"* fill the stadium again.

I grab her shoulder and pull her toward me. "Gotta go. I'm exhausted." I am tired, but it's mostly an excuse to get out of here.

Lena nods and places her hand on top of mine to give it a squeeze. "Get some sleep," she half yells in my ear.

As she releases me, a pang of fear zips through me. The idea of losing all the people I love and care for in this mess becomes too much of a reality.

Love.

The thought of the word burns through me while I blink twice. Hard. I blip out of the sim.

When my eyes flicker to my desolate apartment, the sense of Lena's touch vibrates over my skin. I reach to where her hand was, trying to hold onto the feeling of security. It used to bring stress because enjoying the presence of others was wrong. Weak. Even missing my twin was wrong. I was always terrified of being seen as emotional. Now love and friendship is the only thing that's going to make the risk I'm taking worthwhile.

I log in to the Affinity account from my handheld to check for my instructions. Nothing new has been added other than Adriana's announcement. There's no message from Meyer either.

What if I could find him? He said he could track me. Maybe I can figure out how that works.

My stomach quivers as I secure my desktop system from the network, then link my Flexx and enter the Affinity app through my desktop system. Only a few minutes later, and I find a path into the program. No signs they know I'm in here yet.

It's not long before I'm searching for Meyer's information, but there's too much code to sort through quickly. I blink twice to activate my EP. It should make it easier to navigate, like VR at work.

But inside, it's not like GenTech's VR coding at all.

The space around me goes white. Breathtaking. The simple numbers and patterns of the code have morphed into something like stars in the sky, close enough to reach out and touch. My whole body vibrates with energy as I tap the code. Despite an annoying dizziness, a thrill starts to run through me.

I could get lost in this...

No. This whole process needs to be quick. Find Meyer and leave before they realize I've hacked in.

I use my handheld in the sim to **find Meyer Quinn**, and when it does, I'm caught in the whirlwind of the search. Every part of me breaks apart and reassembles, whisking me to his information. A series of white storage containers presents along with a section labeled *Recordings*. I touch it and up pops a series of files, identified by date. I pull one and activate it. Meyer's voice sounds around me. Then a hologram displays what he sees with his EP when it's activated. I wave away the vid, feeling guilty for seeing it. This is something private. Although, it *would* be fun to watch one of the sims we did together.

Focus, Avlyn.

"Track Meyer Quinn," I say, hoping the program will respond to voice commands.

To my surprise, a file presents itself, and I touch it.

"Download program."

My vision fills with code.

Download complete

The program appears to work. On the right side of my vision, a small icon sits with his name underneath. To find him, I call up a map to the city.

Meyer Quinn Found blinks, then switches to an aerial view of Elore, marking the sectors within Levels One, Two, and Three. The tracker locks onto him in Level One, Sector D. Vitals and all. Just like he could see on me.

He's alive. Meyer's alive.

The excitement burns along the back of my ears, but with the need to get out of the program, I blink twice. I find myself sitting at my chair with much less interesting surroundings.

Meyer, can you talk? I message.

Nothing comes back.

I wait for something. Anything. But eventually my need for rest overrides my frustration, worry, and excitement. So, without changing clothes, I drag myself to bed for a nap. The map still shows in my EP, and I blink twice to turn it off. A ghost of the image remains.

If Meyer doesn't message back by tomorrow, I'm going out to find him.

The thoughts swirl away as a wave of exhaustion hits, forcing me into desperately needed sleep.

CHAPTER EIGHTEEN

My eyes drift open to a blurry room and the vibration of my handheld on the corner of the bed. After a second, I blink to clear the hazy coating on my eyes and roll over to pat for the device. By the time I find it, the buzzing has stopped.

ONE SPOUSE PAIRING MESSAGE ADDED BY A. BARTON.

Scenes from the last few days rush in. The Direction announcement, the Affinity meeting, my instructions.

Meyer.

I swipe away the message and access my Affinity account instead to check for my new mission. My heart pounds while selecting the link.

> *Affinity thanks you for your service. At this time, you are asked to continue on track with your original mission. You may review these instructions at this link.*
> *Thank you.*

That's it? Nothing new?

I know my original mission... training, link my Flexx to retrieve information at GenTech, and continue contact with Aron Barton as a potential pairing.

The spouse pairing message...

I grit my teeth, but still don't look. I check two more times for anything from Meyer, but nothing's new. Then I stare at the screen in hopes something will happen. It doesn't. I log off and resign myself into the account.

ONE SPOUSE PAIRING MESSAGE ADDED BY A. BARTON.

I hover my finger over the link, and it repels like the wrong side of a magnet.

This is it... either Aron accepted my invitation and I can continue my mission, or he didn't and I messed everything up.

Eventually, I tap the screen.

Avlyn,
I apologize for the delay in getting back to you. Work was busy after we met, and you were right. Our first meeting was awkward.

Awkward is an understatement. I got into a fight with him. In *public.*

I have time today at 5:00 p.m. for a few minutes, if you are free. If not, we can reschedule.
Aron Barton

His image, adjacent to the words, partially fills the screen. Golden hair, tan skin, I'd forgotten how good-looking he was.

I squirm in my seat.

And Meyer? I activate his tracker again in the EP. His icon blinks on in my vision, still in Sector D, and he's moving now. My chest clenches at not knowing what he's doing or if he's safe.

But Meyer isn't my assignment right now. Aron is. He's probably doing what he's supposed to be doing, and it's about time I did the same.

In Direction's world, emotions still get me in trouble. Nothing has changed, and the only way it will is by following instructions, not getting sidetracked in silly fantasies. And he *told* me I wouldn't hear from him for a while.

I flick off the EP.

The time?

I look to see that it's 12:28 p.m.... on *Sunday?* What happened this morning, or for that matter... Saturday? If it weren't for the message buzzing, who knows how long I would have slept. After a couple weeks of horrific sleep, I guess my nanos decided more was necessary.

Yes, 5:00 p.m. works.

But not at the café. Meyer mentioned they're not safe.

Let's meet at the park. West side, on the benches.

I hit send.

The bench at the park cools my legs and fingers, which graze the rounded stone edges. After breakfast, I showered and ran sims for the rest of the day. When I finished, I still had close to an hour before the meeting with Aron, so, to get my mind off Meyer again, I left early.

The park is the same as the other times I've come, and a few citizens take advantage of the beauty here through exercise or simply working outdoors. It's the only area in the city to do so comfortably.

A woman runs along the path and disappears around the bend of trees. In the distance, a man sits leaning on a tree and works on a handheld. Then there's me, waiting on a bench for a spouse pairing meeting I don't want, ridiculously consumed with another boy I can't have.

How is it we can go on concerning ourselves with trite problems? At this very moment, Level One citizens are being rounded up to be made into an army under the guise of duty. I've nothing better to do than wait for a meeting with Aron while the rest of Affinity is readying for a revolution.

I grip the edge of the bench, visualizing myself yelling, "*Don't you want better than this? What about the people in Level One drafted for a war they don't understand?*"

I blink and I'm back on the bench. I never moved. The man under the tree sits, staring toward his Flexx device.

"Avlyn?"

I jump at the sound of my name. "What?" I say too loudly.

"Are you all right?" Aron sits by me on the bench, blond hair neatly combed, his hands clutched together on his lap so tightly it's as if he's keeping them from escaping.

"Oh, Aron. I'm sorry. I have a lot on my mind." My second impression is chalking up to be as good as my first. Crazy girl.

"Don't we all?" He gives me a sympathetic smile. "So many changes are going on right now. Syn has upped its drone production, and I've been assigned extra work from home. That's why I couldn't meet until now."

No way can I tell Aron my true source of stress.

"They haven't done that at GenTech yet. Although, I'm sure I'll have my turn on the remote InfoSec team and will pull a few all-nighters." A nervous laugh escapes me. As if I'm not used to all-nighters. "Do you think SynCorp bumped production due to the announcement?"

"Possibly. A few days ago, on lunch break, Director Manning and a few of the level representatives came through. Didn't think much about it until last night."

"I saw him in GenTech, too," I say.

"In InfoSec?"

"No. I was working on data security in the lab. He came in and then went into a secret area."

Aron leans in, giving me a curious look. "Secret?"

A lump forms in my throat. I've said too much. Then again, maybe intriguing him is a good way to keep him interested. And for some reason, I *do* trust him.

"I don't know if it's really *secret*." I try to blow it off a bit. "But they were the only people who went in the two days I was in there."

"Hmm…" He smiles softly, showing off his dimple.

"So why didn't you delete me from your spouse pairing candidates?" I ask, changing the subject.

Aron tips his head. "Why, what do you mean?"

"The meeting was horrible, and you know it." I scratch at the bumpy texture of the bench to work out some of the fidgety feelings I have inside.

"Oh, it wasn't all bad," he says, his blue eyes gleaming. "You didn't seem to mind my sense of humor."

"Why would I mind that?"

"Why do you even have to ask?" Aron chuckles lightly. "My parents always tried to make me tone down and focus. Then I met with a few other spouse pairing possibilities, and while they didn't run out on me..."

He cocks his head toward me and heat flushes my face.

"By the way they stared out the window or kept their mouth full of food so they didn't need to talk, I knew there wouldn't be a second meeting. I'm not sure, but it wasn't my humor that had you running."

I don't know what to say to that, so I keep my mouth shut. Aron seems like a trustworthy person, but I don't want to reveal too much too soon. I've already said enough.

"Well, I went ahead and kept your profile active, just in case. But then you contacted me. I thought about it for a while... and here we are."

Aron confuses me. While growing up, I never considered my pairing would be more than a contract, so I've resisted the idea of even taking one. But he has good qualities. An agreement with him would guarantee security. My life has so little of that right now. So he looks down on the Level Ones... I have too. He could change.

Lose your life and you might find it.

Meyer's words push away the thoughts.

A forced existence would never work. Even if Aron was perfect, to live under Direction's oppression with him could never be right. I'd sacrifice the freedom and rights of others to maintain a sense of false happiness for myself.

Aron is an assignment. Nothing else. I don't even know if Affinity would allow a pairing with him yet. I steel myself and decide to offer up something personal if it makes sense in our conversation. We obviously have some sort of connection here. Let's see if I can work it.

"Sorry about running out on you." I sigh. "As I said, a lot's on my mind. GenTech, then the move into my apartment, and the responsibilities that go along with being a citizen have been... overwhelming. I really shouldn't have started browsing my spouse pairings until I got settled."

Aron averts his blue eyes from mine. "And... I insulted Level Ones and you have a twin brother there."

"Had." Blood begins to rush through my hands and I clasp my fingers together nervously. *Should I tell him this?* "He died, and although I'm not supposed to feel anything about it, I do. I miss him terribly."

"I'm sorry," he says, "but maybe finding someone to share those responsibilities and burdens with could make life easier."

Really? I tell Aron something that's against the Direction Initiative, and he doesn't berate me for it? I always thought it was only me who was dying inside for the want of connection, but maybe I'd found someone else with those same feelings. And if he does, maybe a lot more people do too.

Aron's a Level Two citizen with a high-ranking job, more credits than he needs, and perfect health, but that's not enough for him. Why do Elorians even allow the Direction Initiative to continue? Duty? Patriotism? The illusion that Direction understands our needs better?

"We have everything and still nothing," I mumble.

He leans in slightly. "Hmm?"

I wave my hand in his direction. "Nothing."

"Well," Aron says as he glances at his handheld on his wrist. "Sorry, but I don't have long. I have to get back to my work at home."

"I have a bunch of things to take care of today too," I say, but really, I don't want him to go. Having him near is somehow a comfort.

He stays seated and shakes his head. Stalling? "Do you mind doing me a favor?"

"Sure, what?"

"Can you fill out the rest of the information in your pairing account and give me access?" He gives a shy smile and looks away.

Direction fills in the stats and figures of why we're an acceptable pairing, the important stuff, but none of our likes and dislikes or experiences.

Hearing those words fills me with an energy I never expected. Aron is interested in me.

"Sure," I agree, "if you'll do the same."

At that, Aron stands, and then turns. His lips form into a half smile, and he gives me a wink. I can't help smiling back, but then I turn and focus on the sidewalk. No one has ever winked at me. I look up, wave good-bye, and watch until he disappears into Level Two.

When he's out of sight, I pull my feet onto the bench seat. It wouldn't be dreadful to make a contract with him. Maybe he's sympathetic to Affinity's goals. I'd gain his trust, and we'd work together. It's the perfect scenario, and it's something I can have, unlike Meyer, who's not even a citizen.

A muffled *boom* breaks my thoughts and makes me jump. Looking around, I see nothing but a tranquil park and scattered citizens minding their own business. A few of them are also looking toward the sound. I check for Aron, but he's gone.

The boom comes again from the direction of Level One.

An explosion? What if Bess is hurt?

The thought surprises me, as I never imagined I might even care for her. I could message her to make sure she's safe. I pull out my Flexx, but pause before entering anything.

Affinity has instructed me not to contact her, as it would be out of place and might draw attention. My fingers tremble over to the screen, and the device drops and smacks against the sidewalk. My vision illuminates with information in my EP.

Explosion Level One Sector B
Multiple casualties
Affinity not involved. Do not engage.

I spin and stare toward Level One again. What Sector is Bess in? B or C? I can't remember. On auto, I grab my handheld from the ground and enter my Affinity passcode, activating the app. The same news in my EP repeats on the screen, telling me to go home.

Find Meyer Quinn I enter on my Flexx. The view switches to an overhead map of Level One. My stomach leaps. His avatar is on the move.

Running straight into Sector B.

Creeping the streets of Level One, Sector C, I keep my eyes to the ground. The guards seemed occupied, and somehow I was able to slip in unnoticed.

"Please remain calm and continue to your assigned draft dispatch center." An impassive, disembodied voice coming from the blank media screen announces Manning's orders from last night every few minutes.

Why am I here?

I can't do anything for Meyer, but I also can't go home and wait to find out what's going on. The EP guides me through the streets toward his location. Finally, his avatar stops, and it's a good thing, since my running would only cause more attention.

On the other side of the street, Level One citizens, some in pairs or families, wait their turn for required check-ins at this block's draft center. A few young children are crying, and their mothers or fathers work to soothe them. At the front of the line, an SI checks in each individual citizen.

I try not to stare, but my eyes, as if they have a mind of their own, keep falling back toward them. A human Guardian glares toward one family with a crying child. He moves toward the couple and says something, and the mother with white-blonde, too long hair clutches her son—whose hair color matches her own—to her body and places her hand over his mouth, stifling his cries.

To distract me further, the EP continues to bring up new information of the route to take to get to Meyer and the locations of Guardian and human force. The jitters in my core have morphed into chattering teeth.

You can't do anything about the draft right now. Control yourself.

I fill my lungs with air, hold it in, and then let it out while counting. Eventually, my teeth stop clacking, but the restlessness in my stomach returns.

"No... you can't draft both of us!" a woman screeches behind me. "What will happen to my son?"

When I turn, I see the same mother with the wailing child cursing at the uncaring SI. A man, probably her spouse, steps in toward her, but she shoves him back. Several human Guardians take places around the line of citizens and raise their weapons. The line seems to shrink as the people press together.

Engagement odds of success 0% flashes in my EP.
Do not engage

Another Guardian steps forward and seizes the child from the arms of his shrieking mother while the SI lifts a scanning device. She stops yelling, or doing anything at all. The woman is frozen, mouth hanging open.

Because a woman distraught by Direction separating her from her child is the real *danger to all of us.*

The guard who took the child disappears into a nearby building while another SI emerges and retrieves the frozen woman, its metal tentacles clutching her body like a package. The man she was with follows them willingly into another building.

"Please remain calm and continue to your assigned dispatch center," the voice echoes throughout the sector.

Across the street, a dark-haired woman hugging herself joins the line.

Bess.

I exhale. She's safe. And not in B. Immediately, a rush of relief floods over me.

What will they do with her? Will she be forced into that building too? Be taken away to become a soldier?

I can't answer any of these questions, but I'm relieved she's still unharmed. She doesn't see me, so I hustle along the EP guided path and push away any feelings I have for her.

At the next block, the EP alerts me I've entered Sector B. Nothing is out of the ordinary, at least not today. Some citizens wait in the draft check line while others return home. Then I round the corner.

The lobby to an apartment building is blown to bits, and citizens, people, lie on the ground. Not moving.

This is the blast I heard. My legs weaken, and I grasp for a wall to steady myself.

Why is no one helping or doing anything?

The area where they lie is blocked off by drones, while down the road, a dispatch station checks in more Level Ones.

It's a reminder. Do what you're told, or this will be you.

"What happened?" I whisper as a young woman passes. I didn't intend to speak to her, but still, she stops and leans in.

"The Affinity rebels bombed the building over there. Then they tried to rush the DPF. Guardians surrounded them immediately, got them right in time."

"Are they dead?"

"I think so," she mutters and hurries away.

I thought Affinity wasn't involved?

I check the people on the ground again and hug myself tighter. More lies from Direction.

Meyer Quinn 1 Block North

"Please remain calm and continue to your assigned dispatch center." The announcer's voice has the opposite effect it desires, and a twinge zips through my left temple.

After one more block, I turn a corner.

Meyer Quinn 585 ft. ahead. Continue course

Walking citizens block my view, but the EP continues to feed me his location. My breath quickens as I dodge citizens, and then his dark hair comes into view through the glass of an apartment building. I slow and approach the sliding doors. Someone else is with him.

Lena? Why is she here?

She sees me, then turns to him, mouthing my name.

His head shoots up, and he looks in my direction, then sprints toward the doors, exiting through them, Lena on his tail.

Meyer stops in front of me, scowling. "Avlyn, you need to leave."

I know I shouldn't be here, but it made sense in Level Two. Shame fills me, and I drop my chin. "I... I wanted to help. I was worried."

The veins on his neck pulse and he grabs my arm. He starts to speak, but instead the disembodied voice fills the air.

"Attention, Level One Sector B is now under lock down."

CHAPTER NINETEEN

Meyer's jaw tightens and his nostrils flare. I can tell he must be attempting to form a plan of how to get rid of me.

This was a mistake. I never should have come into Level One.

I flinch as the voice continues. "Level One Sector B citizens, please return to your housing units and await further instructions. All other approved non-Sector B Level One citizens, report to the nearest drafting center and wait to be escorted to your proper sector."

The words cut at my brain. There's no way I can report to the dispatch center. The guards will question why I was here and detain me. I'll most likely be arrested since Manning restricted crossing into One.

Meyer, still grasping my arm, now ignores me while scanning the dispersing crowds and the movement of the guards. After a moment, he lets go and gestures to Lena, who is already outside.

"Back inside, Lena," he grunts and gestures for me to follow. "You, too." Before turning away, his eyebrows knit. The heat of his anger radiates off him.

The second message repeats. "Attention, Level One Sector B is now under lock down."

Head hung and cheeks burning, I enter the building. Never have I been so embarrassed and ashamed. Lena, normally sweet, doesn't even look my way and strides toward the stairwell, Meyer on her heels, also avoiding me. I take up the rear.

We hit the ninth floor and exit. Neither Meyer nor Lena have spoken a word, but they seem to know our destination. I assume they've been here before, or are fed the information in their EPs. Information my EP is not privy to.

A mother, father, and young son scurry past us toward their door. Muffled whispers between the parents meet my ears. The boy looks up, his stare meeting mine. Then they disappear into their doorway. The hairs on my arms are standing on end through my shirt. I work to smooth them, but it's no use.

Eventually, we stop at a unit marked 915. Lena palms the visitor alert. Footsteps sound, and a crack in the door appears as it clicks open. This building is like Bess's and still has old-fashioned swinging doors instead of the modern sliding ones of Level Two.

A man's voice speaks from the opposite side of the door, through the crack. "What day is it?"

"Looks like thunderstorms," Meyer replies.

And that means?

The door snaps shut. Then the sound of clacking metal is followed by the door opening again. A scrawny, short man with reddish-blond hair ushers us into a modest, drab apartment. Apparently, he's aware what "thunderstorms" means. A musty scent overwhelms my nose, and I let out a cough followed by another.

The pale man stares at me as I hack. "Three of you? I'm only equipped to handle two," he says while holding up three, then two fingers.

"Change of plan," Lena mumbles to no one in particular.

"Sorry, Nelson," Meyer says. "We're out of options right now. This will need to work."

Pressure builds in my chest, silently pleading, *just let us in.*

Nelson—I have no idea if it's his first or last name—drops his hand to his side and bobs to stare past us. "Fine, fine. Do what you have to do and leave." He ushers us through the living room and bedroom, then points toward the closet. "You'll find the entrance inside."

"In the closet?" I mumble.

Meyer turns and glares. "Yes, shh…"

I cross my arms and close my eyes. This has to be a dream. But when I crack my lids, the view is the same: a dim, sparse room with four people in front of a closet. And this isn't a sim— it's definitely real. At least it's somewhere to hide.

Lena pulls a handheld from a bag over her shoulder and swipes and pokes the screen. From behind, the door to the bedroom clicks shut. When I turn, Nelson's gone.

I turn back to Meyer as Lena steps inside the closet door.

"Come on," he says.

Meyer and I follow behind her. A gap appears between the few items of hung clothes. He yanks the garments aside and signals me. I crouch and crawl inside. Meyer enters, sits by me, and the panel slides closed. The only illumination comes from Lena's Flexx. She still works on it while scrunched in the corner. My EP seems to be compensating since the room appears brighter than it should.

Nelson was right. He didn't have room for more than two. There's barely room for one in here, just enough to stand without hitting my head, and if Meyer were any closer, he'd be on top of me. I press my back into the wall and slide to sit next on his left. Lena backs up against the other wall, her legs to my right.

"Where are we?" I ask.

"It's a safe house," Lena says. "Affinity has them set up all over Elore."

"Thirsty?" Meyer asks as he hands me a bottle. "It's water."

"Uh, sure." I'm actually extremely thirsty. I tip it back, and the cool water spills into my mouth.

Lena grabs the bottle. "Not too much. There's only a liter in here… and no place to pee."

"There's always the empty bottle," Meyer growls.

"Easy for you to say." Lena rolls her eyes and goes back to work.

I push my back into the corner of the space and massage my temples. After a while, I ask, "What are we doing here?"

"What are *we* doing here?" Meyer spits. "What are *you* doing here?"

At this point, I'm ready to disappear and push farther into the wall. "I told you. I made a mistake. It was just… well…"

"Avlyn, you should know as well as anyone you need to follow orders," he snaps. "Your choices could jeopardize our mission."

"Follow orders?" Lena laughs. "You're one to talk, Meyer."

Meyer narrows his eyes at her. "Shut up. You wanted to be here, too."

Lena raises a hand in the air in surrender.

He returns his attention to me. "How *did* you find me anyway?"

If only I could vanish. Do I lie, or admit I hacked into the Affinity system? Sweat forms on my palms, and I rub them into my thighs, but realize it's no use lying. Why make things worse?

"I tracked you," I mumble.

Meyer pushes his back against the wall, and Lena's eyes dart up from her device.

"You *tracked* me? How? Affinity can't even track me right now, I disabled it."

"Same as you track me. From the EP."

He raises his eyebrow. "Right, but you don't have that capability."

"I do now?" I say as I push my hands into the concrete floor.

Lena drops her handheld on her lap. "What did you do?"

Both stare and wait for words I don't want to speak. The already cramped room presses around me as if the walls are closing in.

"I hacked it," I mutter and pull my legs up.

"You *hacked* Affinity?" Lena asks.

My mind reels with potential lies, but none of them make sense. "Yes, I hacked in to locate Meyer. After, I downloaded the file so my EP could follow him."

"Wait, you *downloaded* my file?" Meyer's voice rises.

"No, only the tracking part." Not that I'm going to tell him I could have, even wanted to.

His jaw is tight, brow furrowed.

"Really, I didn't," I insist.

For a moment, we stare at each other as if it's a showdown, the hot air from the room making me feel ready to explode.

Then Lena interrupts. "Okay... you didn't look. But how did you do it? Affinity's network is incredibly secure. Not just anyone can break the code, not even Direction's finest."

"I'm not sure," I admit. "The design is nearly perfect, but when I downloaded Meyer's file, I... the EP made the route clear."

"What do you mean?" Meyer's voice softens, and his curiosity seems to have taken over.

"Um... when I entered Affinity's network wearing the EP, it was like a real world, except not at all. I can't explain it other than I could physically interact with the code." Some of the stiffness in my body dissipates. "All I had to do was touch the code and think of finding you, and the program brought me to the file."

Both Meyer and Lena stare, mouths slack.

"Isn't that how the EP works?" I ask.

"No, Avlyn," Meyer answers. "No, it is not."

"So, tell me what happened exactly," Lena prompts me.

"Well," I say, "to be honest, I don't really remember, since I just thought that's how the EP worked and I was hurrying to get out. I activated the EP and linked it to my system at home. Then I logged into my Affinity account... and there it was. I didn't do anything specifically."

"This is fascinating, but there's no time for this," Meyer says. "Lena and I are on a mission, which has gotten sidetracked. And *you* are a complication we can't afford."

My chest clenches again.

Meyer pulls out his handheld. "I need time to work out what to do with you."

"Let's take her," Lena says quickly.

"Take Avlyn?" He shakes his head. "No way. It's too risky. She has no experience."

"Yeah," Lena says, "but it's likely a suicide mission, and if Avlyn is the genius hacker she says, it might give us an advantage."

"I'm still here, in case you two didn't notice." Heat burns my cheeks. "Maybe I should have a say in if I'm going on this... *suicide* mission."

Lena takes a gulp of water. "You *should* know what's happening." She nods at Meyer. "Tell her."

"Lena and I are pulling a rescue attempt."

"Affinity is rescuing Jayson?" I guess.

The two glance at each other. Then Lena lowers her eyes. "Not Affinity. *We* are."

"The mission's not official." Meyer sighs. "Right after Direction's announcement in the beach sim, I received intel from a private source. Direction moved Jayson's trial in secret. The judge, probably Manning, declared him guilty, and scheduled the execution, along with a few others."

"Execution?" I ask.

Meyer rubs his eyes. "I requested a team to break him out, but Ruiz wouldn't budge. Too risky."

Lena pats Meyer on the shoulder. "So it's just Meyer and me... and maybe you now."

I suck in air. "Well, what choice is there? I'm either stuck here in Level One, or I go with you guys. Wait... how *are* we getting out?"

"If you want to leave, we can make a plan for you to go on your own," Lena says. "Or you can join the mission. As of now, we're at a disadvantage and can't access full potential of the Affinity network."

"Why not?" I ask, looking between Meyer and Lena. But Meyer is ignoring me, sulking.

"Because Meyer here decided to go rogue," Lena answers. "And if we access Affinity's most recent intel, they'll know what we're doing. I'm just along for the ride to make sure he doesn't do anything stupid."

Meyer glares at her, but then returns his attention to me. "But if you can access security at the detention center as easily as you hacked into Affinity, we might have a better chance… but it doesn't mean I'm telling you to come."

"So what's the chance of *me* getting out of this alive… either way?"

Lena lets out a nervous chuckle. "Sorry, neighbor. Would have been fun to hang out more often." Her smile fades. "Friends are hard to come by."

I press my lips together.

She nods and snatches up her device. "Let me transfer the information we accessed to your device. Study the plan we made, then make the best choice for you."

"Thanks," I say.

Lena gives me a tight smile and goes back to work.

Meyer lifts his Flexx and swipes at the screen. "Everything should be uploaded."

"All right." I turn away and connect to my Affinity account to download the file. The information floods into my view.

Meyer keeps his gaze toward his own handheld. "Use your device to sort what you need."

Maps, information on the facility's security, and Jayson's location—it's all loaded up for me to consider. The compound is 4.4 miles outside Level One. Once out of the city's perimeter, we'll need to break through the security of the detention center, but the codes they have are old, possibly outdated. This would be where I'd come in.

"Is this why you were in One? On your way outside the city?" I ask.

"Partially. I was supposed to be gathering intel on events for Affinity, but I ran into this guy." Lena tips her head toward Meyer. "You know the rest."

Meyer scoffs at her. "Are you coming or not?"

"Depends," I say. "There was nothing in the upload yet about a plan for me to get back to my apartment so I could make a choice."

"Easy," he says. "When we leave, you go the opposite way toward home. Use your smarts and EP to guide you out of One. Oh, and avoid being detained or killed on the way."

"I'm impressed with your tactical planning skills," I mutter. "My odds sound great."

Meyer locks his stare with mine. "If you're going to be a part of Affinity, I can't babysit you."

His intensity fills me with electricity and heat. Everything tells me to turn away, but I don't.

"Why'd you come after me anyway?" he growls.

"You two knock it off. Meyer… you're a mess right now, and not thinking clearly." Lena says. "We've only got a half hour until dark, and after that, curfew hits. Are you coming, Avlyn?"

"We're leaving after curfew?" I break my stare with Meyer. "But security is doubled on the streets."

Meyer smirks. "Oh, we won't take the streets. Not the whole way. The rooftops are more fun."

I gasp.

His eyes soften. "Avlyn, go home. I'll figure out the best way for you to get there."

Desperate to prove myself, I push down the fear working to consume my body. Either way, my chance of survival is likely bad, but I can't just leave them if I have something to offer. I'd come into Level One to make sure Meyer was safe. I can't abandon him, and Lena, one of my only friends, for some dangerous mission on their own. If they're risking themselves, I will too. At this point, I'd rather die than run away.

"When do we leave?"

CHAPTER TWENTY

An hour after curfew sets in, and still in the hiding place, the three of us blink from a practice sim with the EP. The exercise compiled the intel Meyer had on file with several practice runs of getting out of the city and into the compound. At least I feel a bit more prepared, but we couldn't run any with my skills since we can't access any outside systems.

"So, I'm just the backup, right?" I ask.

"Meyer and I have the codes from his source. She's on the inside at the detainment center, so they should be right. There's a weak spot in the defensive shield on the south side."

"And if they don't work," Meyer says, "that's what you're here for. Backup."

I clench my teeth at the thought.

"Guardians are in the building," Lena says.

The same information shows in my EP. My heart leaps. This is it.

Meyer swipes at his handheld, and my vision expands to an overlay of our surroundings. A digitally generated ghostly outline of the space beyond the hiding place appears, like a 3D blueprint.

Two floors below, the EP detects Guardian drone activity. A simple cylindrical shape notes their location.

"Will they come inside the units?"

Lena glances up from rifling through her satchel. "They may. It wouldn't surprise me." She puts on her bag and straightens it. "Ready. Both Avlyn and my trackers are scrambled."

The drones are one floor below.

"Once they pass this floor, we'll go," Meyer says. "Take the stairwell to the rooftop."

Lena and I both nod.

"Clear?" Meyer asks, but neither of us has the chance to answer. "There are five minutes and thirty-two seconds before the Guardians finish. Once out of B, we'll need to move through A. It *should* be less guarded." He eyes me. "Follow the directions in your EP at *all* times."

A pang bowls through me. "I understand."

"Do you?" Lena asks.

"Yes." If I'm going to have any chance of making it out alive, I have to.

Meyer sets our final plan and course.

"Wait, you're both wearing those special suits from the training sim," I say, realizing my lack of any sort of gear.

"Meyer was planning a mission, and I'm always prepared," Lena says, pulling out a pair of gloves from her bag. Instead of putting them on, she sighs and hands them to me. "These will block them from confirming your DNA if you touch anything."

Meyer eyes Lena.

"I won't touch anything that can read me," she assures him. "But if you use your hacking skills, you'll need to."

"But Lena…" Meyer says, stretching on a pair he had hidden in his suit.

"It will be fine."

She turns her attention toward me as I tug the gloves over my fingers.

Lena hands Meyer a stunner and lifts to holster her own.

"Last chance," Meyer says to me. "You could stay here until morning and get home after curfew lifts."

I steel myself to mask the terror that's coursing through me. "No, I'm coming."

He holds my gaze for a second, then lets it loose. "Don't get us killed."

The EP shows the drones nearly complete on this floor, giving us forty-five seconds to reach the stairs after they've moved to the next. Lena clears the panel with her Flexx, and we slip out.

"We're leaving," Meyer whispers as we exit the bedroom.

Nelson's nervous voice comes from the kitchen. "Yes, yes… Do be careful."

After darting out Nelson's door, the three of us are in the hall. Above, the EP displays the ghostly Guardians searching the next floor at the opposite end. I follow Lena and Meyer toward the stairwell, and as we round the corner to the steps, a click sounds from the last door. The boy from earlier pokes his head out, and I duck into the stairwell.

He didn't see. He didn't see, I tell myself.

3 minutes 46 seconds. 45…44…43… counts down in my vision for us to reach the rooftop.

Sweat builds on my temples, and the swaying of Lena's longer hair fastened into a low ponytail makes me wish mine were the same. Instead, sweaty strands of my short bob stick to my cheek.

19...18...17...16...

Meyer is the first to the access door and jerks the handle, but it doesn't give way.

"It's locked," he mutters.

"Well, use your Flexx," Lena answers.

"The building's not upgraded." He pulls out a small gadget from a pocket. "I thought we might run into this."

2 minutes 33 seconds. 32...31...30...

The lock won't budge. Lena bends toward Meyer, swears, and tells him to hurry, but he waves her away and goes back to work. I try to get a better view, but my sticky hair keeps falling in my face.

1 minute 22 seconds. 21...20...19...

Lena taps her foot on the cement floor. "Come on, Meyer."

Back on the floor below, the outlines of the drones creep closer as they sweep the floor, and the outlines of two more figures come into view. Electricity in my stomach tenses me, but I wrench and turn toward Lena.

"New guards. Meyer needs to work faster," I pant. I check again below us, and the guards stand right at the door to the boy's apartment.

55 seconds. 54... 53... 52...

"Lena, the guards are in one of the apartments," I say.

"Better there than here."

"No, the boy might have seen us."

"What boy?"

I tap off my comm so Meyer can't hear. "A kid peeked out the door just as we got to the stairwell. He might have seen us."

20 seconds. 19...18...17...

Lena opens her mouth to speak as the lock clicks.

"Let's go," Meyer whispers.

Lena bolts through the door toward the building's edge and launches herself to the next. I tap my comm back on and follow Meyer and Lena.

At the third rooftop, an alert blinks. The three of us duck behind the stairwell entrance. An upward shaft of light from a guard's work light pierces the sky from the top of the building we left.

4 Armed Human Guardians appears in my vision. They search the rooftop, then return inside.

A Guardian whizzes overhead and continues toward the first building. I press into the wall to avoid being seen or scanned. We stay put for a few minutes until the drone is gone, then move through the series of rooftops.

At the last one, a chasm awaits. It's not a chasm, really only nine feet, but it still seems like one.

91% chance of success

And a 9% chance...

"Just follow the instructions," Lena whispers. "It's like in the sims."

"You first, Avlyn," Meyer says.

I shudder. "Me? Why me?"

"You might get scared, and we'll have to leave you behind." He gestures toward the abyss. Part of me has no idea if he's joking or not. Lena pulls her satchel over her head, rolls it up, and tosses it to the other side. An echoey *thump* sounds when the bag reaches its destination.

Lena shrugs. "See, the bag's safe."

"Fine," I mutter to myself.

The EP instructions are clear. Backtrack nineteen feet and take a running jump over the passageway. Tuck and roll on the other side.

Easy. Right?

I sprint back, bend my knees, and fill my lungs with what could be my last swallow of air.

Don't overthink.

I shoot toward the ledge. The wind fills my hair, and my chest heaves in anticipation of the end. When I reach the edge, I sail through air and over the ghostly EP illuminated blackness below. It's as if no one else exists. I close my eyes, then the EP blinks for me to tuck in.

Thud.

The concrete crushes into my shoulder, and a sharp pain sears my arm. I roll out. Nothing broken, but we are definitely not in the sim anymore.

"I'm all right," I grunt.

"Great, now move," Meyer answers in the comm.

His sails through the air. I tuck my legs in to get out of the way before he hits, rolls, and jumps to his feet. His performance was just about a million times more graceful than mine must have looked.

"On my way," Lena says.

Meyer helps me to my feet as Lena joins us. Now to get down.

The two of them each take out a small tool and release a trigger that shoots cable and anchors onto the bottom of the metal beams of the ledge. Meyer bends to check the security of it manually, but since my EP verifies the safety, I'm sure his does too.

He turns. "You're with me, Avlyn."

I inch toward him. Lena clips in, runs and checks her cable, signals, and disappears over the ledge.

"How are we going to do this?" I whisper.

He flashes a smile. "Carefully."

He stands next to the ledge, exposes clips from his built-in harness, and secures them to the cable. He points at the ledge. "Stand here."

"Are we facing each other?"

"Nope, you have to be on my back. Now get going. The EP will tell you if you're secured," he says.

Meyer turns and backs into me. The EP displays three extendable clips on the back of the suit for me to use as a harness.

Secure flashes in my EP.

92% chance of survival blinks, and my breath quickens.

"Put your arms around my neck."

I wrap my arms around his powerful shoulders, pulling myself in close to him. I gulp. If there wasn't an 8% chance we were going to die...

Meyer hoists us up almost effortlessly with his strong arms and legs and climbs to the top of the rim. He checks his cable again. "Oh, and you probably want to close your eyes." He drops back over the edge with a jolt as he lowers us.

I squeeze my eyes shut and dig my nails into his neck. We don't plummet.

Yet.

92% odds of survival. 93%... 94%...

I gasp for air and bury my head into his shoulders.

"You're almost done," Lena whispers in the comm.

100%

Plunk. Meyer's feet hit the ground, and I open my eyes to Lena jogging toward us. She and Meyer unlatch us, dropping me to the concrete. He presses a button on the tool, and the cable unfastens from the rooftop and reels in as if never deployed. Streams of sweat drip down Meyer's face.

The EP points our destination diagonal to our current location, and we have forty-two seconds before a human Guardian patrol rounds the building.

"Got everything?" Meyer asks as he wipes the moisture away from his eyes.

"Yep, I'm set," Lena says.

They ready their stunners, and Meyer motions for us to go. My hands feel empty and useless.

We make a break for the next block, then round in front of the first building into Sector A. Only a short distance until at least the first part of this mission is complete.

The EP instructs us to slow. Human Guardians wait toward the edge of Sector Patrol, so we're directed to the left and through a narrow alleyway. From there, we can leave the city limits and head northwest.

Meyer leads, and Lena makes sure I don't fall behind. Above is a shadowy chasm much like the one we jumped. From the end of the alley, the destination illuminates past the last building across the road and into the trees. Forty-five seconds from our stopped position to reach the tree line.

Meyer fidgets with his handheld screen. "I disabled a nine-foot section of the electro perimeter. You should see it in your EP.

The perimeter of Elore. I've never been outside the city.

The open section glows in my vision, making my heart pound even faster. We dart out and over the road. I blast forward, trained on the cover of the thick trees beyond.

7 Seconds. 6...5...4...

Meyer cuts through the opening. He disappears from normal view, but not in the tracker.

3...2...

Lena hurls me forward after him.

1...
Human Security Detected

202 ft.

"Halt," yells a stern voice from behind us. When we don't stop, a pulse rips past and slams into a tree. Lena collides into my back, plunging us to the ground, crushing me into the underbrush. A mixture of earth and iron fills my mouth. I spit and wipe away the blood and dirt from my lips.

She rolls off and pulls me to my feet as two guards speed toward us. Lena raises her weapon and fires twice. Frozen, the guards lurch forward, sliding over the thicket, and stop.

"Are you okay?" I pant.

"Fine. Guess the border's getting more aggressive."

Meyer's voice fills my ear as a drone speeds over us. "Keep moving. They probably only think you're an escaping Level One citizen and won't bother chasing you far."

I swallow and tail Lena, who's already on the move.

My legs and lungs beg for rest, but I keep going. The pulses have stopped, or at least I can't hear them anymore. There must have only been the two guards.

"Do you think they scanned us?" I gasp as we slow and catch up to Meyer.

"The EP didn't pick it up if they did," he answers. "But you won't know for certain until you get home."

If I get home.

❀ ❀ ❀

The EP slows us for the remainder of the 4.4-mile trek to the detention center. There's too many ways of falling or being injured on the way if we move too fast. Eventually, an opening in the trees unveils a multi-level stone compound built in a clearing. A transparent electrodome glows over the structure in my EP, and a few Guardians patrol inside. We stay tucked in the foliage cover while Lena works on pinpointing the weak point in the security dome on her handheld, which she's pulled off her wrist and folded the thin, flexible material out into a tablet.

A grid displays over the glow in my vision and the weakness glows bright. A security drone floats across the yard, scanning as it goes until it's out of sight.

"Found it. I'm entering the codes," Lena whispers. "They should open a section of the electrodome so we can get in. Remember from the plan. We need to be out with Jayson in under twenty minutes."

She taps them in, but her expression grows frustrated.

Meyer walks to her and peers over her shoulder. "What's going on?"

"They're not working," Lena grunts.

"Are you sure?"

"Yeah, I'm sure. If they worked the security would be down."

Meyer paces while cursing under his breath. As I watch him, a pit grows in my stomach.

Lena folds her Flexx and snaps it back onto her wrist. She stares at it for a beat before her eyes flick to mine.

"It's your turn, Avlyn," she says. "I'll log you into the detention center. Then you can create a rift in their defense shield."

My eyes widen.

Let's find out if I can really do this.

CHAPTER TWENTY-ONE

Lena cocks her head and pinches her lips together, staring at me. Waiting.

I have no idea how to create a rift in the defense shield, but I'm here and I don't really have a choice.

I sigh. If I'm not going to do what they want, I shouldn't have come.

"Fine, patch me in."

"Great. Get out your handheld and I'll link us up," she says.

I grab it off my wrist and fold it out into a tablet, waiting for the code to appear on the screen. At home, I just touched the system's keypad. Let's hope the same works here.

"The EP doesn't show it, but the electrodome is segmented," Lena says. "Like an orange, except in millions of layers. If you take out a small section for a few seconds, we can slip through, like we did at the border. That's what the codes were supposed to do."

Lena takes out her Flexx and works while Meyer presses against the trunk of a tree. His weapon lifts slightly as the drones hover in and out of view in the grassy area surrounding the detention center again. Each time he looks my way, it's as if a fist grabs my stomach. I swallow down an urge to yell for her to go faster.

"Is it working?" Lena asks.

My heart pounds, and focus lies just out of reach. This whole thing feels like a bad joke. Like I conned everyone, including myself, into doing something I can't do. "No," I whisper.

Meyer mutters something under his breath. "Try the codes again," he growls.

She spins toward him. "Stop it, Meyer. She's just nervous." Lena turns back to me and reaches to clutch my arm with her free hand. "Just relax. You *can* do this. I believe in you."

Just her touch sends an instant calm over my body. And her words? I've never had anyone say them to me.

I suck in a breath, and with a jolt, a wave of sickness rolls over me as my view changes, replaced with snow… no… code. Random. Falling. But staring at it, my mind and body relaxes, and the snowy code organizes itself into patterns. Sparkling, electrical arrangements connecting one to the other. I reach for a sequence and graze over the glowing code. A hum reverberates through my hand and body. Calm. Warm. Like it's alive.

What now?

The last time I just asked for what I wanted.

"Show me inside the security dome."

The code patterns vibrate faster, and a section in front of me brightens. I grasp it, and a miniature, sparkling white hologram of the electrodome appears. Just as Lena said, it's broken into segments. First, eight gigantic ones. Not millions, but thousands of slices within each. Our location illuminates orange beside the closest segment.

"Open the marked segment in five minutes, and then close it sixty seconds later."

Nothing happens. Frustrated, I touch the segment I want and the code flows over and through my fingers. With a light hand, I trace the area I want to open.

"Here," I order it.

As if it were communicating, the code pulses brighter and a countdown displays in my vision. A pleasant tingling sensation spreads from my fingers into my arms.

"Thank you?" After I say it, I feel silly. It's not like this thing is really alive.

Intense light fills my surroundings as the nausea instantly returns. I shut my eyes and hold down the urge to vomit.

Lena sits in front of me when I reopen them. "Are you ready?" she asks.

But I can't hold back my stomach anymore and retch. Nothing comes.

"Are you okay?" Lena grabs my shoulders as Meyer makes his way over to see what just happened.

My stomach returns to normal and I suck in a deep breath. "Ready?"

"What?" Lena asks. "Oh, are you ready to go in?"

"I did it," I say. "We have about five minutes until it clears."

"What? You're done already?" Meyer asks.

"Apparently, she is." Lena shakes her head and swipes her handheld screen.

Meyer shakes his head, confused. "How do you know it will work for sure?"

The reality is I *don't*. This is so new to me. Hacking an app is one thing, this is something else altogether. "I guess you're going to have to trust me."

"Fine," Meyer says. "Let's go. I'm ready to get this over with."

"It's going to work. I just know it," Lena whispers to me.

"Are you getting anything?" Meyer asks Lena.

She shakes her head.

He sighs. "You're leading this one, Avlyn."

I whip around toward him. "Why?"

"Because we aren't getting the same info in our EP as you. Lena and I are blind."

"But we're linked."

"Not for this. We didn't see what you just did, and I'm not getting anything now. Just the thirty-one-second run to the dome we already knew."

"Can you at least see the segments in your EP?" I ask.

"They're not showing, only the dome as a whole. How much time do we have?"

"Three minutes thirty-seven seconds, and the EP estimates a thirty-one-second run to the cleared segment," I answer.

Both Lena and Meyer set their countdowns manually.

A Guardian whirs above. Although under thick cover, we all flinch, waiting for it to move on.

The countdown finally hits one minute ten seconds and I bend to run. The EP blinks, reminding me to slow my breath, although it's difficult when your heart is pounding.

"Get ready," I say.

The darkened night and foliage seem to fall away as the timer ticks down.

"Three... Two... One..." I whisper. "Go."

I hurl myself toward the glow of the dome in my EP. The outline of my chosen section displays a hazy, warm orange. It isn't open yet. Meyer and Lena follow, just steps behind, blind to what I see in the EP, trusting me.

Fear overwhelms me, but I stuff it down and press forward. Tall, wet grass whips my legs. As we near the illuminated segment, the warm, orange hue turns white in my vision. The section disintegrates and clears of the white glow. It's open. Enough for two people to pass through shoulder to shoulder.

"Hit the shield straight on and we're dead." Meyer says in the comm. He still doesn't trust me.

"We won't. Follow me exactly."

I push into the rift thirty-one seconds before it closes. I turn, and both Lena and Meyer make it through. But a *pop* sounds, and Meyer swears, clutching his arm.

"Are you hurt?" I whisper.

"No. Came in too far to the right. Snagged the edge. It was just a shock."

Lena grabs my elbow. "Follow me."

She starts off toward the slate building. The yard in front of the detention center is completely devoid of any trees or plants except the grass, in contrast to the thick forest we trekked through to get here. The EP estimates a twenty-six-second run to our destination, a door on the right side that glows in my vision.

"Jayson and the other Affinity members are in the south wing," she says in the comm, motioning to the left. "We don't have a specific tracker on him, so we'll search manually."

Gasping, we reach the door. It's locked, of course, and a drone patrol alert flashes in my EP.

"Guardian," I say.

Meyer lifts his handheld and starts working on the lock. The security pad shows glowing white in my vision, transitioning to a warm orange. I put my palm to the screen, and the same warm sensation spreads through me, as well as sickness, but I push that part away. The pad glows orange in my EP, and the door turns sparkling white and appears to disintegrate. I gulp and turn as the white floats away like sparks on the wind, but the actual door looks normal.

"It's unlocked," I whisper.

"I haven't gotten through yet," Meyer grumbles.

"Well, the drone is on our tail, and it's open." I wave my hand over the pad, and the door clears.

Meyer shoves the Flexx in his pocket, replacing it with his stunner. "Good job. Let's go."

He checks the hall. My eyepiece says it's clear, but a double-check never hurts. He signals for me to follow Lena inside.

The door secures, and I'm met with a thin corridor lined with stark white walls. The instructions flash, telling me to continue to the right. A human Guardian makes rounds approximately forty-three seconds behind our current position.

We route through a maze of hallways. Only identical white walls and doors come into view until we approach the core of the south wing and come out to a vast room four stories high, clear to the ceiling of the detention center, and descending deep underground at least six more floors.

"Why do they need so much space?" I whisper.

Meyer turns to me. "Since when do you know your neighbors or coworkers enough to realize if any of them went missing?"

He's right. I don't. Direction could take a quarter of the city and store them here and most of us would never notice. Maybe they have.

Below us, some drones escort a few shuffling prisoners, but other than that, this area is deserted. The EP directs me to the left, and Meyer signals the same. Jayson's wing is 118 feet away, and we only have five minutes and twenty-nine seconds to find him and return.

Meyer sprints out first, keeping close to the wall and cell doors since the other side opens to the floors above and below. Lena grabs me, and I follow, but my heart's doing its best to escape again.

"When we get there, you'll disable the lock, Avlyn," Meyer whispers in my comm.

The EP displays there are two more doors until I reach my destination. Meyer skids to a stop, making more noise than he should, but the EP's still green. Once I reach him, he motions toward the pad, securing the door.

"Once we're in, there should be a series of doors to individual cells, but don't unlock them," he says. "We can't risk releasing other people."

I nod and glide my hand to the pad. My eyes shut, then snap to a white, glowing version of the same scene, but I'm alone.

"Unlock the door for four minutes," I command.

The snowy version of the door glows orange, then dissipates.

"And loop the cameras in all detention wings."

The warm sensation stretches through my arm again.

"Are you in?" Lena whispers as I release from the system.

Before I say yes, the door slides back.

"I looped the surveillance."

Meyer's eyes widen. "Good thinking. Let's move."

By now, the cameras are out, but we don't have much time before the guards notice. We all dart through the hall, peeking into the undersized windows on the upper half of each door. Lena and I on the right, since I've only really seen Jayson once, and Meyer on the left. Up ahead Meyer pauses at one, and his eyes brighten, but he moves on. Finally, he points to the tenth door in.

Lena and I race toward it, and no sooner do I touch the security pad than the door clears. The system knows me. I've become a part of it.

Inside, Jayson lies on a cot on the corner. At the sight of him, I go rigid. This man with a swollen, marked face is nothing like the jolly man from before.

"Wha… what are *you* here for?" Jayson slurs. Drugged.

Lena plunges her hand over his mouth. "Shut up. We're getting you out of here."

"You release Jayson, Lena," Meyer says.

"What about you?"

Meyer pauses. "Lena, I need you to. I'm getting Sanda."

Who is Sanda?

"She's *here*? I thought intel said she was dead?" Lena whispers.

Meyer shakes his head and motions behind us. "I saw her back there."

"Get her too," Jayson mumbles.

"I am," Meyer says.

Lena nods a yes.

Meyer squeezes my shoulder, and I suck in air, startled.

"Come on," he says as he pulls me after him. "You'll need to free the door."

I follow Meyer out of Jayson's cell, to the same door I saw him pause at. He stops and nods toward it. I drag my fingers across the pad, and it clears. This cell has no cot, only the balled-up frame of what could be a girl wedged in the corner.

"Who is she?" I ask.

"Go help Lena," Meyer says, ignoring my question.

I hesitate as I watch the helpless girl.

"*Go*," he orders.

"Okay." I sprint back to Jayson's cell. Now he sits on the cot, blinking.

Lena slaps her handheld to her wrist and gazes toward me standing in the doorway. "I gave him MedTech to counteract whatever's in his system. But his nanos aren't functional."

The green cast in my EP wavers and turns a new shade.

"Guardians are en route, probably to check out the camera fluctuations. Time to leave," Lena whispers. Jayson grunts as Lena places an arm under his and pushes up. "Let's go, Jayson."

After she heaves him to his feet, I check the hall. Meyer careens toward us with a diminutive girl in his arms, unconscious. Her face is turned against him, and a mop of dark, curly, gold-tipped hair spills over his arms.

I know where I've seen her. Other than the bright clothing being replaced by a baggy jumpsuit, she's as crumpled as when the drones swarmed and took her away on the street that morning before my placement meeting. She's the one who graffitied the words "Break Free" on the side of the building. The one who stared my way and smiled.

The EP viewer fades to red, and the countdown estimates fifty-two seconds until security arrives in this wing.

Meyer reaches the doorway as the three of us walk into the hall. "Here," he whispers and pushes his weapon into my hands. "I can't use this and carry her."

"Use the MedTech," Lena says.

Meyer shakes his head. "Tried. She's too damaged."

I hesitate. The metal of the gun is heavy in my hands, and feels wrong compared to what we used in the sims. Since I'm the only one not helping another person, I end up leading the group. When we exit the main door to the cell wing, I touch the pad.

"Lock this door and the ones to the unsecured cells."

The system responds with an enveloping sensation, and the EP confirms everything's secure.

Jayson walks ahead of me on his own as the four of them work their way back to the maze of halls we came in through. I race to catch up, positioning Meyer's stunner just like in training.

18 seconds

"Come on." I rocket ahead of the group.

Halt 10 seconds flashes in my view.

I stop and catch my breath. Meyer closes in behind me, but Lena lags with a slumped Jayson. His chest heaves to take in enough air.

As we run, the countdown to move blinks **00**, and we tear out of this corridor toward our exit.

"Take out the segment from the next pad, Avlyn," Meyer whispers as he hoists Sanda. "Make sure to clear the same one. It's marked in the EP now. We're at sixty."

I throw my right hand to the pad to open the door and the segments for sixty seconds.

In my vision, the door disintegrates and floats away in my EP and then I blink. The real door slides back.

Lena tries to pull Jayson along, but he slows down and they both lag behind.

As I turn back to them, my EP switches to red.

Guardian and human security activity.

Meyer dashes toward the cleared segment in the electrodome out of site. My EP shows he's already made it through. Jayson trails twenty feet behind, and Lena drags him by his arm.

"They're coming, aren't they?" Jayson asks.

"I won't leave you," Lena's voice trembles in the comm.

Danger. Warning: odds of survival 19% flashes in red.

"Let's go, people," I whisper, turning back to help Lena, who's now running ahead of Jayson.

We're nearly there. Only a few feet.

A green laser lights up the darkness behind us.

My heart lurches when a flat SI voice fills the air. "Jayson Brant, you are ordered to remain still."

From the left, a drone swoops in, laser still scanning his body, tentacled pinchers ready to seize Jayson. It hasn't detected Lena and I yet.

Jayson freezes, then raises his arms, but Lena's crazed eyes lock to mine. She turns and steps back toward Jayson. A green light from the Guardian snaps on and rakes over her body.

"Lena Maeko Tran, you are ordered to remain still."

I squeeze the trigger of Meyer's weapon and raise it toward the drone.

Lena swings back, her mind returning to reason, and gives me a look that can only mean, *No.* She knows she made a mistake, and doesn't want me to make one too. Then she reaches to her eye and pulls out her EP, ripping it in half and letting it fall to the ground.

Go, she mouths.

At that, the drone emits a blue light and both Lena and Jayson collapse to the ground.

I bolt the other way faster than I've ever run before.

CHAPTER TWENTY-TWO

The breach in the electrodome closes after I dash through. Still feeling conspicuous, I don't stop until the tree branches envelop me. Gasping, I turn. Guardians swarm the yard in front of the detention center. Jayson and Lena are already cleared away.

Are they dead?

Tears burn the corners of my eyes, but I squeeze my lids to squelch them away. The drones haven't detected me yet. Otherwise, they'd be out here.

One drone floats toward the edge of the electrodome and a scanner beam combs over the perimeter. I crouch behind a tree and grit my teeth when the scan reaches the same spot we exited. The light seems to slow when it hits the spot, but then the Guardian moves on and continues to the right. A steady stream of air escapes through my parted lips.

"Meyer?" I whisper.

"Are they with you?" Meyer replies in my ear. "Lena's comm went out."

"You didn't see?"

"I just ran. You all were right behind me." His voice quakes.

"Meyer... I'm sorry."

He curses and the comm goes silent.

"I need to reach you. Can you find somewhere to stop?" I ask. Even though I would have never gotten myself into this without the stupid idea of tracking him, I'm thankful his locator still works in my EP. At least *he's* alive. For now.

"Yeah," he whispers. "There's a spot farther up with better cover."

Meyer marks three minutes fifteen seconds ahead to the southwest.

"On my way."

The EP guides me through the thick trees without too much effort, and by the time I reach him, other than a few scrapes, I'm safe. Meyer is hidden under the foliage of a fallen tree, and I lift a dry branch and climb inside.

He sits with his knees pressed to himself, and Sanda lies on the ground curled up like a child. She's maybe nineteen or so. Her face twists toward me, and my stomach lurches. The skin surrounding both eyes is colored with bruises, and her sable lips and cheeks are marred with dried blood. For a second, her eyelids flit, revealing the brightest, sparkling blue eyes, contrasted with bloodshot whites. As fast as they opened, they flutter shut.

"What happened?" he says without looking toward me.

"The drone came faster than we expected and scanned Jayson." I place Meyer's weapon beside him. "Lena accidently turned back, and the thing scanned her."

Meyer's face falls, the veins in his neck pulsing. For a moment, he stands, silent, but then curses and storms out of the hiding place, leaving me with the girl.

Fear shudders through my body. What if he gets caught? There's a dying person here I have no idea what to do with.

I rush out and find him crouched just outside, his head in his hands.

"It wasn't your fault."

"Yes, it was," he mumbles. "If I would have stuck to the plan, I would have been the one helping Jayson. You and Lena would have gotten out—"

"Lena agreed with you, remember?" I remind him. "Please, come inside. It's not safe out here."

Meyer nods and rises to come back.

"Maybe it was me... I had no idea what I was doing back there."

He shakes his head, looking me straight in the eye. "No... you were amazing. None of us would have made it out if it weren't for whatever you did."

Something about him right now gives me the urge to go to him, hold him, but instead, he breaks our connection and bends to stroke the girl's hair.

I flinch at him touching her. It's stupid, selfish. This lifeless girl on the ground probably won't make it, and I barely know Meyer.

"Who is she?"

Meyer stops stroking her hair. "Sanda... the girl you saw on the street a couple weeks ago. She was captured—"

The feeling in my stomach warns me not to ask. "No, I know that. Who is she to Jayson? He told you to get her."

"Oh. Sanda is Jayson's daughter."

"She's your sister?" Part of me is relieved, but then ashamed at my jealousy.

"Yes, and no. She's Jayson's bio daughter," he answers and returns to stroking her hair. "We grew up together in the Outerbounds. When we were old enough, she joined Affinity and started working missions in and out of the city. A few years later, I followed her. Jayson worried, but he couldn't stop us. We can both be loose cannons. It's why she ended up like this. She wasn't the one who was supposed to do that graffiti work."

My stomach churns, and I squeeze around my middle to try to make it go away. It doesn't work. Thoughts, feelings of loss and desire, swirl in my brain. I've never had to do much with emotions except crush them into the unseen, dark depths. But these… these beg for exposure.

I bring my hands to my face and try to control both the tears and words. Both spill out anyway.

"I just left them…" I breathe. "I didn't do anything but run, and now Lena's going to die too… She *believed* in me. No one has ever done that." Sobs mix between choked gasps. "And we didn't get Jayson out. Then these dumb feelings I've never experienced…"

As the words escape, I slap my hand over my mouth and turn away from Meyer. Heat pricks over my cheeks.

I wipe my eyes and scramble to hide what Meyer doesn't even appear to notice.

"Lena destroyed her EP…" I whisper.

Meyer lowers his chin. "Smart girl," he murmurs. "I already wiped out her Affinity account. It would have taken time for them to break in through her Flexx, if they could, but now they'll get nothing."

I gesture to Sanda. "Did you give her anything yet?"

"I administered the MedTech back there, but it's not working. They must have deactivated her healing nanos, and I have no idea how to get them working again."

I slump and sweep my hand through my hair. The tangles catch and my scalp smarts. For a few moments, we sit there, quiet, but I can't hold in my thoughts.

"What about Lena and Jayson? And how do we get back to the city?" I don't even know if Meyer thought we would make it this far.

He grimaces. "A couple areas around the city are generally easier to pass through. Level One isn't a prime choice. Intel came in on my EP that they've bumped security already. Wouldn't want usable bodies escaping."

"Usable bodies?" I echo.

"Direction can accomplish two things at once by drafting Level One citizens," he explains. "Reduce their population, and rid themselves of Affinity when they convert Ones into soldiers. Now they're valuable assets."

I don't know what to say to this. He's right. Direction has worked for years to dispose of Level Ones, all under the guise of advancement.

"You didn't answer my other question."

Meyer massages his neck. It feels like a long time before he speaks.

"Nothing. We're not doing anything about Jayson and Lena."

No, we can't leave them.

My mouth hangs open, but Meyer's right. We can't do *anything*. Going back is pointless—death.

"But he's your father... and Lena..."

Meyer's quiet. He only goes back to tend to Sanda.

"Where will you take her?" I ask.

"I have to move her to an Affinity camp. One's located not too far from here. The medics should be able to help her, restart the nanos."

"I don't understand. Why disable them in the first place?"

"Simple... to make her suffer."

Sanda moans and her body begins to jerk. Meyer brushes her arms, but the shaking transforms into convulsing. He slips his hand under her neck and raises her head, as Sanda's body continues writhing.

"Is she going to die?" I ask, horrified.

Meyer's eyes radiate a mixture of terror and pleading. "I don't know. How should I know? Medical problems like this don't even *happen* anymore." Meyer grabs my hand. "What if you could do something?"

Panic seeps through me. "Hack her? I can't hack a *person*."

Meyer pulls Sanda over his legs, her body still writhing. "Not her... the nanos. If we can patch you into their system, maybe you can reactivate them."

My gut wrenches. "I... That's a bad idea. I've played a part in enough people's deaths today."

"She could die anyway." Meyer raises his voice, but then looks around and whispers. "It won't hurt to try."

His eyes are pleading. My intertwined fingers squeeze together, and I try to hide my face with them. "I don't even understand this yet."

"Try anyway," Meyer begs.

Sanda's body still writhes, and her lips turn purple.

My mind moves to thoughts of Ben, my twin. If I had the chance to save him, no matter how small, I would go back and do it. This is Meyer's sister. I have to help him.

"See if you can link us."

He picks up his handheld from the dirt and, with a shaking hand, taps and slides over the screen.

"I can't lock on to her due to the deactivation." Meyer mumbles a few curses unknown to me, and as if the whole scene takes place underwater, Sanda's body convulses in slow motion, and the words Meyer mouths refuse to reach my ears.

I scoot in toward Sanda and nestle my fingers into hers. Everything dims. My breath hitches. The underwater experience fades, but now there's nothing.

What did I do before?

My mind is as blank as my surroundings.

"Please. *Please*, make this work."

Nothing. Maybe I'm dead now too.

"Please," I beg. "Please… take me to Sanda's nano system."

White replaces the nothing. I'm alone, and the space shimmers and falls around me. I catch one of the pieces in my palm. It glows, resting in my hand for a moment, then blows away as if wind took it. Along with the one in my palm, the snow disappears and leaves me in a white room. Ten white drones lie on the ground. Instead of long metal tentacles, they have delicate, spider-like legs coming from their bottoms. They're nanos, or at least I think they are.

I dash toward one of them and throw myself on the ground next to it. I run my hand over the top, and a cylindrical panel rises, revealing a small screen. The screen lights, and I jump back when white, scrolling code pops up into the air. After a second, I lean in to watch it pass.

Suddenly, I don't feel well. My lungs can't get enough air, and I gasp to take more in. The white shrouds my vision again, and everything goes so bright I throw my hands over my eyes. Pain shoots through me as a slow vibration takes over.

A scream forms in my throat and sticks there. I have to do this. I can't let her die.

All around me, the room slowly dissipates and scatters.

No, no, no... come back.

But it doesn't. I'm only left in utter blackness. Alone. Fear rips through me. What if I die in here?

The space around fades to gra--

I shoot up and suck in a breath. Meyer bends over me, clutching at my upper arms, digging his fingers into my flesh, his face gone white. Sweat beads the sides of his jaw, and he bites at his bottom lip so hard it might bleed.

"What happened?" he demands, a look of terror still gripping him.

Choking, I sit up and try to remember. "I... I couldn't do it."

Meyer relaxes a bit, and the corners of his lips even turn up slightly. "But you did. See?" He turns me toward Sanda. The seizure has stopped, and her body has relaxed.

I'm not positive, but her face might have softened.

Is she alive?

I grab her and check her wrist for a pulse. *Thump, thump.*

70 beats a second blinks in green in my EP.

"Whatever you did, it worked, but it caused you to have a seizure too. It's like you took it on." Meyer stares at me, eyes wide and glassy. I can't tell if he's grateful, or terrified. "I thought you were dead."

To be honest, I'm a bit terrified of myself at this point.

After a moment, he shakes his head. "I need to get Sanda to a safe location, and you need to get home. Do you think you can stand?"

I nod.

He snatches his device from the ground. "Affinity has a few guys on the inside that should be patrolling the perimeter today. The Level Two entrance to the city is approximately seven and a half miles from here. Guardian security will be high through the forest and at your entry point, so you're going to need to follow the EP's directions precisely. It will alert me when you arrive. Once inside, my buddy will meet you and get you to a secure area. After that, head immediately to GenTech."

Meyer goes back to his Flexx.

"Should be set. The coordinates are uploaded. The viewer will map everything, but you still need the password. I'll send it to your EP."

"Wait… what?" I ask. "You're not coming?"

He tips his head. "I need to take Sanda, remember? Even if you got the nanos working, she needs more medical attention. You can do this."

I didn't even think I would make it this far. What's one more thing?

"Fine," I relent. "Just keep me updated on what's going on."

He nods. "Otherwise you're likely to come after me. But for now, I'm deactivating the comm and your tracker on me. You can't know where I'm going in case..."

He stops talking, but I know exactly what he means. In case I get caught.

Hours later, and without a good-bye, I climb out from the shelter and disappear into the trees. The still-dark sky meets me.

1 hour 39 minutes at current pace to destination

I can't move too quickly since curfew is still in effect, so this walking rate is best. However, with each step, my legs grow tired and heavy. Exhaustion sets in from the night, and any bit of adrenaline my body kicked out earlier has dissipated.

I can't help thinking about Lena. If she made it out, she would have been with me. She'd know what to do. Hot tears sting the corners of my eyes while thick foliage pokes into me. A drone whizzes overhead, scanning the area, and my EP warns me to stay under cover as I skitter next to the nearest tree. As I continue my journey the sky brightens into pink streaks.

Near the entry point, a few more Guardians drift through the sky, probably searching for Sanda. I still have no idea who the guard contact is. I need to trust that Meyer ended up connecting with him, but he still hasn't sent me the code word.

The perimeter is thick with security, but most are SI. Instructions start scrolling for me to run toward the perimeter and a countdown begins.

Don't think. Just do, I tell myself.

I close my eyes for a second and sprint to the back of a guard station, crouching on the left side for my next set of instructions. The counter keeps moving.

Still no code word. No instructions. No weapon. No way this will work. It's not giving me my odds. Probably on purpose.

5...4...3...

I can either turn back or make a break for it.

Human Guardian 10 ft.

Or surrender.

2...1...

I gulp, then stand and start to raise my arms.

"Halt," a woman's voice says from behind me as cold metal pokes my back.

Code from contact: You're in a conundrum.
Answer: Yes, the beach is sandy.

A little too late, Meyer.

"On the ground," the guard commands. I do as she says. I have to dispose of my EP, but I can't do it here without her seeing.

I stiffen as she pats me to check for a weapon, and when she doesn't find anything, she pulls me up and slaps security cuffs around my wrists. Numb, I don't even resist.

"You're in a conundrum," she mumbles, head down.

My eyes widen, and I choke out, "Yes... the-the beach is sandy."

The guard gives me a hint of a smile. "Now shut up. We need to get you to GenTech."

CHAPTER TWENTY-THREE

The human Guardian grips my arm, but I can't even feel it. In a few moments, I find myself stuffed into the back of a security vehicle and told to trust the driver.

"If anyone asks, you were harassed by Level Ones and security aided you. We'll take care of the rest," the guard says before she turns to leave.

After a few blocks, the driver pulls the vehicle up to the side of an apartment building close to GenTech and stops.

"This is as far as I can take you," he says. "Security's too high today."

He swipes his hand over the front screen, and the doors slide back. After that, the driver moves from his seat to the street and takes my arm to help me out.

I slip from the seat and plunk my feet onto the street. "Thank y—"

"Do you need any assistance, officer?"

The cold voice makes my gut sink, and I pivot toward its owner. A metallic Guardian hovers to the side of my driver.

"No," he says. "This Level Two citizen was harassed by several Level Ones. We resolved the issue, and I'm escorting her. The report is in my account."

He holds out his handheld for the drone. A tentacle extends from its body and drifts forward to scan the Flexx.

All I want to do is stare at my feet, but I force my gaze up and straighten my spine. "Please, I'm already behind. There are important duties at Genesis Technologies I don't wish to miss."

The drone finishes the scan and retracts its limb. "Guardian Foley, please return to your duties," the drone says. "Miss Lark, on behalf of Direction, we apologize for your inconvenience. Do you need further aid?"

"No."

"Thank you for your service to Direction," the Guardian drone says before it turns to hover away.

"Anytime," I mumble, but the driver is already in the vehicle and pulling off from the curb.

I droop slightly and grab my handheld from my wrist to check my messages. One from Kyra, and one new spouse pairing request. I swipe Kyra's.

Flexx 35D52G-KLEWIS: I need to meet after work today

I stop and stare at the screen. I'm not even sure how to make it through the day, let alone meet with Kyra. But I do need a friend right now, and she's the only one I have left.

Flexx 682AB1-ALARK: Sure, no problem. Meet me out front of GT.

I trudge to work feeling heavy and dreading the day ahead. My mind wanders to Meyer.

Did they make it?

As I approach, my reflection shows in the glass of the building. Surprisingly, I'm not too disheveled. I doubt I smell great, but no one gets near enough to care. I push my hair behind my ears, enter through the doors, and after a quick trip to the restroom to freshen up, I check in, stomach rumbling.

After gulping down breakfast from the eating area, I ride the elevator to floor eighteen. Inside, I slump into the corner of the lift and drop my head back. When a woman turns toward me, I straighten. She eyes me for a beat more, then resumes her attention to the door, which must be fascinating. At each floor, my mind and body grows increasingly numb, and by the time the chime sounds for my stop, my lids flutter open to an empty space.

Did I fall asleep?

I straighten, take a breath, and step out of the elevator. Daniel is waiting. *Of course.* It's like *this* guy has a tracker on me too. Why did I never set my EP to alert me when he was around?

I move to the side, but he follows.

"Why were you in a Direction security vehicle?" he asks.

"What?"

He crosses his arms, making himself appear bulkier. Probably intended. "You heard me. I saw you getting out of a vehicle."

Without speaking, I intend to make a beeline for the InfoSec suite, but my brain isn't sharp at the moment.

"Nothing. It was nothing," I say, catching his glare. "A Level One citizen approached me..."

Daniel's eyes form into slits and bore into me. The stare brings a lump high in my throat, and I try to swallow it.

"But security took care of it and escorted me to work." I push my shoulders back and look at him. "Direction takes care of Level Two and Three citizens. You, of anyone, should know this."

His body tenses even more. He doesn't break the stare.

My mind reaches for something that will make him leave. "And not that I should tell you this, but I've been commissioned with a special project."

A sneer starts to overtake Daniel's face, but he controls it, and the anger only simmers in his eyes. "What kind of project?" he says through his teeth.

"A special program to help Direction identify angry undesirables before it's too late." I furrow my eyebrows, and I'd swear a low growl comes from his throat.

Daniel steps to the side and toward the closed doors of the elevator.

I start toward the suite, but from the corner of my eye, I see his hand whip up toward the side of my neck.

"What's this?"

I freeze and turn my head enough to see what he holds, but I already know what it is. The necklace. The chain must have come out of my shirt. I grab for the jewelry and stuff it in, but he's seen it, heart charm and all.

"Just a meaningless childhood keepsake," I manage to lie. "Simply haven't had time to get rid of it. I'd forgotten I had it on."

"A keepsake?" Daniel leans in toward me. "Sounds very... undesirable."

"Daniel, unless you have proof I'm doing anything other than maintaining my focus, I'd suggest you worry more about your own distractions." I spin and rush toward my cubicle, but I still catch his last words as I make it through the door.

"Oh, and Avlyn? You stink. Hygiene is important."

I don't turn back. I hurry to my cubicle, slamming my Flexx onto the desk. After that, I launch my GenTech account on the viewer to check the daily projects.

Please, no Daniel. Please, no Daniel.

I scan the list of tasks, finding there aren't any group projects today. The swimming in my head slows. Just a day of tapping away at blissful code, unnoticed, and staying awake.

Throughout the day, the screen keeps going blurry, and several times I catch myself dozing off. At the end of my shift, I'm nowhere near completing the task list, but I need to go home, to bed. I have no doubt that mistakes riddle my work.

When I try to stand, my muscles resist and burn, but I push up anyway, take my handheld, and use the elevator. No stairs today.

Exiting the building, my mind is filled with fantasies of my bed and a shower. Then a vibration comes from my pocket. I pull out my Flexx and tap the screen.

Flexx35D52G-KLEWIS: Sorry, I'm late. I'll be there in a few minutes.

I forgot about Kyra.

Ugh. I could already *feel* the water pouring over my skin.

I shuffle through the other citizens to prop myself on the GenTech building and wait. I could fall asleep right here.

My eyes snap open.

"Thanks for waiting," Kyra says. "I really needed to talk in person."

Something about her is off. The pride I saw in her the other day is gone, and all that's left is nervous energy. Her eyes shift to a passing citizen.

"Are you okay?" I ask, resisting the newfound urge to place my hand on her shoulder. For one, Kyra's not used to being touched, and a public display would be risky anyway.

Kyra hugs herself uncomfortably, looking as if there isn't a place for her hands. "Just get me out of here."

"Where do you want to go?" There aren't many choices. "We could take the long way to--"

"I want to go to your unit."

My eyes grow wide. "But that could draw attention."

"I don't care." Kyra looks at me with pleading eyes. "Talking in the open is not an option."

"Fine, let's go."

Wordlessly, Kyra and I walk the several blocks to my building. She follows me into the front entrance and the elevator. When the doors uncover the hall, I motion to step out, but freeze. Lena's door. I clench my jaw and swallow the lump in my throat.

"What's wrong?" Kyra asks as she steps in front of me.

"Nothing," I reply, but my voice trembles. I force myself toward my apartment door, keeping my gaze from Lena's.

She's not coming back.

"This is it," is all I can muster, gesturing at the door.

She looks back toward the elevator as if to make sure we had not been followed. "Can we go inside?"

I tap the security pad and the door slides clear. Kyra rushes past me straight toward the window, dropping her bag in the middle of the room along the way.

"What an amazing view," she whispers. "My unit is nowhere near as prime."

"Yeah, it's nice. And I'm sure your apartment is lovely." I plop on the couch and let out an unintended groan.

She turns my way. "It's fine. Are you sure *you're* all right?"

"Yes." A flash of Lena crumpling to the ground flashes through my brain, and I shake my head to focus. Kyra wouldn't have come here if it weren't important. "But you have something you wanted to talk about?"

Kyra leaves the window to sit beside me. "I do."

A pained look sweeps over her face but she says nothing else. She's stalling. Why would she risk coming to my apartment and then not tell me why?

"How have your spouse pairing appointments been going?" she asks finally.

I let out a sigh. "You came here to talk about pairings? There's no way that's what this is about."

"I didn't *just* come here to talk about that." Kyra chews on her lip, and sadness darkens her eyes. "Work has been so busy. There's been no time to meet with any of mine."

"I thought you'd be messaging your pairings on the first day, securing the best of the best."

She shrugs. "I did, but I have no time for meetings."

Kyra sits silent, eyes glued to her wringing hands. "Do you have something else you wanted to tell me?" I ask.

Because if not, I'd like to grab a shower and crawl into bed.

"Yes." She lets out a long sigh. "But I don't know where to start."

"You know you can tell me anything."

"And that's why I'm here. There's no one else I could trust." Tears well in Kyra's eyes. Once, I cried in front of her after admitting I still missed Ben. She never said anything about it to anyone, but I've never seen this girl even come close to shedding a tear.

My stomach knots and I straighten from my slouch, feeling immediately guilty I wanted her to leave so I could get cleaned up. "What's going on?"

"Where to begin?" Kyra buries her head in her hands and quietly sobs. "When I started in the Level Two representatives department, it was going smoothly. I actually loved it. But then something happened..."

My first thought is that she could have been approached by Affinity too.

No, not Kyra.

"Representative Ayers was assigning me a lot of responsibility, and so we started spending more time together. The job felt important, right? He told me I'd quickly move up in position. When he started keeping me at the office and calling me in early... he wanted me there just after morning curfew lifted, I was flattered. I'm a hard worker and I deserved to be noticed for my achievements.

"But then one day when I got there early, before anyone else..." Her voice wavers. "When... when I got into his office, he locked the door..."

Suddenly Kyra throws her arms around me, something she has *never* done, and weeps onto my shoulder. The shock of it takes me aback, but I return the embrace and pull her into me.

"Kyra, what happened?" I ask.

She withdraws slightly. "He knew what my parents had done to advance my career configuration. It was illegal, and if Direction found out..." She speaks so quickly I barely get all her words.

It feels a million years ago when Kyra mentioned her parents pulling some strings. I never imagined they would actually be able to change anything, let alone it to be something illegal. It all seemed like talk.

"After that, he wouldn't allow me to leave, and..." Horror blankets her face. "Oh, Avlyn... what if I'm pregnant? I'll never be chosen as a pairing. I'll lose my job."

In my shock, I try to gather my thoughts, tell her something to make this right. "You need to report him... he can't do that."

Kyra's body goes stiff. "He threatened me, told me if I said anything, he'd expose me and my parents. Ruin us. I tried to make him stop by telling him I could get pregnant, but he said not to worry... there's MedTech he could get for it."

Affinity could help her, get her out of the city, but I have no idea if it's a solution Kyra would accept. It might be her only option.

I stroke Kyra's back as she continues to cry, holding back my own tears to be strong for her. "There could be a way to help you."

Kyra looks up at me and opens her mouth to speak just as loud footsteps sound from the hall. She leaps to her feet. "What is that? Were we followed?"

I rush to check the security viewer and find a group of human Guardians with the Direction logo on their uniforms entering

Lena's apartment across the hall. I close my eyes, somehow hoping to will them away.

Kyra stands shaking next to me, staring at the screen. The last of the security team enters and they shut the door behind them.

"I… I don't know why I came." She races back to her bag, plucking it from the middle of my floor. "What were you supposed to do for me? I shouldn't even be here, and now there are Guardians over there. I should go." She makes for the door.

"Kyra," I plead. "Just wait until they're gone. We can figure something out."

But truthfully, all I can think of is that I'm next. They could be in my apartment any second.

She straightens, wipes her eyes, and reaches to smooth her golden hair. "I'm fine. Forget about me. It's best for both of us."

Kyra checks the viewer and slips out my front door. I race to the opening, but she glances back and gives me a look warning me not to follow. Back inside my unit, exhaustion and fear consumes me. I rub my clammy face and park my body right next to the door, waiting for them to take me away, pulse racing.

"What do I do, Ben?"

He doesn't answer.

After about thirty minutes, footsteps sound in the corridor again, and my heart, which had calmed, pounds violently against my chest. I watch on the screen as the Guardians exit Lena's, but instead of coming here, they leave.

I stare at Lena's door through the viewer, guilt pulsing over me.

Why did I leave her?

Finally, I sigh, then shuffle into the kitchen for food. The order display blurs in and out. Hopefully something edible comes out. The timer dings, and a bowl of steaming soup with a spoon inside sits on the tray. Feeling sick to my stomach, I force the soup down in nearly one gulp. The empty bowl clanks to the counter, and then I walk to the bedroom while pulling off my nearly cemented clothes, dropping them along the way.

I grapple in my drawer for a nightshirt and fresh underwear, pull them on, and slump under the sheets on my bed, not even bothering to remove the EP.

Chapter Twenty-Four

Air sucks into my lungs as hands grab my shoulders and force me to my feet.

They're here for me.

A man stands only inches from my body, clutching my arms. I glance around to see how many there are. It's only the one human Guardian, but there's no Direction logo on his shirt.

"Who are you?" I yell.

"Be quiet!" he shouts in my face.

I'm not going down this easy. If they want me, they can kill me right here.

I yank from his grasp and run for my bedroom door. But instead of the door, there's nothing. Nothing other than gray. In my shock, the captor hooks my arm and drags me down. Quick as a whip, I kick him in the shin. No reaction.

"That's enough," a woman's voice says from the darkness.

The man scowls and steps back, leaving me on the floor.

"What's going on?" I pant, stuck somewhere between furious and terrified.

The room lightens, and a woman with an ashen face steps forward. Adriana Ruiz. Her body is stiff, and her dark, close cropped hair is fashioned in tiny ringlets. Past the obvious anger clouding her face, something in her eyes still affords me a sense of safety.

"This could have been Direction, Avlyn," she says coolly. Ruiz nods to the guard, and he exits through a door that hadn't existed before.

"Where are we?" I ask.

"Don't worry. You're safe at home in your bed. The EP allowed us to *contact* you."

The door slides back again, and instead of the guard, Meyer walks through, dark wavy hair hanging just above his eyes, wearing black pants and a similar jacket as the first time I met him.

My heart skips a beat. "You're okay!"

Meyer gives me a tight smile, then looks to Ruiz.

"Please," she says, "if you two would have a seat."

I turn to find two simple chairs a few feet behind me, and walk the nearest one, lowering myself into it. Meyer sits in the one to my left, immediately folding his hands and leaning out toward his knees. I clutch my hands over my body, but stay sitting straight.

Ruiz crosses her arms and slowly paces in front of us. "I want to know everything that happened at the detention center."

Meyer recounts the whole event up to when Lena suggested I should come too.

"And what made *you* think you would be able to handle such an endeavor?" Ruiz asks, stepping directly in front of me. "And you." She turns toward Meyer, eyebrows knit together. "You know better. We lost another good person, and you put everyone at risk.

How are you to know there was not already something planned to get them out?"

"You told me no... It wasn't possible," Meyer says.

"And you think I would fill you in on every bit of information?" Ruiz spits.

Meyer sighs, not answering for a beat. "I have no excuse."

"I'm the one who got them in," I mumble, attempting to take some of the heat from Meyer.

Ruiz scoffs. "Avlyn, your hacking skills are good. We saw it in your tests, and it's one of the reasons we recruited you, but no one's *that* good. Stolen security codes got you in."

"Those were old. They didn't work," Meyer whispers.

"But you wouldn't have known that before you got to the detention center. Why'd you even take her? The safest plan would have been to leave Avlyn in One until morning. You *knew* that. So what is it you aren't telling me?"

Meyer throws me a glance, and I nod.

"She hacked Affinity," he tells her. "Lena thought Avlyn was our best chance. And I didn't stop it."

Ruiz's eyes whip toward mine. "There is no record of a successful intruder recently. We have a few of the best Level Three citizens working to keep the data secure."

"Well," I whisper, "I did. When Meyer went off the grid, I was worried. So, I hacked in to find his location. He'd deactivated himself in the system, but I found it and loaded it to my EP."

Ruiz gives me a skeptical look. "But that still doesn't explain why you escaped detection."

I swallow the lump forming in my throat. "Because... I didn't hack it... normally."

"Normally?"

"Avlyn can immerse with tech," Meyer says. "She saved Sanda by rebooting her nano system."

"What's that supposed to mean?" Ruiz asks, frustrated.

"I really don't understand how it's happening." My voice quavers. "My skills with systems have always been good, better than I've let on, but that's not what this is."

"Then maybe you can tell me," Ruiz says.

"What Meyer called it, immersing, that's a good way to describe it. To be honest, it's a lot like being in VR, except I can actually manipulate the program intuitively. First, I tracked Meyer, then I disarmed the security at the detention center, then I hacked into Sanda's nanos... just by touching her."

"I still don't understand," she says.

"Me either," I admit, "but when I... *immerse*, it's as real as this seems." I gesture around us. "And for some reason, the programs respond to me."

"Show me."

By now it's not a demand, more of a curiosity. I look toward Meyer, and despite his obvious interest in what I'm saying, despair from the loss that still fills his soulful, dark eyes.

"I'll try." I close my lids and envision a better place than this, not that it takes much creativity. The field Meyer showed me comes to mind, but I settle on something more familiar. My apartment.

When I open my eyes, the three of us are relocated to my living room, bright rays of sun shining onto the wall behind, the view out the window as lovely as it ever was. But doing it makes me weak in the knees, and I grab Meyer's elbow to stay standing.

"Are you okay?" he mouths.

I nod that I am. The feeling passes quickly.

"Fascinating," Ruiz murmurs. "However you're doing this... the ability is something Affinity has not encountered. And Direction hasn't either."

She turns away to think, seeming to forget all the trouble we're in. After a moment, she twists back toward us.

"Once we understand this situation better, your current mission may be modified, Avlyn. But in the meantime, we still require your continued pursuit of a pairing with Mr. Barton."

Ruiz blinks twice and vanishes from the sim, leaving Meyer and I alone in the fake version of my living room, my hand still on his arm.

"Sanda made it," he says, not pulling from me. "The medics got to her in time. Another few hours, and I'm not sure... Anyway, thank you for what you did... however you did it." Meyer lowers his eyes and rubs at his forehead. When he looks back toward me, his jaw is clenched.

I know what he's feeling. Guilt. At least it's what *I'm* feeling. How did we get so far and make it out without everyone? Why are *we* alive while they wait for death, or worse?

"What can we do?" I ask.

Meyer flops on the couch, covering his eyes. "Nothing. Lena and I should have never taken the risk we did. Then we dragged you into it."

I softly sit next to him. "The decision for me to come wasn't yours."

Meyer looks over to me, his amazing, dark, nearly black irises filled with sadness. "But if it weren't for my behavior, neither of you would have been there."

In the end, I don't know what to say to this. He's probably right.

Hesitating, I touch my hand to his back. Through his jacket, the outline of defined muscles sends a tingle through my fingers. I've never touched a boy in quite this way. I've touched Meyer's back before, but only because he had to carry me to ground when I couldn't rappel the building in Level One. This is different. Way different.

I push the feelings away, but not my hand, which I leave in place as Meyer breathes deeply.

After a long silence, Meyer sighs. "Who's Mr. Barton?"

Taken aback, I pull my hand onto my lap. Nervousness from the question rolls around in my stomach. "Aron? He's one of my spouse pairing candidates."

"And he has something to do with Affinity?"

"Apparently they have an interest in him."

Meyer's jaw tightens. "Do you?"

"Aron is my assignment, just like I'm yours." The answer is only a half-truth because I *do* like Aron. He's safe, and the path I've always been supposed to take. I sigh and lean back into the couch, shivering. "Can you stay? I don't want to be alone."

The tension in Meyer's body falls away as he nods. "You know you *are* alone, since this isn't real." He leans forward to remove his jacket and gently places it around my shoulders. I pull my arms through and stretch the fabric around myself, taking in Meyer's clean scent.

"True." I lean my head onto his shoulder, taking in a long draw of air. "But it's real enough."

Then I drift.

All too soon, I find myself awake and alone in my bed. Meyer's gone, as if I was never with him.

Spray hits the surface of the shower enclosure, steam rising out the top. After a few seconds, I strip off my nightclothes and slip inside. The hot water pricks my skin. A rush of yesterday's events pours off me as the water flows over my body.

We didn't get Jayson out, and now they have Lena... and Kyra?

I have no idea what to do for Kyra. Helpless, I end up on the floor, my tears mingling with the water. Eventually, I'm able to wave off the spray and stand to turn on the body dryer. When done, I stumble back to my room, grab some clothes, and snap my device to my wrist, but not before checking to see if either Kyra or Meyer have messaged.

Nothing.

I bring up a replay of last night's Direction newscast on the viewer to see if they mention Affinity at all. Instead, a Direction Initiative Message shows with a scroll of words across the bottom, alerting a broadcast will start in three minutes. I don't even bother to see on which subject today. Probably how we should act like mindless SI and know our function.

While it plays, I walk to the kitchen and order a muffin. Any food sounds terrible, but starving myself will do nobody any good.

On the walk back, the Initiative Message has ended, and Brian Marshall's voice echoes through the unit. As I enter, munching on my breakfast, the scene shifts, and a face that is not Brian's greets me on the screen.

Lena Tran

The muffin drops to the floor, and I stumble toward the screen. Displayed under her face are words that make my blood run cold.

Lena Tran sentenced to death for treason and involvement with the Affinity terrorist group.

It's not a live feed, only her identification image. I stagger closer to the viewer and tap her face, but nothing more than the words on the screen appear. Treason. Lena is a traitor.

No... No, it can't be this soon.

The reality of it all hits me again. Her face is clean, raven hair combed. No bruises mar her even skin, but it can't be how she looks by now. Sanda and Jayson were in appalling shape.

The screen switches to Jayson's image, and under his are similar words to Lena's.

The image disappears, and Brian's face returns. "The execution is scheduled for a mandatory live viewing Friday at seven p.m.," he says.

A *live* execution? Direction has never executed people on a broadcast.

I can't listen to anymore, and wave off the screen. Numbness drags through my shoulders.

From my wrist, my device vibrates with a message alert in my Affinity account. Just an auto reminder to contact Aron. I rub my hands over my face and log into my spouse pairing account. Another potential has requested a meeting, and I hide it and the other three options. Aron's profile now requests the additional information concerning me. My likes, my dislikes, the information he asked me for... before everything happened.

Aron's likeable. He seems kind, and I can just make out the spot where the dimple on his cheek sits. His ice blue eyes sparkle, even on the standard ID image, but he knows nothing of me. Nothing of the turmoil my life and this world is in. Frustrated, I shake my head.

I steel myself. I have a duty to Affinity. Aron is my assignment.

With a sigh, I enter the information he requested and, to be polite, remind him to do the same.

For some reason, Daniel is out my entire shift. It's strange, but I don't want to question or think about it. I engross myself in security code, but my mind isn't really in it. My thoughts are consumed with Lena and Kyra. At the end of the day, I hurry downstairs and onto the street, jogging the blocks toward the Level Two Representatives building.

When I reach the front, I message Kyra.

Flexx 682AB1-ALARK: I'm out front.

Nothing comes back, so I try again, trying to conceal my worry from the other workers exiting the front.

Flexx 682AB1-ALARK: I need to speak with you.

The device buzzes against my wrist, causing my heart to skip a beat.

Flexx 35D52G-KLEWIS: Full-fledged citizens are advised to break contact with any childhood relations during the transition to complete configuration.

Heartbroken, my mouth falls open. Kyra copied and pasted the passage from the citizen welcome letter. My chest stings as I gasp for breath. My instinct knows she's still stuck inside that building, terrified. She could be protecting me, not wanting me to be involved.

Unable to force her without making the situation worse, I wipe away the message and trudge to my building. At my floor, a pang sweeps through me again. I focus on the ground to avoid Lena's door, finally retreating to the mock safety of my unit.

CHAPTER TWENTY-FIVE

A golden micro drone zips in and past me when I open the door to head to work.

What in the world?

Butterflies skitter in my stomach as the thing buzzes twice around my head until I swat it away. It hovers over and settles on my dining room table. I wave the door shut and follow the piece of tech.

The tiny drone could fit in the palm of my hand perfectly. I cautiously approach and step back as a tiny circle dilates on top of the device. From it, a hologram of a face appears. Aron's face.

He clears his throat. "Um, just field testing my new project, and... um,,,"

My lips curl into a small smile. "Hi, Aron."

He doesn't respond. It's a recording only.

Aron's blue eyes sparkle, even on the hologram. And that dimple... well, I don't know how I didn't notice it the first time I saw his image on my account.

Anyway, its appearance when he flashes a silly grin reminds me of the wink he gave me before I got myself trapped in Level One.

I shake off the feeling. This is no time to be worrying about boys.

"Well, I read the information you sent, and... What I was wondering..."

Something about his nervous demeanor makes me clench my jaw.

"I was wondering if you would be interested in making a spouse pairing contract?" His words spill out quickly. "No need to decide now, but I wanted to ask."

My heart skips a beat.

"The pairing is good for a few reasons," he continues. "Firstly, our career configurations are to protect Elore. You at GenTech, and me involved in drone production. Secondly, Direction rated us a 98.5% pairing for producing Level Two or higher children."

He clears his throat and leans in a bit.

"And... not that this is terribly important, but I think we could be... content."

Aron gives another nervous smile before the hologram blips out and the button snaps back into the drone. The little orb takes a whirl around my apartment and ends at the door, hovering as if it's waiting to be let out. I activate the door and watch as it disappears down the hall.

Would I settle for content? Is that all Aron and I would be?

However, just knowing I've succeeded on this part of my mission sends a thrill through me. I send off a quick message in my Affinity account to let them know I've gained Aron's trust and he's asked for a pairing. Almost immediately, my device vibrates with a message from Affinity.

There's only two words.

Accept it.

My heart plummets.
Really? So soon?
My thoughts move from Aron to Meyer.
Should I tell him?

A wave of guilt that I don't understand shudders through me. I have nothing with Meyer other than friendship. We shared a terrible experience which bonded us, but that's normal. There can be nothing between us any more real than the moment we shared in the simulation last night.

I sigh and re-log into my spouse pairing account, tapping into Aron's profile.

I accept.

At my cubicle, I link my Flexx to sign in, ever aware it's still collecting information for Affinity. I attach my headset, then login to GenTech's server. The real world falls away, leaving me isolated in my virtual office.

ASSIGNMENT: SECURE WORKSTATION 519 displays in the headset.

Corra's station again.
What's up with that?

Chemist reports when she tried to archive work the system crashed and would not reboot.

I sigh at the fact that it's not really in my job description to fix crashed systems, so there must be a security concern. I access the workstation from here and scan the system for any viruses, all while running system diagnostics in the background.

Hours later, I haven't found anything of substance, but my assignment still tells me the system is not secure. This should be a simple fix, but for some reason, it's not. Each time I fix a small issue that may be triggering the security alert, another minor issue is caught by the scans.

My stomach groans, and I check the time. Lunch. The diagnostics and malware scans continue as I rip off my headset and eat a sandwich I packed this morning.

After lunch, I'm still not getting the information I need, and request to work onsite in the lab. The approval comes almost immediately, and Corra is notified I'll be there soon. I bundle up my bag and headset and slap my handheld on my wrist before moving through the InfoSec suite.

Just as I walk by, headset removed, Daniel swings his chair out halfway and eyes me. I ball my fists, but continue past.

The lab chems are so focused on their work that I'm not noticed when I arrive. Corra works with a sort of liquid today in a beaker, and although it's cool in the room, seventy-six degrees Fahrenheit, according to my EP, sweat flecks her forehead. She's probably trying to prove her extraordinary ability and receive a promotion. I snicker at the thought, but quickly lower my head so no one notices.

I scan the door to the *secret lab*. It's still closed.

I spot the appropriate work station. On my approach, Corra turns, and I gesture toward her chair to work with her system. She moves to a table with another project. I attach my headset, sync it to her viewer, and begin the diagnostics again. As they run, I lean back and wait.

While I'm waiting, my Flexx buzzes with a message. I snatch it and tap the screen. Aron.

I'm so appreciative you got back to me so soon. Can we meet this evening to discuss the details?

I guess so?

This whole spouse pairing thing is moving too fast with Aron. If we make a contract now, we'll be living together by next week. Paired for life.

When I move to answer, illumination in my EP snaps me up in my seat.

Avlyn Lark: Instructions for Modified Mission

My heart quickens as the words scroll on the bottom of my vision.

This will only be available for viewing one time. Please memorize your instructions.

Focus. Breathe.

Your current assignment is to disable the security of lab 1008B of GenTech at precisely 5:56 p.m. in a manner that cannot be detected using access from workstation 517402. When complete, exit the lab suite, leave the building, and return home. Await further instructions. Do not make any modifications to these instructions.

Send an alert only if you CAN NOT complete the project.

My gut forms a knot, and I comb the room, making sure no one else realizes what I'm seeing. Of course they can't though, since the words are from my EP.

If I can't do this and am caught, I'm finished. There will be no leniency from Manning. The pressure from my heart crashing into my ribcage makes my lungs ache for air. I close my eyes and concentrate on slowing my heartbeat. I remember the beach sim with Meyer, visions of the slow waves lapping onto the shore rolling through my mind.

Finally, it slows to a manageable rate, and I lift up the headset and open my lids. Nothing has changed in here. Corra still works and sweats in the corner, and the other chems buzz about like drones.

I check the time and note the countdown in my EP.

4 hours 32 minutes

I can only hope this project takes me that long.

5:33 p.m. It's almost time. I make a last check over the system I'm working on and sort through the information to make a few final patches to security, but it's still telling me the system's faulty and unsecured. I'm not even sure I'll finish this today.

Should I start another set of scans today or wait for tomorrow?

I rub my hand over my face and wipe the perspiration beading at my temples. It's not hot in here, but it is to me.

Thinking about my options, I brush over the touchpad on the desktop. A sting strikes my arm. The EP goes white, and I'm in. It's not time yet... but I'm in.

Security for floor ten, room 1008B, I think.

Warmth surges through me, and the lab transforms to glimmering white. All the chemists are gone.

Inside the system, I stand and walk to the secret door. With the tips of my fingers, I touch it. Nothing happens, and I put my hand on the security pad.

The door slides back, revealing the same equipment to that in the real lab: enlargers, viewers, and tables, only they're digital, not solid.

As if my feet work on their own, I step into the virtual lab. This is a bad idea. My assignment is to simply unsecure the room and leave, but instead, I walk around the tables and into a second attached room where I see them.

Ten human forms lie on top of tables, each enclosed in a clear, dome-like case. They're shimmery white, as is everything else in the room, with no facial details. When I tap the clear dome, it displays information, including an identification image.

VacTech test subject 3043

I stare at the image. I've seen her before... on the street. The woman with the long, nearly white hair that security took away in Level One the other day. The one screaming they couldn't take both her and her spouse and leave their child behind. They never drafted her as a soldier, but took her here as an experiment.

"What are they doing?" I mumble.

As if the system's responding to my question, the answer immediately appears in the form of information, scrolling across the bottom of my vision. I flinch.

Development Project for Aves Virus Stage 2 - Project Ectopistes
Goal: To create a mutated version of the original Aves virus and the accompanying VacTech to be administered to Level Two and Three citizens and select Level One citizens. Elimination of all non-essential Level One citizens.

Choking for breath, I wave away the information and jog out of the virtual room. Even inside the system, my lungs burn. Manning is testing subjects pulled from the draft, seeing how their bodies respond to the virus to release it on a large scale.

A sickness washes over me, making my head spin. The room begins to dissipate.

No, no, no! my mind screams. I can't leave before I'm sure the mission is complete.

With a groan, I push away the sensation and the vision returns to normal, but it won't hold for long. In my mind, I quickly program the door to secure again while coding a timer to unlock it at 5:56 p.m. I blink twice to end the experience and am met with *DIAGNOSTIC COMPLETE* in my headset. Along with it, my EP is flashing **ERROR** in the corner.

Great...

I scour the code and make the repairs with trembling hands.

This can't be happening.

After ten agonizing minutes, the viewer flashes, *COMPLETE.*

It's 5:51 p.m. Five minutes until the timer releases the door. I reach up and grasp at the headset and pull it from my face. This needs to be returned to my cubicle. The instructions are to exit straight from the lab, but taking it home isn't an option. It's against regulation for me to take my headset home, or even leave it in here. I nod to Corra to alert her the repair is complete, grab my bag, and head to the elevator.

At my InfoSec station, I force my shaky fingers to logout of my GenTech account and return the headset. The line back down has gotten long, but the elevator is still the fastest way to go. When my turn comes, I board and move to the back, keeping my arms crossed and head lowered.

We make a stop back at the lab floor, and people get on and off, but I stay tucked in the back, head down. Corra tucks in and slides up next to me before the door closes.

"You have to come back to the lab," she whispers.

"What? Why?"

The cab stops and chimes. Floor three. Corra grips my arm, pulling me forward.

What is she doing?

"They need you up there. Come back."

Corra releases me and bumps her way through the people in the elevator. I don't want to create a scene, so despite my reservation, I follow.

"Why did you go upstairs?" she pants as we hustle through the corridor of floor three.

"I had to return my headset."

"Those were not your instructions."

I shake my head, confused. "Instructions?"

"You weren't supposed to go back upstairs. It wasted too much time. We need to take the service stairs *now.* They're waiting for you at the bottom of the elevator."

"*Who?*" I choke out.

"Direction."

"How do *you* know?"

"When they saw your EP had an error, I got a Flexx message to escort you from the building."

Questions reel through my mind. *Corra* is working with Affinity? But if she's right about Direction guards waiting downstairs, there's not much choice but to follow her.

Instructions loading alternating with ERROR blinks at the bottom of my EP.

We race the three flights down, successfully avoiding a few other GenTech employees.

"Keep your head low and stay behind me," Corra instructs.

At the bottom of the stairwell, we disappear into a group headed toward the exit. Through them, I see the guards waiting near the elevator, scanning the departing workers. One of the dark-suited men with a Direction logo on the right side of his chest glances my way, and I tuck my chin down and fall in behind Corra, who leads me down a service corridor and out the back.

As we hit the street and tuck into the crowd, it hits me.

This is it... I'm not going back home.

Nausea wells up my throat as I realize I won't see Kyra again... won't have a chance to help her. A picture of Aron's face finding out what happened to me fills my mind, and to think, he offered me a spouse pairing.

"Where are we going?" I ask. I'm still not receiving directions in my EP.

"Level One."

"What? Why? What about the increased security?"

"It's been reduced," Corra replies sharply. "Level One is subdued... Don't you watch the news?"

The EP finally kicks in and starts directing me on which streets to take.

Keep north using Tenth Avenue to Sector A

The two of us hustle down Tenth as the sky darkens, fast enough to move from sight, but not so much as to stand out from the clusters of citizens returning home.

When we hit the first street of Level One in sector C, I see Corra was right. Security has returned to nearly normal. Guardian Drones buzz above, and an occasional human patrols the street.

As we bound through C, the EP words flash red with each new direction, but still assure our location is secure. We press into Sector C, silent, except to let Corra know the directions since it's easier than constantly checking her device.

We pass Twenty-First Avenue, and I slow as we near Bess's building. Something tugs at the back of my mind to go there. Bess is my last real link to Ben. Maybe I need answers. When Lena was captured, I didn't do anything but run. Now she's going to be executed Friday. I can't let that happen again.

I can't message her a warning... It's probably monitored by now.

"We need to keep moving," Corra says.

"You don't have to stay with me," I tell her. "I can find my way."

"No, my order is to escort you to the destination."

Figures I'd be stuck with the girl who's always trying to prove herself.

"Then I guess you're going with me," I say as I sprint across the street toward Bess's.

Corra catches up as I enter the lobby. "We're not supposed to be here," she whispers.

"I need to see someone."

"No way," Corra hisses. "I'm to make sure you're safe. Let's *go. Now.*" She turns and motions over her shoulder for me to follow.

"I'm going upstairs. Either come with me, or don't." I move toward the stairs without turning back and bound up. Soon after, a second set of footsteps closes in.

"You're coming?" I ask.

"Just following orders to escort you," Corra's frustrated voice sounds from below.

We rush from the landing on floor four, and I knock on Bess's door.

Corra grasps my arm and yanks me toward the staircase. "No one's home. Let's go."

I tear from her grip, pull back, and rap again. "Bess?" I say into the crack of the door.

"Avlyn, there's no one here. Now let's *go.*"

"Knock it off, Corra. This is important." I spot the lock pad to the side of the door and set my hand on top, but use my body to block what I'm doing from Corra.

The door clicks, and I bump it open to a darkened room. Night vision on my EP kicks in. Inside, the space illuminates in my vision, looking absolutely ransacked.

"Bess?" I call. "It's Avlyn."

I step over a few pieces of overturned furniture and manually switch on an intact lamp in the corner.

"Careful, stuff's everywhere," I say, remembering Corra doesn't have an EP to lighten up the room.

She shuts the door behind her and one tiny auto light flicks on. "What happened?" she asks.

"I have no clue. Haven't spoken to Bess for weeks."

"Who's Bess?"

"My bio mother."

I wander into the bedroom, and it's in shambles too. The room is strewn with bedding, and every one of the drawers is pulled out, their contents littering the floor.

"Well, she's gone, and this isn't exactly the safest spot for us to stay."

"It's safe," I hiss. "The EP would tell me about any danger if there was surveillance."

Corra skulks in the doorway, wordless, for once. When I push past her for the living room, her glare burns into the back of my neck.

"I'll just be a minute," I say. "Then we can go."

All the drawers are pulled out in the living room too. Bess's mementos are either ripped from the walls, broken, or both. Over near the dining table, the mostly smashed animal figurine lies on the floor. I walk over and kick away some debris, finding the head of the deer figurine. I pick it up, stroke the intricate details, and return it to the shelf.

I spin around and head straight to the office next, Ben's old room. The door is open, and the desktop system gone. The desk it rested on is overturned and partially smashed. Quickly, I scan the floor for any hint of the paper I found in the hiding place under the baseboard. Not that they were mine, but Bess's letters are some kind of link to my past. After today, I'll have nothing.

"Do you see any papers?" I ask.

Corra walks inside the doorway and glances around the room. "No. What would you need paper for?"

"Help me move this." I grab the corner of the desk and push it. It makes a sharp scraping sound across the floor. Corra stands behind me, doing nothing.

"Thanks a lot," I mutter.

She scoffs, still not moving.

The desk is pushed aside enough for me to get at the loose baseboard piece and pry it up. Once it's out, I reach my hand into the opening to check for anything. Disappointingly, the stack is gone, and so is the stuffed rabbit. I stretch my fingers to the back of the hole and the tips catch on something.

I grab it and pull out a small, folded sheet of paper..

"Find what you were looking for?" Corra asks impatiently.

"May have."

She walks over, but I pull the note against me and glare back at her.

Corra throws her hands up in the air and shakes her head. "Whatever," she says and sits on a broken chair she's overturned.

I unfold the note.

Avlyn,

You will probably never find this letter, but in case you do, I have to tell you something.

First, I know what you found. Please understand what Devan and I did was out of love for you and Ben. We had no idea of our mistake until it was beyond too late. We deeply wanted the best for the two of you, and were deceived into thinking the research project would ensure your futures. The credits were always to make sure of that.

Please, forgive us.

I also felt you deserved for me to tell you why I left. I didn't message you because I wasn't sure how you felt about me, and it wouldn't be safe for me to explain myself that way.

I never knew my bio mother or father. I was raised by Level One parents and told nothing of my past. Even the nano scans revealed no answers. Over the years, I've pieced together rumors and evidence and believe I now have answers, but if Direction finds out, it will not only put me in danger, but you as well.

Disappearing is the best thing for me to do.

I love you, I always have.

Bess

What? This is ridiculous. Who knows why I bothered with this? I crush the letter into my pocket and turn to Corra. "Let's go. There's nothing here."

Chapter Twenty-Six

Corra stares at me, eyes narrowed. "That's it?" she huffs. "You see some letter, and now we can move on?

I don't answer. It doesn't concern her, and it means nothing. I'm not sure what I'd hoped to find. Answers, I guess, but now there are only more questions.

"I don't know why Affinity cares so much about you," she mutters. "You can't even follow orders."

"Well, what about you?" I scoff. "You've always been miss 'follow all the rules' and here you are working for Affinity. It makes no sense."

There's a sorrowful look in her eyes that instantly fills me with guilt. "You wouldn't understand."

"Try me," I say. With everything I've been through lately, I don't think much would surprise me.

Instead, Corra averts her eyes. "Let's go."

This time I allow Corra to lead the way to Sector A under the night sky. I'm sure it's in my head, because my EP doesn't warn me of any specific danger, but people seem to stare as we pass. I keep ten or more paces behind her to try to ward off attention.

After close to twenty minutes, we make it to A, and my EP instructs us to enter a brown brick building, taller than most in Level One. Corra goes in first and I follow, but not before turning for one final check of the street. All clear, hopefully.

Inside, we enter the elevator and place our hands on the pad inside. The cab jolts, and my heart leaps as we drop down, like the day Meyer took me to meet Jayson. I shut my eyes and try to squelch the feeling that today could likely turn out the same for me as it did for him.

The elevator clunks to a halt and the doors open. Corra motions for me to exit. I'm led through a corridor to a secured door, and I run my hand over the pad. The door slides open to reveal a room of people working. Most busy themselves quietly on viewing screens, tapping and swiping away. At a table in the corner, nine people sit in what appears to be a heated discussion.

Meyer's among them, and my heart flutters into my throat. If he hadn't deactivated his tracker, I would have known he was here.

I leave Corra in the doorway and rush to the table.

Meyer raises his eyes from the conversation. When he sees me, they brighten, and the corners of his mouth turn up into a smile.

My stomach leaps, and the urge to barrel into his arms races through me. But as quickly as the smile came to his face, it disappears, replaced with a serious expression.

My pace slows to a walk while my arms curl around my torso. I tighten my jaw. From my right comes Adriana Ruiz, as if to stop me.

"Corra, thank you for the safe delivery of Ms. Lark," Ruiz says. "Your instructions are uploaded. Please return home and review them."

"Yes, ma'am," Corra's voice replies from my left. For a second, I forgot she was there. "Good-bye, Avlyn."

I somehow manage a nod. "Thank you."

And she's gone.

"Ms. Lark," says Ruiz, "first, I'm relieved you're safe. But the little stop you made along the way... From here on out, we *require* you to obey orders. Keeping you safe is our highest priority."

I cast my eyes down and stare at a spot on the floor.

"Meyer will accompany you on your next assignment," she continues.

Upon hearing his name, I glance at Meyer, who's come up behind Ruiz, but his attention stays toward her.

"Are we clear?"

My eyes whip to her. "Yes, ma'am," I say.

Ruiz's voice softens. "Now, there's business to attend to."

Some of my tension drains away, and I glance toward Meyer again. This time he gives me a slight smile.

"We need an hour before we're ready," she says.

"Ready for what?" I ask.

"I will inform you in an hour." Ruiz's eyes flick to Meyer. "Please give Avlyn the tour."

Meyer glances my way, then back to her. "Yes, ma'am."

He motions for me to follow. Nervous, I exhale and leave without making eye contact with anyone. The door opens as he approaches it, and I trail behind him into the corridor.

At the end of the dimly lit hallway, we pause in front of another door, and Meyer opens it.

"Let's just eat for now," he suggests. "I have to get my mind off things, too."

The idea of dinner is a welcome relief. "Fine by me."

Scattered throughout the plain room are a few tables. A couple sits eating odd, square-shaped food.

Meyer guides me to a long table with benches. "Have a seat. I'll be right back."

He turns and walks toward a break in the wall. While waiting, I activate my handheld. No messages from Kyra or Aron.

Aron... ugh. I guess I won't be meeting him tonight.

I stuff the device away. Meyer's returned with something which most definitely does not appear to be dinner.

As if he read my mind, he says, "They're meal bars. Ruiz doesn't trust the instafood from the printers... or at least she doesn't trust the stuff Direction uses to make it."

He holds out a clear package containing a brown bar. Cautiously, I extend my hand to accept. "What's it made from?"

"Oh, partially chemical nutrients, like printed food. But in the Outerbounds, we grow crops, some areas more than others, so real food is mixed in too."

I stare at the package resting in my palm. Real food has always fascinated me since I've never had anything but printed meals, but this bumpy bar isn't what I envisioned.

"It's not terrible. It's not great either," he says, tearing off a hunk of the bar with his teeth. "But it lasts. You won't be hungry for twenty-four hours or so."

I unwrap the clear packaging and break off a tiny piece. The morsel rips away, appearing to be chewy. First, I sniff it. A type of pastry? I place the portion into my mouth and chew.

"Yeah, it's passable," I agree after a moment. "Sweet. Somewhat of a disappointment, though." I split the bar in half, trying and failing to identify a chunk of something inside.

Meyer cocks his head and pulls his lips together in a tight smile. "Because you always wanted to try a meal bar?"

I chuckle. "No, *real* food. I've always wanted to try real food."

"Oh. Well, if we happen to make it out of this mess, real food... *real food,* tastes way better than this. Sanda's a great cook, given the right spices." Meyer leans back in his seat and continues eating, lost in his own thoughts.

"What are... spices?"

Meyer snaps his attention to me. "Herbs and stuff. I'll show you someday."

I still don't know what he means.

The pair across the room stands and disappears out the door.

"Ruiz has decided to discuss a rescue attempt," Meyer says. "But it can't happen until Friday morning. She told me so I wouldn't do anything stupid again.

My heart leaps. Lena and Jayson might actually have a chance.

"But that's the day the execution is scheduled," I say.

"It's cutting it close, but it gives me hope."

"Me too." I smile.

I swallow the last bit of the bar, surprised to find it feels as if I've eaten a substantial meal. Maybe it will last twenty-four hours— if I even live that long.

Meyer's eyes meet mine. Under the light, I notice his ebony irises are actually brown, and their depths swallow me until I wrench free and cast my attention to the table.

Meyer crumples the bar's clear packaging between his fingers. He reaches and takes my wrapper, gets up, and throws them into a receptacle. "We should do sim training. It will still be a while."

"Sounds like a good diversion."

We find an empty room. It's a perfect place for us to stay out of the way. Meyer programs the new sim while I have a seat on the floor.

"I'm unsure what they're planning, but target practice is always helpful," he says. "We also have a new suit for you for later."

My ears perk up. "The special one you have?"

"Yes."

This means I'm in. I'm really a member of Affinity. For once, I belong somewhere.

I push up on the concrete to stand and skip toward Meyer. "Thanks for at least a little more positive news." Without even thinking, I stretch up and kiss his cheek. His warm skin and the roughness of his unshaved face sends a brief shock into my stomach.

Meyer almost drops his Flexx, but catches the device as it flips through the air. His face flushes red, and it must be contagious because mine does too. "Why'd you do that?"

I jump back and inhale. "I... I'm not sure. It seemed... nice?"

He laughs uncomfortably. "It seemed *nice*?"

I inch away from him, and the heat continues to creep over my face.

His shoulders relax. "It was just... unexpected. Let's do the sim."

He swipes his handheld, and the next time I blink, we're outdoors. A holstered stunner sits at the waist of my suit. I sweep my hand over the metal, and reality presses in. In a few hours, I'll use this for real. Any embarrassment from the kiss flutters away.

"Remember, the weapon is set to immobilize unless changed manually," Meyer says. "Don't take this lightly. We don't want to kill people."

"I remember." Since the weapon and the EP are interlinked, I confirm it's on the lowest setting.

Ten tiny black targets are set up on the grass. Could be difficult to hit, but not with the EP's help. I unholster my weapon and take aim. The EP locks on the mark, and as I'm ready to squeeze the trigger, the EP guide blinks out.

"What...?" I lower the stunner and turn toward Meyer, who's messing with his Flexx. "The guiding system's not working."

He glances from the screen with a sly smile. "I don't think you need it."

"But..." I protest.

"No. You're a quick learner, and I have a hunch."

"A hunch?" I echo. "Tell me."

"No." He studies the ground and kicks a foot into the dirt. "Not until I see if it's right."

I turn back toward the targets and set up again. As I do, Meyer steps from behind and gently places his hands under my arms. The sensation of his touch blanks my mind, and I can only manage one thought.

"Well, this is unexpected," I whisper.

His face grazes mine, and I can feel his upturned lips. "Arms a bit higher... don't overanalyze it. Just fire."

He backs away, and I inhale, then squeeze the trigger, moving from target to target. The pulses shoot and display on the ten marks.

"Let's go check," Meyer says, motioning for me to follow.

Bullseye. All ten.

My gaze moves from the targets to Meyer.

"The hunch was right." He turns and looks me straight in the eye. "You were right too."

"About what?"

Without breaking eye contact, he says, "It *was* nice."

CHAPTER TWENTY-SEVEN

A hot jolt runs through my center. I kissed Meyer. He ignored it, but now he's telling me he liked it. Or, at the very least, that it was nice.

"But it's not smart to start the mission distracted," Meyer says. "Full focus is imperative if we have any hope of living."

He's right, but if I'm honest, I'm feeling sidetracked.

"If you don't want me distracted... don't tell me the kiss was nice."

Meyer gives me a grin, then turns toward the marks. "Ready for my hunch?"

I tap my foot impatiently. "Yes."

"Without further study, it's still only an idea. But I think your brain might be more complementary to your internal nanos than the average person. It's like your body and brain have made an organic connection with the bots. It's allowed you to communicate with systems, even control them. What I don't know yet is why it's happening, so Ruiz is planning to run some tests on you soon."

My mind moves to the experiments on Ben and me.

Could that *be why?*

"But why did the ability surface now?" I ask.

"Not sure yet. Could be the EP allowed your brain to put it together."

Or that last MedVac update... Strange things started happening after that.

"What if I didn't have the EP, though? There's no way I'd shoot that accurately."

"For now, you'll probably still need the EP for guidance outside the sims. Until we can test it further, we won't know."

"It seems crazy that I could do some of this on my own."

"Says the girl who sent Direction into a frenzy with the detention center escape," Meyer says.

"I sent them into a *frenzy?*"

"You did."

If only it had been more successful.

"We should continue the training," I say, but the EP flashes green.

Return to the council meeting.

"Time to go," Meyer says.

I blink twice and return to the crisp, empty room. Back to reality.

Meyer leads us to a new location at the opposite end of the corridor, to a concrete room. To the left are a few people working on viewers. They appear to be scanning the city, as different locations are on each screen. The table has only enough room for the eight council members and us. Ruiz stands in the doorway waiting for us.

"Please, have a seat," she says. As she says it, a man comes up from behind her.

"I need to speak with you ma'am," he says.

Ruiz gestures to us to sit. We walk toward the last of the empty seats, not at the head of the table. I slowly round the table, struggling to listen to what the man has to say. He lowers his voice, but I still pick up a few of the words.

Michael and Darline Lark... Representative's office... Detained.

My parents have been arrested because of me. My hands begin to shake, and I look up to eighteen eyes.

Ruiz locks her attention on me and gestures for me to find my seat. I shuffle around the table, keeping my gaze low. I drop myself into the spot and chew at my upper lip. The man across the table stares at me, a concerned look on his face. He's older than me, maybe in his thirties.

"Ruiz?" I ask.

"Yes," she says.

"What was that about?"

"Nothing you need to concern yourself with at this time."

"My parents—"

She crosses her arms, frustrated. "Yes. Please understand we are working on it, but need you to focus on greater problems."

How am I supposed to focus knowing this? My parents never did anything wrong, *ever*, and now they may have to suffer for me. I push away from the table with a jolt, the legs of the chair screeching over the concrete.

Everyone's attention snaps to me again. Meyer tips his head and eyes me, indicating we should talk later.

"Sorry..." I mutter, but anger and concern still race through me.

From the other side of the room, the Direction News chime plays. The viewers display the spinning Direction logo. The symbol disappears, replaced with Manning in front of the Direction Center in Level Three. Now, instead of on me, everyone has their attention fixed on the screens.

"Citizens of Elore," Manning says. "First, we are proud to announce the hard work and dedication of Direction-appointed security. This includes the man-hours of our new Direction Preservation Force, as well as the work involved with drone advances from SynCorp. The combination of technology and manpower allows us to continue our focus on a thriving, highly intelligent human race with superior health and almost nonexistent crime.

"But, as you know, in weeks past, a terrorist organization has attempted to spread among us, to deceive our citizens with lies. They are just as dangerous as the virus which nearly destroyed humanity. This distortion works to destroy everything we have achieved, and will result in death for ourselves and our children.

"Just as our VacTech has protected us from deadly viruses, Direction will keep you safe from this threat. We have detained multiple Affinity members who have attempted and succeeded in not only damaging our way of life, but also murdered many of our top Level Three citizens.

"These individuals have been tried and convicted of involvement in the movement. Despite our best efforts in re-educating and retraining these individuals, they have resisted. We are left with no other choice to keep Elore safe."

The scene switches to one I don't recognize. It could be anywhere, since it's just a blank room.

I stand to get a better view, and the drones march them out. Jayson and Lena, plus a group of unknown others. I feel dizzy, but catch myself on the lip of the table and fall back into my seat.

This isn't supposed to happen until Friday. Meyer said Jayson and Lena would be rescued. They had a chance.

Everyone around the room sits frozen, eyes wide, watching the broadcast. They're unprepared too.

Jayson and Lena actually look better than I'd expected. Gone are Jayson's bruises and his overall haggardness from when I last saw him at the detention center. All I can guess is that Manning turned his healing nanos back on to erase the signs of torture— Direction's attempt to appear as if it is above that sort of thing.

Sickness rolls around in my stomach. First Bess is gone without a trace, then my parents are in custody... now this. Everything is falling apart.

The screen scrolls information concerning their "guilt" as the prisoners stand, noiseless, awaiting their sentencing.

I gently rise from my seat again and drift around the council table to where Meyer is. The air in the room feels thick, viscous, as if I have to wade through the space to reach him. When I finally reach the back of his chair, Manning speaks again.

"Jayson Brant, you have been sentenced to death."

Manning moves on to outline his crimes, then does the same for Lena, but by now I'm only picking up bits and piece while my mind grasps for ideas to do something.

"What… what if I can hack… immerse into the network and do something? Maybe if I disrupt the coverage it can buy time?" I reach for one of the viewers, but Ruiz grabs my upper arm.

"Avlyn, we have not done any testing yet. We have no idea if your hack will reveal our location. We can't risk it."

She releases me. I open my mouth to speak when the scene on the screen changes and pans back.

An unseen voice continues to list off their "crimes", starting with a woman at the end trying her best to appear brave, but the terror in her eyes is obvious. At the end of her judgment, a green scan rakes over her. She instantly goes limp and crumbles to the ground. Dead.

One by one, the unseen voice names the next person's crimes. The scan murders them all until they finally get to Lena. My friend. Tears cascade over her smooth skin, her long raven hair pulled back into a ponytail, just like the last time I saw her.

I press my hands to my ears to block out the sentencing and squeeze my eyes tight. I can't see this. I know after this it will be Jayson, and I turn toward the back wall and hug myself, holding back the tears that threaten to overwhelm me.

From behind, I hear Jayson's voice. "It wasn't your fault."

At that, my knees buckle, and I grab Meyer's arm. I'm fully aware that statement was for Meyer alone. Reluctantly, I swing my head back toward the viewer just in time to see his body fall to the ground. The scene flips back to Manning. His mouth is moving, but I don't hear him since the room has erupted. Everyone is speaking at once.

"Turn it off," Ruiz's voice rings out, and the viewers shut off one by one. Everyone goes silent.

Meyer rubs his eyes and starts to speak, then pauses. "I need some air."

He pulls away from me and heads from the room. I start to follow him, then look to Ruiz. She nods.

"Just go."

In the corridor, Meyer stands leaned against the wall, head in his hands.

Numbness creeps over my body, and I have no idea what to do. I want to be anywhere but here.

"Is your EP on?" I ask.

Meyer nods and rises.

"Give me your handheld."

He tips his head. "Why?"

"Just do it."

He reaches into his pocket and places the device into my palm.

With it, I jog toward the same room we used for training earlier and clear the door. As if in a trance, Meyer follows. An auto light illuminates the stark room as I pull my Flexx off my wrist and place it and Meyer's together.

I close my eyes. Code swirls in my mind and forms a destination. Before I open my lids, the sound of crashing waves fills the air and the wind kisses my face.

Meyer releases a long sigh, his eyes brimming with moisture.

"Anything's better than that bunker," I say as a pink-and-orange-streaked sky greets us.

Meyer nods and walks toward the edge of the water to step into the surf. The water and foam drifts over his feet, and I watch as he releases the tension from his shoulders.

After a few minutes, he sighs and turns toward me, tears streaking his face. "Jayson loves it here. We go sometimes just to talk."

I glide toward him and stand at his side, tracing his jawline in my mind and working up to eyes filled with sorrow.

"I could have done something," I say.

"You don't know that," he sighs. "Ruiz is right. It was too risky."

"They have my parents too."

"I know... I'm so sorry," he says as his gaze moves from the painted sky to me.

Meyer's body remains still, solidly alongside me, but from the corner of my eye, I can see he's returned to watching the sun recess into the horizon. Heavy tears stream down his face.

Without a word, I slip my palm into his and interlace our shaking fingers. A warm calm seeps through me. "Thank you for being my friend."

Meyer's hand squeezes mine. "Friends are what make Lena's and Jayson's death's worth *something*."

The EP flashes. They need us to come back. Even though I ache to stay, I let go of the sim in my mind, blink, and Meyer and I stand in the empty room. The heat of his palm still burns on mine, even though we're not holding hands anymore.

I hold out his handheld and he takes it.

"Thanks," he mutters. In real life, his face glistens with tears too.

"For what?" I ask.

"For remembering that place."

I square my shoulders and look him straight in the eyes. "Now, let's go do something."

When we enter the makeshift headquarters, the room already bustles with activity. The people working on viewers are back, swiping and moving information, furious as ever. Whatever they're doing appears important... and urgent.

Ruiz motions the two of us back to the council table where the others have returned, but neither of us sit.

"Unfortunately, there is little time to discuss what just happened," she says. "Each one of those people is a huge loss, both personally, and to Affinity. But there is urgent business to attend to. So many more lives are at stake."

She looks around at the silent council.

"All the intel has arrived," Ruiz continues. "Avlyn, the project you worked on this afternoon at GenTech was successful."

Upon hearing her words, a minuscule amount of hope spreads through me and I fall into my seat. It's something. Maybe this means they can focus on getting my parents out.

"We got what we needed, but unfortunately, it wasn't enough," Ruiz says.

My hope turns cold and rigid.

"As much as I desire to remove Miss Lark from the city and explore her... *ability*, in order to proceed with the next phase, I can't. Manning has advanced his timeline, and so too must we."

She turns to Meyer.

"Quinn, you're leading the team with Preston." The guy who showed me some concern before snaps to attention when she says this. "It is imperative you get Ms. Lark in and out of Genesis Technologies tonight."

My mind reels.

Affinity is sending me back into GenTech?

CHAPTER TWENTY-EIGHT

Every ounce of confidence I just had with Meyer in the sim dwindles away to nothing.

"I can't go back in," I protest. "They'll be on high alert." I'm up again, and don't remember standing.

"Please, sit." Ruiz's expression is flat, but frustration brews in her eyes.

I fall back into my chair with a *thump*.

"You're unaware of how dire this situation is."

"Well, fill me in," I growl, tipping forward with rapt attention and my own irritation.

The side of her neck twitches. "Direction wants to prune its tree, so to speak…"

"GenTech is developing a new virus," I say. "Something called Project Ectopistes. Most of the people in Level One will not have immunity. Manning is wiping them out."

"Yes, but how do *you* know this?" she asks, her eyes flicking to Meyer.

"I didn't tell her," he says. "I understand it's need-to-know information."

The stares of the council sting. "I read it," I admit. "When I unsecured the lab."

"You *read* it?" Ruiz asks.

"Through the GenTech server. In the lab, I could bring up the information on what they were doing," I explain.

"You were only supposed to disable the security, not enter the project," Ruiz says.

Heat builds in my entire body, but I lock my gaze to hers. I'm not going to justify myself to her. "You didn't even let me try to get into Direction's network for Jayson and Lena, and now you're trusting me to go back into GenTech to stop this inhumanity?"

Ruiz leans back and folds her arms. She makes eye contact with the woman sitting to my right who says, "The mainframe doesn't allow access from the outside. This means we need you *in* the building to do it. At this point, options are limited, time is of the essence, and your ability to immerse and destroy the project quickly is our best hope. This part of GenTech's system doesn't extend outside the building, so you will need to physically be there. Meyer is one of the best, and as you know, your ability guided you out of the detention center. It was impressive, although sloppy..."

She trails off. The reminder of Jayson and Lena proves too disquieting.

"So?" I ask. "What *does* Manning know about me?"

"By now, GenTech must realize the lab was breached, and may suspect you," Ruiz explains. "And it seems another placement filed an anonymous report on you recently. Someone thought you were up to something. That's why Direction was waiting for you today."

Daniel finally made his move.

"But, according to intel," she continues, "Manning only believes you to be a hacker, albeit an amazing one. A pawn for Affinity. If he truly understood you were more, he would have sent in more than a couple officers. You never would have escaped." She narrows her eyes for a moment, thinking. "Does anyone outside this room know about you? Your parents?"

The mention of my parents feels like Ruiz reached over and grabbed my heart through my chest, knowing Manning has them.

I push back away from the table. "No," I mutter, anger stirring in my core. How can this woman be so calm? My life, the way I knew, has ended. My parents may be killed. And Kyra? What will become of her?

"At least it buys us time. Anyone else?"

The rousing fury shoots up my spine at her question. "No, only the people around this table, and the other one who just *died*!" I yell, slamming my fist on the table and jumping from my seat.

My gaze darts to Meyer. I didn't mean to say it… not like that, but he's a stone.

Ruiz gestures with a nod to my chair. "Please, calm yourself."

Preston, the guy who is apparently coming with Meyer and me, at the other end, sits quietly, but the white on his knuckles on top of the table isn't the most encouraging sign.

A dizzying sensation fights to better me, but I drop into the chair again and try to focus.

"We've run the stats, probability, drone schedules, and anything else to determine the best course of action to take," Ruiz continues. "Of course, there will be variables, but the EP should help guide the team. Ideally, you'll be in and out."

"What will I be doing exactly?" I ask.

"Meyer will be escorting you to the mainframe access, where you will be completely wiping Project Ectopistes."

"And someone more experienced can't do this?"

"The speed and accuracy you have will better ensure the mission's success," says the woman next to Meyer. "Preston will be destroying the actual lab, and Bates, Davis, and I will be targeting anyone who worked on Ectopistes."

I whip my head toward Meyer. "Targeting? What does this mean?"

The look on his face tells me I already know what it means.

"This is a war, Avlyn," Ruiz says. "There are hundreds of thousands of lives at stake. Our first step is to stop this project."

"What are the chances this will play out accurately?" I mutter as my foot taps under the table. No one responds. "You're confident?" I ask, louder than before.

Ruiz's gaze falls on me. "I am. I *must* be. And you need to be certain too. At this point, you're our only shot, because if the information brought out earlier is as disastrous as it appears, confidence in this team is all we have left."

"And it's only the three of us in GenTech?" Meyer asks.

Ruiz nods. "Sending in more seemed like a better option, but in every scenario we ran, your team strengths and capabilities ranked the strongest. The best chance of completing the mission and getting Ms. Lark out alive is with a limited squad."

I gulp. What about Meyer and Preston?

As if she sees into my brain, she says, "The team mission is get you in and out of GenTech... no matter what."

"What do I do when I'm in?" I ask.

"You'll be given the code for a system virus to upload directly within GenTech to wipe out the research." Ruiz leans onto the table. "Your ability to immerse should allow you to make immediate modifications if necessary. Doing this will set them back considerably, and buy us time."

The memory of the Level One woman who only wanted to stay with her child comes to mind. "Real people are in that lab," I say.

"Yes." Ruiz lowers her gaze and shifts it to the man sitting on the right. "This mission will be at the expense of the test subjects' lives as well. If we fail, most of Level One may become infected if Direction finishes their work."

She's right. So many can't be put at risk to save a few...

"When can we review the whole operation?" Meyer asks.

"Instructions are uploaded. Study it to help you prepare," Ruiz orders.

"One thing that should be interesting," Preston's deep voice finally pipes in, "is getting there."

I picture another race through the darkened city and dread the increased security. How in the world will this work?

Meyer leans back and folds his arms. "What's the plan?"

Preston smirks. "Drones. We're riding in the package compartment of three drones."

My stomach lurches.

I can't fly. I hate flying.

Even the thought of riding in the public air shuttles gives me the shivers, and now *this?*

"This means go time is in less than thirty minutes," Ruiz says. "The team needs to be out of here while the building is still receiving packages for nighttime deliveries. The drones have new, modified Direction technology programmed into the hull. On the way in, the drone will appear as an Aerrx, and on the way out, a Guardian. Once they drop the team at the lab, the drones will maneuver out and onto the rooftop and circle the city until you are ready. Get inside, complete the task, exit, and they will dispatch your team to a safe location."

"Back here?" I ask.

"No, Avlyn. Affinity needs you out of the city as soon as possible," Ruiz says. "The risk of your ability falling into the wrong hands is too great."

My chest constricts. "What about my parents?"

"Please focus." She stands. "I understand your concern, but Affinity is doing what it can. Unnecessary risks are dangerous for everyone, including your parents."

I open my mouth to argue, but the words die in my throat.

She's right. I wanted to help, and I'm only being selfish.

Ruiz motions at Meyer. "Quinn, get Avlyn out of here and ready to go. Preston has the new suits. Council adjourned." She sighs, then turns and strides toward the door.

Meyer rests his hand on my shoulder. "Come on. Let's suit up and review the rest of the mission."

Preston walks to the door, and Meyer and I follow, leaving the council. I'm headed to do something more incredible and meaningful than I've ever done, but all I feel is smothering dread. How is it that stopping a deadly virus that will affect most of Level One, and one not unlike the one that killed Ben, falls on me? A girl who not much more than a month ago wanted to disappear into the crowd?

We spend the next twenty minutes fitting the suit and gloves. The letter from Bess is still crumpled in my pocket, and I smooth it out and tuck it into a secret compartment inside the chest of my suit. I get a chance to review the virus code, and Meyer uploads the contained version to my nanos.

There's only time for a quick mission review. After our trip in the drones, we will be scanned in as a delivery. The drones will drop us near the mainframe access, where I can upload the virus. Preston is loaded with a small, but powerful set of explosive devices he will set off in the lab once we exit on the roof, hitching a ride to a safe location.

My teeth chatter, even though the air in the room is warm. Meyer and Preston check the weapons and other equipment to ensure all is in working order. I'm a ball of nerves, just anxious to get going. If I'm going to die, I want to get it over with.

"Where are the drones?" I ask.

"Waiting on the roof," Preston replies. "We'll ride the elevator to the top floor. It's completely secured. Then we'll take the stairs to the rooftop. The drones calculate liftoff depending on the patterns of the ones already in the air, so you won't have to do a thing until we arrive at GenTech. The one downside is the drones have no defense system. There was no time to build it."

Which means if they discover us... we're going down.

Meyer glances from his handheld, then folds and stuffs it in his pocket. "It's time." From the table next to him, he grabs the two gray stunners, holsters the first to his side, and then tosses me the second. I catch it. The metal is heavy and cool in my hands, and I attach the equipment, trying to convince myself it could very well stay unused.

When we exit the room, I half expect Ruiz to be in the hall to fill us in on last-minute details, but it's just the three of us.

On the rooftop, three large model 3000 Aerrx delivery drones sit parked, the evening sun glistening off their metallic hulls, each big enough for commercial-size packages. I'd never imagined a human could actually fit inside a drone, but why not? The packages for GenTech and other companies are sometimes sizable. A person *could* fit in one... barely.

The cargo panels of the pods slide up as we approach. The holding space is even tighter than I imagined. I stop in front of the cavity and lean over to peer inside.

Preston chuckles. "It's roomier than you might think."

I swivel toward him. "You've done this before?"

He smiles. "Oh, once or twice."

Out of the corner of my eye, I catch Meyer shaking his head, a slight grin on his lips.

"What?" I ask.

"Nothing," he says, then pulls his Flexx from his pocket and swipes the screen.

My hand finds a spot to rest on my hip. "You've never done this, have you?"

Preston knits his eyebrows together and starts to say something, then stops. "Just trying to make you feel better. You look green." He ducks to peer into the cavity, then straightens to turn his attention to me again. He forces another smile. "I have to fit myself *and* this pack inside."

He stuffs in a backpack that must contain the explosives needed to destroy the lab, and I shake my head, willing down the sickness from the thought of flying welling up inside me. Since the ride won't be long, comfort isn't a huge priority.

Closing my eyes, I steady myself, and the EP comes alive with information.

Brace for liftoff flashes green.

Are you kidding?

I'm so wedged in here that no bracing is necessary.

"Ready?" Meyer's voice sounds over the comm.

Preston grunts, "Yeah."

"As I'll ever be," I groan.

The drone whirs, and my gut drops when the unit defies gravity and lifts from the concrete roof. In the EP, the walls of the transport appear to fade away in my vision, giving me a full 360-degree view of our surroundings. I gasp and throw my hands to the metal interior as the buildings of Level One appear below.

"I didn't know that was going to happen either," Meyer says. "Sorry, would've warned you."

"Nice view." Preston sighs. "Better take the time to enjoy it."

I don't even want to consider the meaning behind the words, and instead focus on the night sky.

"The moon is so big tonight," I say softly.

"It won't be the last time you see it, Avlyn," Meyer assures me.

The comm goes silent. Not because of a malfunction, but because there are just no words left to say.

Our three drones join in with a group of others, a mix of both Guardian and Aerrx on their last evening runs. The EP alerts that we've dropped into Level Two and are approaching the GenTech building. My teeth grind together as I clench my jaw. A drop of sweat forms and trails from my neck into my suit collar.

The words Genesis Technologies move across the top floors of the building, and we glide toward them. My stomach flips, either because of the descent, or the sight of our destination. Probably both.

"This is it," Meyer whispers.

The streets below are deserted, save for drone activity and a few human guards. The transports maneuver to the building's rear service entrance. A few other units hover in the modest bay, waiting to be scanned for entry into the main structure. We fall in line, and my heart thuds.

"Step one," Preston whispers through the comm.

"One hundred to go," I mutter.

Meyer's drone floats in first to receive the scan. I let out a breath when the screen on the front of the SI attendant glows green and the bay door clears. Preston's next and does the same.

My drone propels forward and the scanner moves over the front.

It's fine... This will be fine.

The AI's screen turns bright yellow, and I clasp my hand over my mouth to halt a yelp that tries to work its way out.

Delivery item description missing displays across the screen.

No, no, no... It *can't* end here because of something stupid like a missing description.

The SI reaches out toward the pod with its metal claw. I wince and press my hand against the inside of the tiny prison.

What would I be if I were a delivery?

My mind races and pulls up an image of a beaker I saw Corra working with in the lab.

The machine manually rescans the front of the unit, and this time, the screen glows green.

50 beakers for Lab Suite 1008 are the words displayed while I waft through the now-open door onto the main level. I relax as the wide space comes into view, both Meyer's and Preston's drones hovering high above through the exposed ceiling.

The drone makes its way to the seventh floor, to the office of Margo Yates, the president of GenTech. Intel maintains Yates should be gone from her office. Even the president can't be here after hours.

I thought we'd just be returning to the lab to finish the task of destroying the research. The idea made sense in my mind, but the mission overview explained the easiest access to the mainframe was through Yates' system.

My drone sails over the half-open wall lining floor seven and follows the corridor to the office. The EP confirms the other two have arrived safely as well.

Floor 7 Suite 752, Arrived flashes in the EP.

It alerts me to no immediate danger, and the compartment door slides free. Fresh air envelops me, and I shake my head as I squeeze out from the oppressive inside of the drone. The compartment seals, and the drone immediately whirs back the way we came, leaving me in the corridor, exposed and alone.

10.27 minutes before next security check displays in my EP, and a countdown starts.

Preston and Meyer round the corner.

"Where were you guys?" I whisper.

"Waiting for you." Meyer eyes the security pad beside the entrance to Suite 752.

I hold my breath and press my gloved hand onto the surface, then I close my eyes. Blank. Nothing happens.

"Is she in?" Preston mumbles.

Hands shaking, I squeeze my eyelids tight. It's gone. Again, I try, this time with my other hand, calming my mind…

But nothing happens.

Maybe the ability was a fluke, and if it's dead… so are we. I snap away from the pad as if it's hot and swing around toward Meyer.

"It's not working," I hiss.

"Well, something's happening because no alarms have triggered yet," he replies. "If I touched that pad, security would be blaring."

Preston turns away and rakes his hands through his hair. "This won't work," he mumbles.

"Listen," Meyer says. "You fully understand the stakes this time, and you're scared." He holds my terrified gaze. "But don't make it more than it is. You've done it before, and you can do it now. Avlyn, I believe in you."

Intently, I drink in his concerned face as a wisp of his dark hair falls in the middle of his forehead. A feeling stirs inside me that I've been trying to push away.

I love Meyer. I have no idea if he loves me, but he believes in me… just like Lena did.

I can't let either of them down. If I have to die, so be it. At least I finally have a glimpse of understanding the gift of love Ben wanted for me.

The feeling consumes me. Love for Ben. Love for Meyer. Kyra… my parents… Lena… even Bess… the Level Ones whose lives are at stake and don't even know. It's my responsibility to love them more than my own life. To give my all.

I inhale deeply, focusing my mind on the heart necklace encircling my neck under the collar of my suit, a symbol. After three deep breaths, I slow my heart rate and lower my palm to the pad. Dizziness engulfs me.

The door to the president's office slides back with a soft whir.

CHAPTER TWENTY-NINE

I steady myself, and the three of us hustle into the sparse office. The door closes. Preston stands guard at the entry while Meyer pulls out his handheld and monitors security. Yates' large system sits on the desk, and I slam into the chair in front of it. I fumble for the data port to the side and struggle to relax. My heartbeat pulses under my skin.

I take a quick glance at Meyer, hoping for one of his signature grins, but he's still engrossed. No doubt with something extremely important... like keeping us *alive*.

"Your security is confirmed," Meyer says to Preston.

"I'll lay the explosive, then meet you up top."

Preston rounds out the door, pack on his back, and disappears. The EP displays the countdown.

8 minutes 55 seconds

I force air into my lungs and grip the port. I shut my eyelids and the room falls away, my vision glowing hot white. Then, the vision dissolves, leaving me in a vast, empty space, trying to will away the lightheadedness that threatens me again.

"I need access to Project Ectopistes."

The files flutter in, filling the blank room, surrounding me. It's the same as Meyer's files, except there's much more information. Thousands of tiny cabinets of labeled information from the mainframe wait for me to access them.

Where to start?

This project is huge, and the EP shows less than eight minutes for me to complete it. This needs to be a mass wipe. Manning wanted a virus, and I'm going to give him one. The InfoSec remote crew will be standing by, so this will need to be quick.

I call up the Network virus and brace to release it into the system. Heat moves from the tips of my fingers and climbs my arm. Gently, I place my palms onto the surface of my vision of cabinets.

Release, I think.

The code flows from my hands into the system.

The symbols move out in circular patterns as I will them into correct placement. When the last pattern configures into place, my brain and hands surge. Despite the urge to back down, I force myself into the collection of files, collapsing, straining.

Gradually, the fire ripping through me moves forward into the data. Bright, red-orange shapes glow from the spot under my hands. The orange bleeds out from the marks and spread deeper and wider over the file containers. I concentrate on targeting and overwriting the Ectopistes files with new, random data, destroying every last bit. As the hue envelops each repository, it dissolves and floats away.

"Estimated time for the completion of the destruction of Project Ectopistes?"

3 minutes 18 seconds

I have 58 seconds more than I need. At least I can pay my respect.

Floor ten, lab ten-oh-eight b, I think.

The white room filled with the half-ruined files dissolves, a shimmering, generated version of the lab replacing it. Glass domes containing human research subjects in comas and numerous climate-controlled units housing vials line the back wall.

I study the unconscious Level One woman's dome. There's nothing I can do for her, even if this was the real lab.

"I'm sorry," I whisper as I stroke the top of her encasement. Her only desire was to protect her child, but instead, she ended up unconscious, strapped to a table under a dome. A mutated virus eating her from the inside.

"What was her name?" I ask the system.

Naomi Jensen. Level One, flashes across my vision.

I make a mental note of it, thinking of her son, how he cried for her. If I live through this, I will find him, tell him that his mother was brave and loved him. He should know.

Nausea waves over me, but it's not as bad as the last time. Maybe my body is adjusting to immersing. The counter flashes red, alerting me it's time to go. I inhale deeply and blink my lids, opening them to Meyer's face.

"Nothing like waiting until the last second," Meyer growls.

I shove the chair backward and surge to my feet.

Weapon in hand, Meyer forces me into the hall. I grab my stunner and position it the way Meyer taught me, but the weight still feels off. Combat is not something I'm made for. The EP display shows a Guardian drone arriving seconds behind us, and Meyer motions me into an alcove. It passes and floats out over the balcony ledge behind us into the exposed space in the middle of GenTech.

Human security detected. ETA 29 seconds.

"I'll meet you at floor ten," Preston whispers in the comm. "This is taking longer than I thought."

"The drones are waiting. Hurry," Meyer replies.

We continue toward the stairwell. We've got to make it up seventeen floors to the roof and meet up with Preston without being spotted. However, the EP still indicates we're in the clear, and the security guards seem to have rerouted from our location.

As we work the stairs, my head throbs with each step.

At floor nine, the EP flashes red.

Immediate human security alert
Exit stairway and retreat to floor 9

Meyer checks above and below us. "I don't see anything yet." He runs ahead of me and bursts into the corridor of nine. "Are you getting this, Preston?"

No answer returns.

I follow Meyer's lead, stunner in hand, as the footsteps reverberate below us in the stairwell. The security team must be a few floors below. We crouch against the wall, Meyer inches behind me, until the rumble of feet meets our level and continues. The EP says it's safe. Meyer's rapid breath hits my neck, reminding me to slow my own.

Continue to rooftop, flashes green.

"Preston, come in," Meyer says, urgency in his voice.

Still no answer.

"Be on alert and have weapons ready," Meyer says.

Climbing the stairs again, I keep my gaze fixed above and push forward. When we pass the entrance to floor ten, I peer down the corridor to look for Preston.

"Maybe he's already there," I say.

The EP goes instantly red, sensing unknown danger. The door to the lab bursts open. On instinct, I raise my weapon and train it on the person exiting.

Preston.

Meyer flanks me and lowers his stunner immediately, as do I.

Preston rushes to us. "We need to move. Something went wrong. The timing's all off." He grabs my arm and pulls me forward.

A rumble from the hall echoes and builds. Suddenly, the door to the lab explodes and slams into the corridor wall. Flames erupt through it and hurtle toward us. I'm knocked to the floor, my heart racing.

I scan to find my team in the smoke-filled corridor. Meyer crouches behind me, and Preston still stands, gripping the hand rail. A loud crack splits the ceiling, and I cover my head to shield myself from the falling debris.

"Let's go before this thing blows again," Meyer says. "Security has to be on the way."

Meyer stands and extends his hand. I catch it and pull myself up. As we take the stairs up, Preston in the lead, another explosion sends us off kilter, and flames lick at the stairwell above.

"The pressure must have gone up and out on eleven, too," Preston says.

He starts toward the stairs again when I reach for his arm. "It's not safe."

He glares back at me. "Stop wasting time. It's not safe to go either way, and the EP still says to meet the drones on the roof, but not for long."

Meyer pushes against my back. "Go, Avlyn. The suit is fire resistant. Just cover your face."

The EP lights red. Company is on its way. I gather myself and vault forward. At the landing of the next floor, water gushes from the ceiling, and an alarm blares, nearly deafening me.

Water rushes over my suit, and drenched hair clings to my face and scalp, but it's better than being burned or blown to bits.

On our way to the roof, we have to exit onto floor seventeen to wait out a passing Guardian. According to the EP, the rest of the commotion is still below us. By the time we reach floor twenty-five, we're doused in a mix of sweat and water.

Preston arrives first to the exit. It's locked, but the door has a security panel to the side.

"Got it," I say, jogging past Preston and leaving Meyer on the last of the stairs. I put a palm to the panel and the door skates back. Cool air from the rooftop blankets me and sends a chill through my wet suit.

Preston throws his arm out in front of me. "Wait here." He inches out onto the platform, weapon poised. "Looks secure, and nothing's showing in the EP."

When we step out, a drone whooshes by above us. I instinctively duck until it passes, my heart pumping wildly.

"Keep alert," Meyer says. "We're not out of here yet."

The three Guardian drones sit parked, waiting for us.

"You're first, Avlyn," Preston whispers. "Meyer and I will cover you."

Panic rips my body, and I turn back toward Meyer. He nods for me to go.

Weapon ready, I dart toward the silver pod and reach for the open package compartment. Wedging myself into the tight space, I suck in my chest and stomach as if it will make me more compact. Once I'm in, the hatch closes, the EP artificially dissolving the metal walls, showing the surroundings again.

The rest of the team enters their transports, and the panorama view provided by the EP engages. We all lift from the rooftop. My breath hitches from the weightless sensation, and a smile turns up the corners of my lips as we move away from the top of GenTech.

My pod keeps the lead, but both Meyer and Preston's transports show in the EP view. We sail through air and over the high-reaching buildings of Level Two. Our heading is east, toward the closest exit of the city.

"We did it—"

Pop, pop. The drone vibrates. Drowsiness threatens me, followed by a start. In my vision, I catch the end of a green scanner trailing through my body. I shake off the sensation and whip my head around to try to see what's happening, but I can't see anything.

I throw my hands against the inside of the unit, asking, "Did they scan us?" But no one replies.

Preston's drone takes a dip, and then careens to the side.

"Meyer!" I screech. The comm is dead. My breathing goes erratic, and my mind races, but I have no solutions. These drones aren't even armed. In the silence of the pod, I can hear my pulse drumming in my ears.

Meyer's drone still flies behind mine, but breaks formation and moves to the side.

My chest seizes, and I thrust my hands onto the metal again, hoping for a chance to connect and control the flight pattern.

The EP lights red too late. Three jumbo model 4000 Guardians surround us.

A hefty drone dives in above our transports, tentacles and pinchers extended. My pod jolts, and metal against metal screeches in a deafening howl as the tentacles intercept me.

Meyer's drone pitches and swerves to avoid the clutches of his pursuer, then rights and somehow speeds out of sight, but his tracking still displays in the EP. One of the drones shoots after him…

And then Meyer's gone.

The second drone clutches Preston's pod, and a green light glows around the surface in my EP. The tentacles retract to release him. The pod pitches and languidly spins, dropping to the ground. A terrifying, high-pitched whine follows it as it plummets.

"*No!*" I scream and thrust forward, my pod still trapped in the clutches of the Guardian.

Far below, fire and smoke plume up, extinguished as promptly as it lit. An echo of the impact meets my ears as Preston's drone tracker blanks out.

They… they blew him up…

CHAPTER THIRTY

Shaking and gasping for air, I wait for the same to happen to me. To be dropped to the ground and exploded into tiny bits…

But it doesn't come.

Unsure what to do, I rake my hands through my wet hair. The dampness coats my palms and I drag them over my thighs, but it's no use. I'm sodden. My hand curves over the edge of my Flexx on my other wrist. I pull the device off, access the Affinity app, and message Meyer. There's no way he's making it out of this alive… but just in case…

It was worth the risk.

Then I run the self-destruct operation to wipe the account, but not before I will the app to download to my nanos. They won't even know how to look for it if they tried.

Next, with a shaking hand, I rip the EP from my eye, blink, and the illusion of seeing outside the drone goes dark except for a tiny light from the internal panel. Everything's gone; the starry sky, the buildings and streets below, and the Guardian which clutches me like I'm a package to be delivered.

Everything but the simmering dread in my gut telling me I'll die soon.

I sob and crush the EP, then tear the tech in half. It's nearly dark, and I can't see it, but the device shrivels and dissolves in my palm.

Clunk.

The air's knocked from my lungs when the drone comes to a stop. I clutch the stunner pressing against my hip. I'd be stupid to shoot, no matter how skilled a shot I am in a sim. This is not a good time to test Meyer's crazy theories.

Pop, pop.

The drone vibrates again. I flinch. It's the same sound and shudder before Preston crashed. I rub my face and the back of my neck.

The vibration stops, and then there's nothing. If I didn't expect I'd be shot, I'd pop the hatch to see what was happening.

A new, muffled voice breaks through the confining metal, sending a shudder down my spine. "If you want to live, throw any weapons, your Flexx, and any other tech from the hatch."

The hatch clears. Bright light and a waft of fresh air dizzies me. Hesitating, I reach for my stunner. I hate just handing it over, but I yank the gun from my side, sigh, and throw it, then the Flexx, out. The two pieces clank onto hard concrete, one after the other.

"Now, come out. Slowly," the male voice instructs. "We have our own weapons, and no one wants to use them. They're supposedly painful."

I poke my head out. The barrels of twenty pistols are trained on me, which I'm sure are not set to stun, and the faces of those who hold them are blank. Hollow. These are not the standard human Guardian squads. By the DPF logo on their chests, these belong to Manning's Level One army, now under control.

My gaze flits between the faces when an older, but fit, man dressed in a white smock steps between two of the soldiers. Just the slightest smirk blankets his face, taunting me.

Manning.

"Avlyn Lark?" Manning nods his head toward me. We lock eyes. "We've been searching for you. For a Level Two, you've become somewhat compelling."

I hold his gaze, and my tongue, for that matter. But when I force myself out of the compartment of the drone, I glance away, trying to ignore the guns trained on me.

"This is a bit much for one girl," I say, feeling bold for a split second, feet hitting the floor of the bay.

I raise my hands to show I'm unarmed and nod to the Director, who's only a few inches taller than me. His expression remains poised, but something in his eyes tells me a scorching blaze lurks inside. Not seconds after I step from the transport, several of the sentinels holster their weapons and descend on the pod. The commotion pushes me toward Manning, but I don't turn. They won't find much.

My hands raise higher as I inch forward on shaking legs, boldness gone. A female guard with shiny dark hair and russet colored eyes steps up with a type of scanner. She looks a lot like Lena... possibly on purpose.

A reminder.

The white beam trails over me and beeps. My heart jumps when it hits the spot where I hid Bess's letter.

I never should have brought it.

"She's free of any weaponry, Director Manning." The guard lowers her device and steps back in line with the others. They aren't looking for paper.

"So," Manning continues, "do we need a few guards to accompany us, or could you join me of your own account?"

He's not stupid. Whether these guards come or not, I'm secured in some way.

"Do what's best for you, Director," I say.

He eyes me and presses his lips together. By the tightening of his jaw, he seems to be grinding his teeth.

"Troops dismissed."

The men and women of the guard retract their weapons and exit the bay.

"Well, Ms. Lark," he says, attention still fixed on me. "Please, follow me."

When Manning speaks, his tension dissipates. Maybe years of practicing repressing emotions have been a success. Manning motions for the door, and I take a step forward. His face now displays a strange smirk. When I reach him, he steps toward the door and I follow, checking behind me one last time.

"I have been informed you were recently placed at Genesis Technologies… in information security."

I nod, but keep turned from him.

"Ironic." He chuckles. "Your assignment was to protect the interests of both GenTech and the people of Elore, and you have performed the opposite."

"I *am* protecting the interests of Elore," I mumble.

He steps slightly in front of me and brings us both to a stop. His cold, gray-eyed stare bores into me and holds my body in place as if he'd reached out and grabbed me. Everything in me wants to yank back, but I don't dare.

"Says who? You? What do you understand? Only the lies of a few dissenters." A crease forms between his eyes. "Direction has spent years... *decades* studying possible outcomes for this society." The words roll from his tongue as if we were having an everyday conversation. "The Direction Initiative gives us survival in a world without crime, with reduced pain and loss, and a naive *little girl* comes along and suddenly thinks it's still not enough."

He gives one last look and moves to the side as if to let me pass. An argument builds in my throat, but I know my words would be wasted on him. Instead, I study the neutral walls of the inside of the building, wondering where exactly I am.

Manning starts walking again. "Prior to Aves, life was different. Wars, hate, crime, violent atrocities. The virus was dreadful, but in the end, it saved us. It saved us from ourselves."

We pass a door labeled with an unknown name. I still don't know where I am.

"And setting your own virus free inside Elore *isn't* an atrocity?" I spit.

"I'm not a monster, but sacrifices must be made in order to return the Initiative to order. I will not return to the world that existed before the Collapse."

REPRESENTATIVE MITCHELL AYERS is displayed on the next door. Ayers, Kyra's supervisor. We're in the Level Two Representative building. Mother and Father are, or were, here. My pulse gallops with the possibility, but I shift the thoughts away. For now.

"Sacrifice?" I echo. "It's our own people."

"Oh, *child*. The problem of the undirected population is so much greater than you know. The Outerbounds has gotten out of hand, Ms. Lark."

"You're releasing this virus outside the perimeter?" I ask. "Are you truly that amoral?"

"Amoral? This concerns *survival*, not morality. What is more important?"

I clench my teeth, willing away the disgust skittering over my skin. "By killing anyone who thinks differently, or is unworthy?"

Manning tsks. "Oh, Avlyn, you comprehend so little. And to be honest, Direction knows little concerning you. But my intention is to become much better acquainted this evening."

He stops in front of a door and activates it. A conference room with a long table and chairs and a viewing screen behind glass on the wall greets us. The room has no windows, and another door sits on the left.

The door shuts behind us when we enter, and Manning gestures to the table. "Have a seat. Food will be delivered soon."

Ruiz didn't trust Direction's food. I'm keenly aware they want information, and they have other ways to get it, but I won't make this any easier for them.

"What about my parents?" I mumble. "They've done nothing but follow the Initiative."

"We will see," he replies. "If you decide cooperation would be worth your time, we might discuss Mr. and Mrs. Lark further."

I glare at him and walk over to the corner of the room, my back to the door.

"Ms. Lark, Direction is aware of your involvement in the terrorist activity against GenTech earlier today, and then again tonight. There is also suspicion you had a connection with a recent detention escape. You know these crimes are now punishable by death."

I wince, but still say nothing. He knows something about me, but how much?

"Well, no matter. With some re-education, someone with your skills could be useful to us. For that reason, Direction might be willing to overlook the fact you destroyed years of research so near to completion."

My lips turn up to form a smile. The Director could be lying, but there's a chance we succeeded.

I spin toward him, willing the expression away. "You got the wrong person. The guy that did that crashed to the ground when you brought me in."

Manning stares at me as if he sees right through the lie, tucking his arms over his body. "If you choose death over working with us, it will be a tremendous waste, but any actions will not extinguish Direction's resolve to do what is best for the people of Elore."

I let out a scoff. He still doesn't know the extent of my abilities. They think this is simply expert system hacking.

"Where... where is this *Direction*?" The words spew out before I can stop them. "I see only you, Director Manning."

"Elore trusts *my* judgment." Manning steps close, inches from my body. "And Ms. Lark, I suggest you do the same."

I recoil from the simmering energy radiating off him, falling back into a chair behind me.

Manning takes a step backward and straightens his white smock. "Now, if you are ready to listen?"

I cross my arms and turn away.

His voice has returned to its usual calm. "Because of your hacking skills, we are prepared to upgrade your status to Level Three."

"Level Three?"

"Yes." Manning's eyebrow raises as he stares at me. "And you will be given a new position."

Hate burns in my belly. Does he think I can just forget what he's done and is willing to do?

"And my family?" I press.

Air softly expels from his lungs. "I don't understand why you care… but, yes. They will need some… *work*, but if cooperative, Mr. and Mrs. Lark will be released."

My gaze darts from him to the floor. The offer sounds tempting, but I have no reason to trust him.

"What if I don't take the offer?" I whisper.

"Then you die. They die."

The finality of his words knock the breath from me.

"But I can wait for an answer," he adds. "At least for a while."

Manning turns and exits. Before the lock clicks shut, I'm already searching for a way out, but other than beating a hole in the wall, there are no options but the main exit. The other door just leads to a bathroom. There's no windows, and no accessible tech, so nothing to hack.

There's a crackle from behind me. The glass encased media viewer is playing. The Direction logo spins, then fades away. Images of death and destruction float across the screen. A young child cries in his mother's arms. A gaunt man wastes away from starvation.

"For thousands of years, the earth was riddled with pain, greed, and corruption," the deep voice of a narrator drones. "Direction has risen above this destiny with focus and determination. Join us in being part of this solution."

I cover my ears. But the vid only plays again, louder.

The vid plays. Over, and over. So many times I stop hearing and settle into the corner, arm over my head. I lay with my face shoved against the wall, and my tears soak into the fabric of my shirt.

When I wake, the vid is still playing. The dull lights illuminate the room, and their meager glow stings my eyes. By the door sits a tray of uneaten food and a glass of what looks like water. My tongue sticks to my mouth, and my head is pounding. In hopes of improving the pain, I rub on the back of my neck as I sit up. My internal nanos are not helping fast enough. There's water in the restroom, but… no, it could be tainted too.

A light scratching at the door makes my breath catch and I leap up, expecting Manning. Instead, a girl with golden hair rushes into the room.

Kyra.

My eyes widen. "What are you doing?" I whisper.

"Giving you a chance to leave." She flips back toward the door. "I have some time before I'm missed. The guards are changing now, so you have a few minutes."

Kyra reaches into her satchel and pulls out a handheld and stunner.

"I stole them from Ayer's office," she says. "Manning stored everything in there last night."

"But how'd you know I was here?" I ask.

Kyra tips her head, a look a pain washing over her face. "Ayers is careless around me. I saw the vid feed in his office."

My hands tremble as I take the device. Kyra's hands tremble, too, and she turns again toward the door.

"Hurry, you don't have long." She glances at me, and then averts her eyes. "The next guard will be here any second. Hardly anyone's in the building."

"Thank you so much." I throw my arms around her and squeeze. "Please, stay safe."

"Avlyn, I'm sorry…" Tears fill her eyes. "Sorry I couldn't do more. I have to go, before I'm late and Representative Ayers reports me missing." Kyra pulls from the embrace and starts for the exit.

"Do you know where my parents are?"

She thinks for a second. "If they're being held, it's probably in suite ten-thirty-eight. I've seen others kept in there," she says without turning as she rockets away.

Following her, I dash for the door, but she's gone, a wisp of blonde hair disappearing around a corner. No one else is there.

I pull back into the room and grip the stunner. It's activated and on the lowest setting. I then slap my handheld to my wrist and immediately reactivate the Affinity app I downloaded to my nanos.

Meyer is my only chance. Although I have no clue if he got away or not, I send a message.

We need help. I'm getting my parents.

Easing out in the corridor, I place a palm on the security pad and wince for the alarms, which don't come. They're not reading my presence.

Suite ten-thirty-eight, I think.

A layout of the building forms in my mind, showing my current location in relation to Mother and Father. It's close. In my mind, I link into the surveillance system. Sure enough, two frames are huddled in the corner of the room. I tell the system to loop the surveillance in the entire building as well, setting it back fifteen minutes, to when I was still asleep. This way makes it so Kyra won't be seen either, but it won't take them long to notice. The quickest route to my destination is a service entrance at the back of the building, and Suite 1038 is not too far from it.

When my hand lifts from the pad the door seals, and I continue down the hall, weapon poised. I take the corridor and turn two rights. I'm about to round to the left when I hear voices and stiffen.

I tuck into the first doorway I see, stuffing the weapon into the back of my suit and pulling out the Flexx. I poke at the screen and try to look busy.

The two citizens early to work at the Representative's building pass me without a glance and continue out of sight.

Three doors ahead, I see the suite numbered 1038. I rush toward the door while pulling out my weapon and sliding my hand onto the pad.

"Open," I whisper. I'm met with a dark room, the only light spilling in from the hall. Two faces peer toward me from the ground, and I make out the outline of Mother's bobbed hair.

"Mother?" I choke.

"Avlyn?" Father's voice comes from the shadowy figure next to Mother.

I step in, holster the weapon, and activate the light on my handheld. "Let's go."

Mother holds her hand to her face to block the light.

"Are you all right?" I ask.

But she's not. Her lips are swollen, and an angry cut mars her cheek. Purple tints the skin under her bloodshot eyes. My stare swivels to Father, and he looks similar, but not as bad since his dark skin hides it.

"What happened?"

"Never mind that," Father says. "You can't be here."

"Doesn't matter. I'm likely dead either way." Weapon in one hand, I grab Father's arm. "It's time to leave."

If I'm going to die, I'm at least going to try to save my parents.

CHAPTER THIRTY ONE

Mother and Father don't move. My mind races for the right words they need to hear so they'll come with me immediately, but this is not how they do things. They still believe Direction will save them.

"You're going to die either way," I tell them. "You might as well try to make a run for it and force them to kill you here instead of televising your deaths to further their propaganda."

"Manning is after *you*, Avlyn, not us," Father says.

I lock onto his eyes. "He dragged you two in here and *tortured* you. If you think either of you will see the light of day again, you are sadly mistaken. Believe me, if I thought for one second you'd be safe, I'd leave you. Manning will probably televise your execution for all to see, letting them know how you were spies for Affinity. Manning's a liar."

Mother throws me a look that only tells me she knows there's no other option. "She's right, Michael." She takes my offered hand and pulls herself up from the floor.

Father grimaces, but deep down, he knows too. "Fine."

Whatever happened to them must have been bad for him to back down this easily.

Squeezing my stunner, I peer into the hall. "It's clear."

The three of us run into the long, neutral hall, but quickly slow as to not look too out of place. Since Manning offered me a deal, I can only hope the news of my capture has not been televised.

Every sound makes me flinch; the tapping of our shoes on the slick tiles, muffled voices from behind closed doors. There can't be much time left before this area is filled with citizens who work at the Representatives building.

I glimpse back at my parent's sunken faces and shudder. There's no way for them to blend in. Manning must have disabled their nanos too. If I had time, I would reactivate them, but it's too much of a risk. Father's normally strong jaw quivers slightly, and the dark streaks under Mother's eyes make her look frail and exhausted.

I whip the thoughts away and replace them with a memory of the building layout. Not far now. Up ahead should be the service entrance bay. I make for the door, Mother and Father huffing behind.

I twist and activate the secured bay door, willing it to open and hoping no one is on the other side. We duck inside just as two guards, clothed in dark uniforms, the Direction emblem on the chests of their jackets, whip our way. I pull up the stunner and fire twice as the door slides closed behind us.

The closest guard freezes, stunned, but the other withdraws and pulls up his own weapon, followed by a burst of light and muffled blast.

"Get down," I yell, aiming again and shooting.

A grunt comes from behind me. Mother's on the ground, clutching her arm.

"Darline!" Father springs to her. I've never seen him with so much concern for another person on display.

I force my attention to the guard, who now stands frozen in time like the first, weapon still extended. His teeth are bared at us in a silent, fixed growl.

Mother groans again and I pull my thoughts from the guard back to my parents.

A cascade of blood flows from the singed tear in her sleeve. Seeing it makes me dizzy. How are we going to get out of here now?

"Can you stand?" I ask, kneeling at her side.

She glances from her wound and nods. Father clutches her around the waist and pulls.

"Wait," I say. I know we don't have the time, but we can't go onto the street with her bleeding all over the place. She *can't* die.

I grab her hand and a snowfall of white engulfs my vision. I command the nanos to reboot. In seconds, I emerge to see the bleeding has slowed. Already her face looks improved, the bruising reducing.

"You need to cover the injury," I tell her.

"What did you do?" Father asks, looking a bit confused.

"Nothing..." I lie. "It must not be that bad."

I scan the room to find something, anything, to cover it, my gaze falling on the guards.

"Help me get his jacket off," I say, gesturing in their direction. We run to the first guard and remove the black jacket from his stiff body. In a flash, I turn it inside out to hide the security logo.

In one of the few tender moments I've ever seen my parents share, Father gently wraps the jacket around Mother's shoulders.

458 N. 36th Street Unit 582
I think it might snow.
If not today, then on Tuesday.

My heart leaps with joy at Meyer's message. Not only is he alive, he's given us a way out. The stuff about the snow must be the code to give the person at the unit.

"There's a safe house a block away," I say. "You only have to make it that far for now. Ready?"

Mother nods. She looks nearly healed by now.

I stroke the security pad and the door shifts back, allowing the morning light to stream into the bay. I tuck the weapon into the cuff of my suit.

"To the right," I whisper.

We move out onto the sidewalk and quickly blend into a group of citizens heading to work. Somehow, none of them acknowledge us, too engrossed in habit.

Drones zip overhead, and each time one passes, I wince. We reach the apartment front and scan the surrounding citizens one more time, but nobody is watching us.

We sprint through the entrance and up the stairs to 582. The inside of the building is similar to my—or what *was* my-- apartment. Sleek and modern, the contact must be a Level Two working in the prestigious sector.

The corridor is empty, but I check behind us for the hundredth time, activate the visitor alert, and wait. Leftovers of this morning's headache resonate behind my temples. The contact could be at work already. I reach for the security pad, waffling between the idea of breaking in or waiting.

Click.

I yank back as the door to another unit opens and a young man steps out. He walks the opposite way, toward the elevator, ignoring us.

I sound the chime to 582 again.

"No one is home," Mother whispers.

We can't stand out here in the hall any longer, so I reach for the security panel and will it to open. Mother gives me a confused look as the door slides back and the three of us hustle inside.

"I need to clean this up." Mother pulls off the jacket hiding the wound and glances back at me. "It's not serious. Just a nick. Looked worse than it was."

I don't think she realizes I healed her yet.

Father wraps himself around her and shepherds her into the unit from the entryway. Then, for some reason, he squeezes my shoulder and disappears with Mother down the hall to the back of the unit.

The touch bites. It should be a comfort, but instead serves as a reminder we have so far to go and so much to lose. Rubbing off the sensation, I find a seat in the living room, but the rigid armchair offers no relief while I check the handheld and find a missed message from Meyer.

Supplies on the way. Instructions to follow.

Supplies? Just get us out.

The door chimes, my heart leaping into my throat. But if Manning tracked our location, he wouldn't ring the chime and ask to come in.

I stand to check the security feed. An Aerrx floats outside the door, releases a package to the ground, and glides away.

The Flexx vibrates, and I wince.

Answer it.

Father rounds the corner of the living room, his face white. "Who is it?"

"Uh, supplies? How's Mother?" I ask.

His wide eyes relax. "She'll live. Cleaned it and grabbed a new shirt from the closet."

I nod, then open the door where a sizable, unmarked package sits outside. The drone is gone, so I pull the parcel into the unit, and the door secures.

"What's that?" Mother's voice sounds from behind. She's tucking the fresh shirt into the waist of her pants. She almost resembles herself again. Her disheveled, caramel-colored hair is now neat and tidy. Forgetting the package, I rush toward her.

"Careful," she warns.

I stop and embrace Mother gently. No doubt the wound is still healing, but she seems to be okay for the time being. Surprisingly, she accepts it. In the past, she always shrugged off any affection I showed. Maybe it's taken almost dying for them to see what's important.

We stay for a moment until Father clears his throat. The package lies torn open at his feet, and he's holding a stunner and three light jackets with hoods.

The handheld vibrates again.

When ready, call for a secured taxi.

A link to page the cab is directly on the screen.

"Tell me when you're ready to go," I inform them.

Father hands us each a jacket, and I put mine on. Then he holds out the stunner for me.

"I have no idea how to use this," he says.

I nod and take it. My first one stays holstered under the jacket, and I tuck the other into a pocket as Mother and Father don the coats.

"Let's go," Mother says.

I hit the link Meyer sent and a message pops up that the cab will arrive in one minute. It's 6:45, fifteen minutes before most citizens need to be at work.

On the street, the taxi waits. I pause and watch the drones buzz above.

Are any of them searching for us?

Not wanting to consider the possibility, I scurry to the front as my parents load into the back.

I then message Meyer.

We're coming.

Out the window, the crowds of morning citizens on the street has thinned. Thirteen excruciating minutes later, the cab enters the upper sector of Level One, where the Affinity bunker resides. I grit my teeth from the stress of looking conspicuous if we don't make it by seven.

"Are we going to make it out of here?" Mother whispers.

I straighten, fill my lungs, hold it, and exhale. "Yes." I have no idea if it's true, but I have to believe.

The vehicle stops to the side of our destination. Of course, no one greets us. A straggler citizen rushes by, and the ever-present drones litter the sky above.

Exiting the taxi, I rush to the lobby door. My parents trail close behind, their footsteps in time with the pulse racing inside my ears. Inside, we pass a harried-looking man with a scrunched face, no doubt late to work and soon to be docked credits.

The elevator doors whoosh back and the three of us move into the space, taking turns skimming our palms over the inside pad to confirm our identities. The door shuts, and the cab starts its journey down. Mother stands in the corner and hugs herself, and Father produces a thin smile. I can't even return the meager expression until we're safe.

The cab rattles when it bumps against the bottom floor, and I propel from the wall toward the exit. The door skims back.

Meyer. He's coming toward us, his strong shoulders held high, but a glimmer of worry shadows his face.

I race into the corridor and clutch him around the neck. His arms lock around me, and I melt into the heat of his body.

"I knew you'd make it," he whispers into my ear.

Any uncertainty we'd fail washes away. I pull back, only inches from his face. His hot breath makes me gasp slightly for some air of my own.

Meyer loosens his embrace and clears his throat. "Mr. and Mrs. Lark?"

"Yes," Mother answers, sounding slightly annoyed.

I let go and spin around. "This is my... friend. Meyer. He's with Affinity, and is going to help us."

Both my parents have a look of shock on their faces, most likely because they are becoming more and more aware I'm working with rebels.

"Uh... yes." Meyer plants his feet and gestures down the hall. "Ruiz is waiting."

"You made it," Ruiz's voice calls from behind our little group. "Are you all uninjured?"

Father glances toward Mother's arm, but looks away when she announces, "Yes, we are all fine."

After, we settle in a cramped room with a table, and everyone sits except for Ruiz. The leader of Affinity faces me, clothed in a white, loose top, her head full of short, perfect, dark curls.

"Congratulations are in order," she begins. "The work you did at GenTech was successful. The outcome gives us time to regroup and formulate a plan, but this won't stop Direction forever."

At her words, my parents stiffen, shock further overtaking them. Father looks as if he's holding in a breath.

"Breathe, Father," I say.

He does and gives me a look that lets me know the significance of me needing to tell him to breathe is not lost on him.

"Thank you," I mutter and glance at Meyer sitting next to me. "Preston didn't make it?"

He frowns. "No. He did not."

A sharp pain stabs in my chest, and Meyer shifts his eyes away from Ruiz. I don't know how close they were, but it's another loss for him.

"Preston was an informed soldier willing to make the sacrifice." Ruiz lowers her head. "But it doesn't make the loss less painful." After a moment, she raises her chin again. "I am sending my captain to pick you and your parents up. You can't return to Elore, so we must get you out of the city. The transport should arrive within the hour."

I begin to speak, but Ruiz's expression has changed. Her small mouth turns into a frown, and her eyebrows have pulled together.

"Repeat?" she says to no one in this room, apparently hearing something in her ear comm.

Her eyes flit my way.

"Sources indicate our location has been discovered. Prepare for an imminent attack."

CHAPTER THIRTY TWO

"Attack?" My gaze zips toward Meyer, but he's in as much shock as me.

"Are you *sure?*" Ruiz says to whoever is in the comm.

Father clutches Mother around the waist while the five of us wait silently, hoping a mistake has been made. Ruiz nods, then focuses her attention back toward us.

"Meyer, get these three out. Manning is wasting no time, and there's no time to wait for backup. Use tunnel fifty-six."

Her reminder of Manning jogs my memory. "That virus we destroyed, it wasn't just meant for Elore. He was going to use it on the Outerbounds."

Ruiz's gaze snaps to me. "*What?*"

"When I was detained… Manning told me," I say.

She goes quiet for a moment, thinking, before saying, "You need to leave. *Now.*"

"Yes, ma'am," Meyer says as he stands.

Mother reaches across the table and grasps for my hand. Fear clutches at every inch of me, but I push it away, squeezing her fingers.

"Show us. We're ready," I say, catching Meyer's dark eyes and rising from my seat.

Meyer makes for the door and pilots us into the hall, leaving Ruiz behind. The halls were relatively vacant less than fifteen minutes ago, but they now bustle with activity. Equipment from the conference room is being moved out as people railroad past us.

I catch up to Meyer. "There's a tunnel out of the city?"

"Several."

"Why didn't you have me use one when I had to get back into Elore?"

"I wasn't authorized."

I chuckle. "Did that matter?"

He doesn't answer, but his hand brushes over the small of my back, giving me a small sense of hope.

We reach the end of the corridor and enter into a plain room lined with opaque containers. One wall is completely free of them.

"You're coming, right?" Father asks Meyer.

"Yes, sir," he replies. "Orders are to escort you out of the city, and I'm the only one of us with an EP."

"Don't remind me." I hated the EP at first, but after using it these past few weeks, the lack of information in my vision is disconcerting.

Meyer cracks a smile, but it's gone as quickly as it appeared. He takes out his handheld and looks to be punching in a code.

Something odd about the wall catches my eye. A shimmer. I leave the others to step toward it. The shimmer grows stronger, and I reach out. Upon touching the glow, an electric pulse zips through my muscles and I jump back. The illusion of the wall dissolves and a metal panel slides back.

342

"Should have remembered you might be able to do that," Meyer murmurs.

Mother's mouth hangs slack, and Father's face is blank.

"Why... why can you do all these things?" she asks.

I shrug. "There's not time to tell you now. Follow me."

A *crack* sounds from overhead. I grab the side of the panel opening and duck while swinging around to check with Meyer. Mother lets out a yelp and Father steadies her.

"Is anyone else coming?" Father asks.

"No," Meyer says. "There's a larger tunnel on the other side of the build--"

His face goes white as his voice fails. He must hear something in his comm.

"They're right on top of us." His eyes snap to the ceiling. "We need to get in and seal this thing." Meyer ushers us down the stairs and stops to reset the panel, hopefully to recreate the illusion of the wall on the other side.

The staircase is tight, and longer than I envisioned. The dull auto lights overhead barely break through the blackness. An explosion sounds again and the lights flicker. Fire races through my skin and muscles as we pound down the steps. Our panting breath echoes through the space, interrupted by the battering overhead.

The bottom of the stairs reveals a long, narrow tunnel. There's only enough room for about two or three people to stand shoulder to shoulder.

"How far is it?" I scan the walls, and they feel as if they're compressing around me.

"It's a ways," Meyer's voice rings out, cut short with another blast. "Keep moving."

The four of us jog through the tunnel, and the noises stop.

Father slows ahead of me. "Might be far enough away from the bunk—"

Crack. Part of the ceiling crashes to the floor in front of us. We skid to a stop, tumbling into each other.

"Keep moving forward!" Meyer yells.

I dash past the crumbling material and queasiness burns my stomach. To keep it down, I swallow hard.

Thunder fills the space. A split forms on the roof and chases toward us. There has to be at least ten feet, probably more, of concrete over us. If this collapses... we're dead.

"Manning knows our specific location. They're following us!" Meyer yells. "How?"

I stop and he clasps my arm to pull me forward.

"Keep moving!"

Fear explodes and rips through me. Tears blaze in my eyes, then blur my vision.

"Did they give you anything?" he demands. "Do anything?"

In my panic, I go blank. "Uh…"

Meyer yanks my arm, and a rumble sounds again overhead, bringing me back to reality.

"No... nothing happened. I didn't even eat or drink." My body churns and shudders. "I... I remembered what you said about Ruiz not trusting Direction's food. The only thing I took was the Flexx from Kyra—"

Meyer goes rigid and his eyes widen. "I assumed you escaped on your own. Let me see it."

I rip it from my wrist under my sleeve, holding the device out in front of Meyer. "This one… the one Kyra delivered…"

Meyer stares at the handheld. "It's got to be bugged."

I snatch it back. "But... but Kyra *helped* me."

With my mind I access the processor and find it. Sure enough, we're being tracked. Revulsion spreads from my palm and worms its way through my arm, and I throw the device to the ground as if it stung me.

Meyer crushes the Flexx with the heel of his boot as he curses under his breath. At first the thin, transparent screen bends, then cracks in two.

"Kyra gave you this to track you," he says. "It's why you could escape so easily. Manning wanted you to."

Mother keeps pace behind us. "Oh, Avlyn," she moans.

I never could be what they wanted. Even now I'm a disappointment.

"Why would Kyra do that?" I slow in my confusion. We've been friends most of our lives. I've always trusted her, and she trusted me with her secrets.

The mass of confusion makes everything hazy, jumbled. Meyer grips my shoulders, shaking them and snapping me back to reality.

"It's done. We need to keep going." Quickly he pokes at his Flexx. "I'm sending out a new signal to misdirect our location, but it will take a moment to engage."

Meyer grabs my shoulder and propels me forward. My feet strike the concrete and drive any thoughts other than escaping away. A roar like thunder fills the shaft and I hurtle forward to get away from it. Crumbling bits of ceiling pelt us as we pass, dust catching in the little bit of light the emergency fixtures emit. The tunnel roars, and the breach above us widens, propelling dirt and concrete ahead of our group.

"It's going to give!" Meyer yells.

And with that, the ceiling breaks free. The four of us turn on our heels and tear in the opposite direction, back to the bunker. The walls rumble, and a barrage of debris slams down behind us. Shattered pieces of concrete fly past, cutting into my skin. I plow into the wall after someone pushes me forward, throwing my hands in front of me, palms scraping against the rough surface. Blood beads wet across my skin.

Father's fallen beside me, and I try to choke out words to make him stand. Up ahead Meyer's wide eyes peer back toward us. I spin and look behind us.

"Mother!" I scream, scrambling back through the rubble. An enormous, jagged chunk of concrete pins her to the ground. She's not moving. She must have pushed me out of the way. Then it hits me; she saved me.

I push against the chunk, but it doesn't budge.

"Mother? *Mother!*" I shriek.

Father's voice breaks through the rumbling. "No, no, no!" he cries. He's joined me and digs frantically in the debris.

Mother coughs and groans.

"We're getting you out. You'll be fine." I touch her face and smear blood from the side of her eye into her hair.

"Go," she murmurs. "Leave."

Meyer brushes me on the shoulder. I flinch.

"We can't stay." He kneels beside me. "The EP's telling me she's pinned in tight. Even if we could get her out, she wouldn't make it long. Her chances... they aren't good."

I twist toward his pleading eyes and growl, "We're getting her free."

"If we don't leave now, none of us will get out." Meyer looks toward the woman who raised me. He grabs my arm, but I yank away and whirl back to dig with Father.

"Michael... you need to stop," she mumbles. Her face is covered in dirt, and more blood trickles from her hairline. With sudden intensity, she locks eyes with Meyer. "Get Avlyn out of here... She's important."

The words sting. I never believed I would be important. And not to her.

Father collapses next to me and stops digging. His dust and tear-streaked face falls forward toward hers. The two share hurried whispers I barely hear, then Father rises, their clasped hands ripping from one another, and he walks behind Meyer, back turned from his spouse.

"Avlyn," she whispers.

I lean toward Mother and lower my face to touch hers. Sweat and blood connect us.

"Mother—"

"Shh... love you. Never forget."

Pain tears through my abdomen. She's telling me good-bye. "I love—"

"I know you do. I'm so sorry we couldn't tell each other until now. It took this for me to see it." Mother's voice falls so low I can barely make out the words. "Avlyn, this world is both beautiful and broken." She closes her eyes, and her breathing slows. "Make more beautiful moments than broken ones."

Pressure grips my arm, and someone pulls me through the disintegrating tunnel trap. I spin around to Meyer. "No!" I yell, pulling away from him. Just as I do, another explosion rips the crack in the concrete ceiling further, debris raining over us.

"Go," Mother chokes.

Meyer jerks me to my feet and drags me forward. "I love you… I'm sorry!" I wail. Any words Mother might have left are drowned out as we leave her behind.

Father, Meyer, and I rush through the haze of dust and dirt, hands covering our mouths, dodging falling chunks of concrete. The dust kicking in the air hurts my lungs, but the dim emergency lights ahead silhouette the staircase to the tunnel.

What will be out there?

Meyer readies his weapon and starts for the steps. I take the one from my pocket and hold it to the side.

"I've lost my comm," Meyer says.

I have no idea how long he's been out of communication with Affinity, and I don't ask. I push between them and race to the top of the stairs, touching the panel.

"Ready?" I ask without turning.

"Yes," Meyer answers.

The panel slides open to reveal the slight storage area, but this time many of the containers are smashed and toppled in the space, spilling their contents. There's no Guardians though, human or drone.

"They've definitely been here," Father whispers. Tear stains streak his dust-covered face.

I close the panel and reset the illusion, then we skid behind a pile of overthrown crates. Meyer's eyes flicker. He must see something in his EP.

"Drones," he murmurs. "Stay here while I clear the hall."

He advances to the door and triggers it. Meyer pauses and looks out, weapon extended. The pulse light on the barrel illuminates and an electric vibration sounds from the hall. I lunge forward, but Father catches my shoulder. His eyes are pleading.

"No unnecessary risks."

Meyer pops back in the room. "Now. Go."

Father pushes me up, and the two of us escape the mess of containers. At the door, one drone is taken out, crushed and smoking on the floor.

"There's an emergency escape across the hall," Meyer says.

We follow him into the next room, where a body lies slumped over in the corner. I freeze and stare. To me, the man appears as if he's asleep. Meyer hooks his arm around my waist and propels me forward, but my eyes stay glued to the man and the pool of blood I can now see seeping from his body onto the floor.

Meyer releases me. He and Father pull a vent cover from the upper half of the wall.

"Get her in," Meyer says.

I gulp. "And you?"

"I need to cover you two. Go. I'll follow."

"Come on, Avlyn," Father whispers.

I follow his direction, pull out the stunner, and dive into the vent. It's wide enough for one person to fit through at a time. As I glide through, my arm scrapes against bent metal and heat flares at the spot. I wince but bite down, willing away the pain.

Father follows me inside, then the clunk of the vent being closed indicates Meyer's in as well. We press on through the shaft around ten feet until it opens up above us. A ladder affixed to the wall bids me to climb. My sweaty palms slip on the rungs, but I push forward.

Meyer's voice sounds from below. "The exit's one floor up."

The panel above comes into view. At the opening I ready my weapon, shoving the vent cover open with my shoulder. Thumping and popping sounds echo from outside the room. Part of me wants to hide in the safety of the shaft. Instead, I crawl out onto the floor of another cramped work room. The hole is partially blocked by a pair of shelves.

I squeeze through and kick them forward. They slide along the smooth floor. I kneel and grasp for Father's hand to pull him out. Meyer emerges after.

"My comm's back... for now," Meyer whispers. Three loud *pops* sound, and he holds his hand to his ear. "Philly has sent in an army." He sounds surprised. "A hovership is coming for us. The bunker is cleared and they're holding Direction back."

Meyer clears the space outside the door, and the three of us start toward the lobby, stunners ready, toward the sound of shooting. The beating of the explosions reverberates through me as we sprint toward freedom.

Hopefully.

"The lobby is the only way out from this location," Meyer says. "As far as I know, we're good, but don't let your guard down. My comm and EP's on the fritz, so I might not know what's ahead."

Rounding the corner, repulsion swirls in my stomach. Bodies litter the floor, what must be a mixture of Affinity members and the DPF force.

A micro drone, similar to the one Aron sent to my apartment, zooms into view, and without thinking, I aim and fire. Bullseye. The thing explodes and smashes into the wall behind it. My sick sensation is replaced with a flicker of excitement.

But the feeling disintegrates when dozens more tiny drones, no bigger than small birds, fly around the corner and stop directly in front of us. One stops inches away from my face. I recoil slightly.

A blue beam emits from several of the drones and our stunners wrench from our hands and fly across the room, hitting the floor with a *crack* before skimming away.

"Freeze."

A black-masked, armored soldier with a lean frame appears, looming ahead of us. The spark in my gut explodes. I raise my hands, and Meyer and Father do the same. For some reason, he's not killing us. Yet.

Another beam shoots out from one of the drones, destroying our weapons on the floor, shattering any hope of escape.

The drone in front of my face shoots a ray of light toward my torso, filling me with electricity. My arms cement to my side.

The male soldier points his weapon toward us. "If you try anything, these drones are equipped to kill." Then his voice softens. "Let's go."

Something sparks inside me as we obey the soldier's command.

I know this voice.

"Aron?" I ask.

"Move," the soldier repeats more forcefully this time. "I'd rather arrest than kill you," he mumbles, motioning with his weapon toward the lobby.

"Aron, let us go," I plead. "Manning is going to kill us."

The soldier steps closer, his pained blue eyes looking straight into mine. He sighs and unlatches his mask. "Avlyn, I don't have another choice." His caramel hair sticks to his head with sweat, and his cheeks flush pink. "When the report came out that Direction was trying to bring you in, I panicked. I thought the whole thing had to be a mistake, so I volunteered to help bring you in with my new drone project... I'm the only one who knew how to run them. It was stupid, but I thought maybe I'd find you first."

His eyes are pleading when he looks back at me.

"But when I got cut off from outside communication and Affinity took over the building, I hid. Then I saw you..."

I want to reach out to him, but I can't move my arms. "What did you do to us?"

"I made your nanos control your muscle groups and lock your arms in place," Aron says. "I'm sorry. If you just do what Direction says--"

"Who is this?" Meyer sneers.

"His name is Aron," I tell him. "He's a friend."

Just the guy who asked me to be his spouse. And I said yes to.

"Aron Barton? Your *pairing*?" Meyer asks, whipping his head toward me.

I don't answer.

Aron raises his weapon toward Meyer, causing me to step back. "Listen," he snaps, "you could be dead right now."

"It makes no difference," Father mutters.

"Let's go." Aron eyes me and mutters something into his comm. The diminutive drones glide overhead and take a place behind and to our sides.

Numbness spreads through me. I'm unsure how my feet are actually working right now. I turn to check Father and Meyer. Tension radiates on Meyer's face, but maybe *he* has a plan.

Aron whispers something in his comm again, and half of the drones zip away. "On the wall!" he yells.

I smash myself to the wall and onto the floor alongside Father, who reeks of powdery dirt. Sweat. Blood.

Mother's blood...

The memory smarts, so I shove the thought away. If Aron takes us in, Father and Meyer are dead. And me? Probably worse...

From the ground, the micro drones hover over us, and something scrapes against me inside my jacket. The other stunner. If I could only get to it, I could stun Aron before he does something to us.

Remembering how I hacked Sanda, I close my eyes and visualize my nanos.

Set me free, I think.

I tug at my wrists, but they're still stuck. I focus on my goal, to save my father and Meyer. They are all I have now, and I can't let them die.

Set me free.

With a snap, my arms release.

Aron glances nervously back toward the lobby, and I turn toward the wall and gingerly reach for the weapon. I feel the cold metal graze against my fingers. Wrapping them around the grip, I twist, throwing my arm out to fire at the remaining drones. The blast hits each directly, flinging the dead devices toward the wall as I lunge toward Aron, who's just now bringing up his weapon toward me. My stunner ends up inches from his head.

I like Aron, he's a good person, but I can't let him bring us in. "Drop it," I snap.

From the corner of my eye, Father inches back toward the wall, but the heat and tension of Meyer's body is not far behind my shoulder.

"Avlyn, at this close a range, your stunner will do more than stun him," Meyer growls.

I don't move.

Aron stands wide-eyed as he inches his hands up and drops his weapon. "You can't do this..."

"I'm not who you thought I was," I whisper. *I'm not who I thought I was.*

From behind us, a group of soldiers burst into the corridor. An electric blast sounds, and then another. Their weapons are not pointed at us, but at Aron. I lower my stunner as Aron pushes back against the wall, his focus moving between them and me.

One soldier speaks into his comm. "Yes sir, the building and area is secure, and Lark is located."

I turn and touch both Meyer and Father on the shoulders, releasing their arms. Relief rushes through me, but my stare flips to Aron, who now has his hands in the air.

"Don't hurt him!" I shout and charge forward.

An arm clasps my waist, and I twist toward Meyer.

"Let's go," he says.

"But..." I turn back to Aron. Terror blankets his face. For all he knows, Affinity is a group of terrorists... a virus. A deadly virus, like Direction said. A pang shoots up my center for shoving a gun in his face.

"It's time to leave, Avlyn," Father says.

The two escort me forward into the group of soldiers in a daze. Father falls behind, and my arm accidentally brushes against one of the soldiers, whose back is toward me.

A jolt pops at the spot where we touched. It runs up my arm and seizes my chest. A wave of pain rolls over me, then subsides. With a gasp, I turn, pulling from Meyer's grasp. I tear back to the brown-haired soldier, taking hold of his shoulders and spinning him around. His straight, dark hair falls into his hazel eyes.

I stare at his face and my mind screams, flooded with a white wave of long-forgotten memories. A laugh. A cry of lament.

"Do... do I *know* you?" I choke out, nausea swirling in my gut.

He looks away, his deep voice quavering. "Quinn's right. You don't have long."

Meyer jerks me forward, but I stay focused on the scattering of freckles over the soldier's nose until he's blocked from view.

"That boy back there," I say to Meyer. "Do you know him? He knew your name."

Meyer shakes his head. I stare into his eyes, convinced he's telling the truth, but still utterly confused as to what's going on.

When we reach the lobby, there are no bodies to be seen, only chunks of the walls scattered over the powdery tile. The glass of the entrance is coated in a layer of grime, and long cracks spider out over its surface.

I pull away from Meyer and rush to the exit. It's stuck, but the slider is cracked a few inches. I wrap my fingers around the frame and pull it open, wedging myself through the gap.

The roar of what must be a hovership reverberates from the front of the building. The sound sends an ache through my ears, and I throw my hands up to dull the pain.

The massive black pod lowers itself to the ground, kicking up a cloud of debris. Our soldiers circle the building around us. When the hovership touches down, a hatch opens on the side and expels a rush of air. A ramp descends and kisses the ground.

Meyer and Father jog past me and onto the ramp. I race to catch them. Once inside, the ramp pulls in and the hatch shuts with a hiss. Inside, there's nothing to see but a cramped loading area which has four seats attached to the walls.

A middle-aged woman with high cheekbones and a muscular build pops her head through a doorway. "Welcome. The captain will be with you in a minute. Please have a seat and get ready to take flight. We are so glad you're safe."

The three of us sit in silence until footsteps bring a dark-haired man speaking on a comm into the loading area. "Yes. Yes, we have the four... no, three of them secure."

Father's face goes white. He starts to stand, but a jolt from the ship plops him back into his seat.

Pictures... no, memories continue to dance in my mind. A run in the park, a secret gift given in haste. I don't need anyone to tell me what I already know in my heart.

That was Ben back there. Ben's *alive*. Somehow, impossibly, it's true. The news should fill me with joy, and there, but tainted with loss.

This isn't how it should be.

I catch Father's sad, hollow eyes and bend forward to squeeze his hand. He forces a smile and surprisingly clasps mine back before he pulls it away.

The three of us stand and follow the captain into the middle of the ship. It's the size of my living room, and three people work at stations lining the perimeter. At the front, a pilot sits behind a wide window, steering us to safety.

"Where will we go?" I whisper.

A voice sounds from behind. The captain. "We're on course to New Philadelphia."

I have no idea what, or where New Philadelphia is, but don't ask. Instead, I shuffle toward the vista out the window in front of the pilot.

Meyer steps beside me. His fingers slide into my palm, and I take them gratefully. His weary face and eyes seem to indicate that he wanted to do more, but a meager smile is the most I can manage, and I focus forward.

The viewing glass at the bow of the ship devours the cityscape of Elore and rushes into the enigma of the Outerbounds. I pull out the heart charm from beneath the collar of my suit while Mother's last words burn into my conscience.

This world *is* both broken and beautiful.

I draw closer into Meyer's body. Off in the distance, a single, humble brown bird, maybe a lark, swoops and dives against the horizon.

Beckoning.

Book one of Avlyn's story is at an end, but you can find out what happens next in Immersed (Book 2 in the Configured Trilogy).

Dear Book Lover,

Thank you SO much for your support. I am truly humbled. As a new writer, I would be incredibly grateful if you took the time to **leave a review on Amazon**. Short or long is JUST fine. Your review will make a big difference and help new readers discover **The Configured Trilogy**.

I would also love it if you joined my book club at **JenettaPenner.com**. When you do, you will receive a FREE printable Configured YA coloring book, as well as YA book news and information on upcoming releases. You can also follow me on **Facebook** and **Twitter**.

XXOO,

Jenetta Penner

ABOUT THE AUTHOR

I'm Jenetta, and I am a lifetime lover of Sci-Fi (thanks Dad). I had a weird LONG stint (declaring HOW long would give away too many age secrets... and eh-hem... a girl never tells) where I read almost no books for pleasure (the horror!). Near the end of 2014, I picked up Hunger Games, and I was off like a rocket.

That next year I read about 40 YA books (mostly Sci-Fi/dystopian) and a couple months into it, got the idea to write a book (with no prior experience or even desire) about children who were not allowed to be raised by their biological parents. You see, I am an adoptive mama of two lovely daughters from foster care. That story grew into what Configured is today.

It has been a HUGE journey with a lot of ups and downs, and it took WAY longer than I anticipated, but it is finally here.

FINAL THANKS

Firstly, I want to thank my husband, Jon, for coming with me on this journey of writing. It has not been an easy one and I still have a long way to go. Thanks to all my other supporters, including my mom, the wonderful writers at Critique Circle, Jud Neer, David Bernstein, and Anna Atkinson, who helped with tech and computer information. Thank you to my Street Team and blog readers who have come alongside me even prior to publishing. And a big thanks to Derek Murphy and the AAYAA group for all your encouragement.

And to Emma. I didn't know you personally, but have thought of you often over the course of writing Configured. **To learn more about Emma's life, and to pass on kindness, click here** (www.agiftfromemma.com).

Made in the USA
Monee, IL
17 May 2021